PENANCE

THE REDEMPTION TRILOGY

AJ SIKES

GREAT WAVE INK
PUBLISHING

GREAT WAVE INK
PUBLISHING

Cover Design by Elizabeth Mackey
ElizabethMackeyGraphics.com

GREAT WAVE INK
PUBLISHING

This book is dedicated to America's service members.

A portion of the author's proceeds from sales will be donated to the Iraq and Afghanistan Veterans of America, and to the Lieutenant Michael P. Murphy Memorial Scholarship Foundation.

Foreword
by
Nicholas Sansbury Smith

Dear Reader,

Thank you for picking up a copy of Penance by AJ Sikes. This is the second of the Redemption Trilogy, and opens at the harrowing moment when Jed Welch is unable to save Meg Pratt from the Variants who have her trapped in the sewers.

Originally published through Amazon's Extinction Cycle Kindle World, Penance became a reader favourite in the Extinction Cycle series side stories, and transcended to far more than fan fiction. Unfortunately, Amazon ended the Kindle Worlds program in July of 2018 with little warning. Authors were given a chance to republish or retire their stories, and I jumped at the chance to republish Penance through my small press, Great Wave Ink. Today, we're proud to offer Penance in paperback, audio, and to readers outside of the United States for the first time ever.

For those of you that are new to the Extinction Cycle storyline, the series is the award winning, Amazon top-rated, and half a million copy best-selling seven book saga. There are over six *thousand* five-star reviews on Amazon alone. Critics have called it, "World War Z and The Walking Dead meets the Hot Zone." Publishers weekly added, "Smith has realized that the way to rekindle interest in zombie apocalypse fiction is to make it louder, longer, and bloodier... Smith intensifies the disaster efficiently as the pages flip by, and readers who enjoy juicy blood-and-guts action will find a lot of it here."

In creating the Extinction Cycle, my goal was to use authentic military action and real science to take the zombie and post-apocalyptic genres in an exciting new direction. Forget everything you know about zombies. In the Extinction Cycle, they aren't created by black magic or other supernatural means. The ones found in the Extinction Cycle are created by a military bio-weapon called VX-99, first used in Vietnam. The chemicals reactivate the proteins encoded by the genes that separate humans from wild animals—in other words, the experiment turned men into monsters. For the first time, zombies are explained using real science—science so real there is every possibility of something like the Extinction Cycle actually happening. But these creatures aren't the unthinking, slow-minded, shuffling monsters we've all come to know in other shows, books, and movies. These "variants" are more monster than human. Through the series, the variants become the hunters as they evolve from the epigenetic changes. Scrambling to find a cure and defeat the monsters, humanity is brought to the brink of extinction.

We hope you enjoy Penance and continue on with the rest of the Redemption trilogy, and also the main storyline in the Extinction Cycle. Thank you for reading!

Best wishes,
Nicholas Sansbury Smith,
USA Today Bestselling Author of the Extinction Cycle

— 1 —

5 May 2015
Upper East Side, Manhattan, approx. 1140 hours

Jed stared at the gun in Rex's hand, wondering how he'd kept it hidden, and what he was thinking by pulling it out now.

"What the fuck, man? What the absolute—"

"Keep it down. They could be anywhere and they'll hear you." Rex motioned with the gun for Jed to start moving. "We have to go. We have to find some place safe."

Jed took a step back and froze in place. The ruins of New York surrounded them, with wrecked cars, shattered buildings, and mountains of debris filling the once proud streets. Jed felt his own pride covered in filth as well. Meg had gone down the open manhole between him and Rex. She'd fallen into the sewer, with the monsters.

He'd tried to help. His protective suit snagged on a car hood, and he'd fallen over a body as he spun to the side to get free. He was almost at the manhole when Rex had shoved him away and pulled the gun.

Rex had pushed the manhole cover back in place while

Jed stared at him in shock.

"We can't leave her down there!"

"Keep it down," Rex said. His eyes twitched left and right behind the visor of his CBRN hood. Jed felt the closeness of his own mask and suit, constricting and tugging no matter how he stood or tried to hold himself. Every inch of his body screamed to be let out of the damn *body-condom*, but if he got a speck of tainted blood on him...

Jed still had his axe from the fire station. He could probably knock the gun out of Rex's hand—

Meg's scream from the sewer split the air. Rex shook his head like he had a bee under his hood. He stepped backwards, dropped the gun, and took off running. Jed watched him go and thought about picking up the gun. Then he saw it didn't even have a magazine in it.

Motherfucker played me.

Meg was still screaming from the sewer, calling for help, but a loud hiss and shriek spun Jed around. He came face to face with two of the creatures sitting on top of a car. Their sickly pale white flesh glistened, even in the weak sunlight. Spit drooled from their open gaping mouths as they flicked ropy tongues around their bulging lips. Veins stood out from their flesh in dark lines that looked like rivulets of oil.

Jed backed away, holding his axe in front of him. The monsters paced side to side, and then sprang forward. He caught the first one with a chop through its face, dropping it to the pavement where it landed and thrashed at the wound with its clawed hands.

The second one landed awkwardly beside Jed. It held one arm at its side, like the shoulder was out of joint. Jed reared back to swing the axe as the monster whipped its good arm at his legs, tearing a gash into his CBRN suit, but missing his flesh beneath. He tripped on his own feet and fell backwards, still holding the axe in front of his chest. The monster shrieked and sprang forward, crashing on top of Jed.

He drove the axe head into its bad shoulder. The thing screamed and jerked away, sliding off of him. Jed rolled onto his hip, bringing the axe down again and again until the monster was dead.

The other one had tried to slink away, holding its hand over the slice Jed put through its face. He went toward it as it tried to squeeze under a car. With a solid swing, Jed ended the beast. He staggered back, yanking the axe free. The weight of having survived for two weeks in the hell of what used to be New York pushed on Jed's shoulders. The city seemed to breathe around him, like the streets and ruined buildings were all calling him to just lie down and die.

Can't. Not yet. I got something to do still.

Jed went back to the manhole and stared at it. He couldn't hear any screams. He went down hard on one knee, using the axe handle for support. The CBRN gloves made his hands feel like flippers as he gripped the axe and tried to lever the manhole up using the blade.

The manhole lifted away from the pavement and clattered back down. Meg's voice trailed up from below, in a weak cry for help. Jed ripped his gloves off, no longer caring about anything but getting Meg out of there. He worked the axe head into the crack around the manhole, cursing as the blade slipped. He jammed it back in and called to Meg as he struggled to raise the cover.

"I'm coming, Meg. I'm sorry. Gonna get you out. I'm—"

The cover bucked once under his hands, then again, pushed from below this time. Jed shifted on his feet so he was ready to stand. The cover flew upward and flipped onto the street with a *clang!*

Bulging lips and spiked teeth filled Jed's vision. He spun away from the manhole, feeling the axe torn from his hands. He looked back to see one of the monsters throwing his last and only weapon across the street. Jed lurched to his feet and fled, running with all his might away from the hungry shrieks and scraping claws on the asphalt. The fabric of his CBRN suit tugged and pulled, but he pumped his legs as fast as he could and heaved in a breath with every step. He could still hear them. They'd catch him. He knew this was the end. He'd tried to go back for Meg, but it just wasn't meant to be, and maybe Jed wasn't meant to be anymore either. But he just couldn't take the easy way out and let the monsters dog pile him from behind. He had to keep running.

He flashed a glance over his shoulder. Four of them followed, leaping from cars to the pavement, scrabbling along the streets and sidewalks.

Flying as fast as his feet would carry him, Jed whipped past wrecked cars and leaped over bodies lying in pools of dark, dry blood. He spun to the side as a wiry monstrous figure emerged from another manhole directly ahead. Claw marks shredded its arms and a bite mark stained the pale white skin of its chest.

Are they eating each other?

The monster reached an arm out, like it wanted to stop him, but he easily dodged around it. He stumbled off to the sidewalk and stared at the thin creature standing in the middle of the street. A second later it disappeared from sight as two of the monsters chasing him landed on top of the thin one. The whole mass of sickly white flesh dropped back down the manhole to the sound of howls and screams. The remaining two monsters hovered nearby, flicking their tongues and twitching their heads back and forth, looking at Jed and looking down the hole.

Without missing a beat, Jed sped around a corner and down the sidewalk.

The dead lay in his path like a blanket of gore covering New York City's streets. He jumped some of the bodies, then tripped and fell face first into a pile of the corpses. Most of them were monsters, but some had been human still when they'd died. Remembering how he, Meg, and Rex had survived in the fire station, Jed quickly pulled a body on top of himself and curled his legs up so he was in a fetal position, tucked into a tangle of death.

If it weren't for the hood he wore, he'd have spilled his guts from the stink all around him. It still got in a little bit, and he had to hold his chest and throat tight to keep from heaving. He angled his neck so he could see behind him, back to the last corner he'd rounded.

If this is my time, I gotta at least see it coming.

At the corner, one of the beasts squatted on top of another small pile of bodies. It's greasy white skin made Jed think of a toy he'd played with as a kid. Some action figure with crazy muscles, all pale glossy plastic. But Jed knew the thing at the corner was no toy.

It moved like it had spotted him, whipping its head around from where it had been looking at a nearby building. The sucker mouth popped open, and it let out a hiss as it scrabbled forward, coming over the corpses and shattered glass littering the sidewalk. Thick webs of saliva spread across its bulging lips and it flicked its tongue at the air, like a snake tasting a scent. Jed cowered in his hiding place, praying the thing hadn't really seen him. It wasn't looking at him, just at the pile of bodies he was hiding in. His legs hummed with a need to flex and kick, but he forced himself to stay still as the monster crawled forward. Its joints clicked, and it roved its gaze back and forth along the sidewalk as it came.

Jed squeezed his eyes shut. In a heartbeat, he realized the thing might see him pinching his face up, so he quickly relaxed his cheeks and just kept his eyes closed. If it was his time, it was his time, and now he knew he'd rather not see it coming.

There was nothing he could do about it anyway.

A clawed hand came down on his right thigh. Jed swallowed a whimper of terror and held his stomach tight. He couldn't risk pissing himself now. The thing would smell it and then it'd be all over.

Another clawed hand grabbed Jed's shoulder.

This is it. It has to be it. This is the end, Momma. I'm sorry I didn't do better by you.

The weight on his leg and shoulder stayed where it was, pushing Jed down into the mound of death he'd chosen as his last resting place. Then he felt the monster's weight lift. A second later, the thing had moved over the pile of bodies. He felt it crawl down the other side of the pile, driving the corpses tighter against his hiding spot. Then it was gone. The clicking of its joints faded from Jed's hearing.

He stayed there for a while, waiting, praying it was

safe. Finally he opened his eyes and saw the sidewalk stretching out in front of him. Bodies, dried blood, and broken glass still covered everything Jed could see, but the monster was nowhere in sight.

Jed risked flexing his legs. They'd gone numb from being tucked and bent for so long. His feet were stiff, and his arms ached from holding himself still against the concrete.

Meg would probably give anything to feel this good. But now she's under the street. She's down there. Dying.

Because you left her. Because you ran away.

The woman who had rescued him on the street in front of her fire station was now just another corpse in a city that might as well be a morgue. She'd helped him survive the past two weeks. After the Air Force dropped those chemical bombs, she agreed with Jed's idea that they should go looking for more survivors. Fucking Rex was scared shitless, said they should stay put. Maybe they'd all still be alive if they'd done like he said. Most of the monsters *were* dead now.

But not all of them. Some of them made it by hiding in the sewers, or by being strong enough. And you let them get Meg.

Jed held in a sob. Meg had been the closest thing to a true partner he'd ever had, someone to look out for you and watch your back while you watch theirs. Rex was about as ate up as a guy could be. Nothing but muscles under his shirt, but he was a cowardly lion if Jed had ever met one. Fucking candy-ass—

Rex. He may have been a wash out, but so were you once. His name was Rex.

And her name was Meg.

With a scream, Jed shoved the body off him and

to use knives or guns, at least not that he'd seen. And he doubted they'd just kidnap someone instead of eating them on the spot.

New York had another kind of enemy in it now, and it was one Jed could beat.

With his heart pounding, he continued heading north into Harlem. Central Park was a couple blocks to the west. If he had to, he could probably find a place to hide there, at least until he got hold of a weapon. He thought about that as he moved through the city. If he could stomach the idea of looting the bodies of fallen soldiers, he could arm himself pretty good.

Gotta do right by the dead, though. Can't just take their gear and leave 'em lying there.

The street cleared up a bit the farther he got into Harlem. It seemed like most of the action had been in the Upper East. Or maybe that was the only part of Manhattan that Jed had seen since the world ended two weeks back.

The fuck do I know about what's going on? A whole lotta nothin'.

Jed stopped in the middle of the street and turned in a circle. Cars had been driven into storefronts and office lobbies, like the drivers were trying to avoid something here in the roadway. The drivers hadn't got very far. Bodies were lying half in and half out of their seats in most of the vehicles in the area. The back seats and passenger seats were all empty, and some of the seat belts were sliced up just like in the first car he'd checked.

But these were civilians, just people who had probably been trying to get away. And they'd been shot. Every one of the drivers had been taken out with a round to the head or the heart, and sometimes both.

And the blood doesn't look that old. This happened last night, or early this morning.

The rattle of small arms fire snapped Jed's attention away from the dead people in the cars. He whipped his head left and right. The CBRN suit pulled against his shoulders, preventing him from getting a clear look at his surroundings.

Swinging around where he stood, he scanned the shattered buildings. Gunshots popped again from a few blocks away. It was hard to tell with the CBRN gear muffling everything from sight to sound to touch. He crouched by the nearest car's front grill.

The gunfire sounded again, this time from back the way Jed had come running. He looked over the hood of the car and automatically locked his eyes onto the dead person inside.

"The fuck is happening? Why'd they kill you?"

Great, now I'm talking to dead people. What's next for Jed Welch?

Jed lifted a hand like he'd wipe the sweat from his face, and he had to laugh when he felt it bump impotently against the suit's hood.

At least I can still laugh at my own stupid ass.

He thought about heading back toward Queens, but he'd seen enough of his old neighborhood on the trip into Manhattan. That was the hot zone everyone had run away from.

"We were supposed to be safe here," Jed said to himself, huddling by the car's grill and no longer laughing. The clouds had come back and cast deeper shadows around the area.

The monsters like the shadows.

More small arms fire rattled nearby. Jed darted his head left and right, up and down, trying to spot where the shots might be coming from. Then a scream echoed through the dead streets, followed by the howls and animal shrieks of the monsters on the hunt.

— 3 —

Gallegos and Reeve shared a quiet meal, tossing their empty MRE wrappers through a hole in the floor. They'd blown the hole with the last of their demo. She closed her eyes and rocked gently where she sat, remembering that night. It had been a nervous damn twelve hours of waiting for explosions out there in the city. The Air Force was letting something loose, and it was killing the sucker faces. But she'd seen some of them crawling away, like they were unaffected by whatever was falling out of the sky.

I thought for sure they would find us that night. Thought for sure we were over and through.

But they'd lived, and Mahton had been fast with the demo triggers, setting the charges off so the noise would be drowned out by the explosions outside.

That was doubly important with the collaborators only two blocks away. Gallegos was the first to spot the black truck driving slowly through the surrounding neighborhoods. The driver had to be braver than any man she'd ever known or just plain stupid. At least, that's what she'd thought at the time.

Then Reeve spotted the prisoner swap. He'd called her

"*Pinche*— Fuck it," she said and leaned over to scoop up Reeve's trash and toss it down the hole.

The remains of their flashlights were scattered nearby. She scraped them into the hole, too. She had hoped the red lens lights wouldn't attract the sucker faces, but she hadn't counted on their vision being as good as it was.

Any kind of light at all. Any movement. Any noise. They'd see it or hear it and they'd come running.

Reeve had smashed the flashlights while the flyboys were dropping the chemical bombs. He'd needed to smash something, and she figured why the hell not.

What's left to care about anymore? Why not just smash it all to pieces? Isn't that what we've done?

"I was gonna rack out, Sergeant. Rah?" Mahton asked.

"*Errr*," Gallegos answered. The shorthand was easier now, even though she knew that open communication was the key to keeping them all alive. She worried about what would happen if they started grunting at each other and doing nothing else.

Is one of them gonna snap first, or will it be me?

After two solid days of staring at the same dead city and watching the same horrors play out on the street below, Gallegos wasn't sure how much fight she had left. They'd lost the rest of their company in Operation Reaper. They'd lost most of their platoon finding this bus depot.

They'd lost Gunny Pacau running from the sucker faces, not five minutes after they got into the depot.

Now it was just her, Reeve, and Mahton.

Three US Marines against a city of the damned.

Gallegos reached for her MRE wrappers. Her hand automatically shifted direction and latched onto her weapon when a shriek ripped through the neighborhood outside. The pop of small arms fire came next, and Gallegos was on her feet, racing to Reeve's position and shouting for Mahton as she ran.

***

Jed rushed away from the wrecked cars and into the neighborhood around him, toward the firefight. He was done hiding out and knew that if anyone in New York City still had a weapon, they knew how to survive in this hell that had taken over his world.

Or maybe they're just damn lucky.

The monsters still split the air with their violent cries and shrieks. He couldn't see them anywhere, but he shot a look left and right, up and down, as he moved.

Nothing. Where the fuck are they? Where are they hiding?

Jed stumbled up against a storefront and thought about ditching into the building. The thought vanished as quickly as it came when he heard a man shouting.

"Pull back! Menendez, keep 'em down! Sustain—Shit, right flank! Right flank!"

The familiar cadence of a leader's command, followed by the chatter of a SAW, spurned Jed to action. Another surge of strength pulsed in his veins. Someone who knew how to fight was still alive in this city, and they needed help. Spinning away from the storefront, Jed ran again toward the sounds of battle and soldiers in need.

"I'm coming!" he shouted, hoping someone would hear him. The firefight raged on and it had to be only a block away. Storefronts and bodies blurred in Jed's vision as he ran. The pops and rattles of automatic fire came wounded man.

The one on top was dead with two bullet holes in his back. He hadn't been wearing any armor. Jed moved the body off the wounded soldier and found a young man lying on the ground. His face was dark with grime and blood. A dark pool slowly spread under his back and stained his uniform around his left shoulder. Jed quickly put his hands on the bloody jagged hole under the soldier's left arm.

"Hey man. Hey, I'm Welch. PFC Welch. What's your name?"

Jed felt the blood's warmth as it flowed between his fingers. He pressed harder, but he knew the wound was too severe for him to be any help. The soldier's time had come, and Jed couldn't change it.

A weak voice croaked out of the young man's lips.

"Pivo—Pivowitch. Spec-4—"

He coughed twice and blood frothed around his lips. He didn't look much older than Jed himself. But the scars of war ran in deep lines around his eyes, like he'd had to squeeze them shut too many times. Jed kept pressure on the wound and did what he could to make it easier for the man whose life he knew he couldn't save.

"You been in the sandbox, Pivowitch?"

"Yeah. Used to be."

"What unit you with? I was in the corps."

"You a jarhead?"

Jed chuckled. "Now ain't the time to be talking shit, rah?"

The wounded man tried to grin, but it slid off his face as he said, "Hey man, can you—"

A spasm pulled Pivowitch away and Jed had to lean

forward to keep his hands pressing on the wound. The blood still flowed and Pivowitch's face looked almost as white as the monsters' skin. Jed nearly let go, but he fought the impulse. Pivowitch wasn't turning. He was dying.

"What do you need, man?" he asked, scooting on his knees to stay close to Pivowitch in case he jerked away again.

"Can you pray—for me? Don't wanna die without that."

"Yeah, of course, man," Jed said, wondering if God would hear a single thing he had to say. It had been years since Jed bothered thinking about prayers much less making them.

"He don't..." Pivowitch said.

"Who doesn't?"

"Tucker. Heard them call him Tucker. He don't...he's the one...did this—"

Another spasm sent Pivowitch's head rocking back on his neck, flexing his shoulders. In that position, Jed couldn't keep his hands tight over the man's wound, but a second later that didn't matter. Pivowitch flopped onto his side and went limp against the asphalt.

Jed sat with the dead soldier for a while, just staring at his face and the creases around his eyes and mouth. With a sigh that he felt all the way to his toes, Jed gently closed Pivowitch's eyes and rolled him onto his back. He set his hands over his heart and said a silent prayer for his soul.

Taking his time, forgetting about the monsters and half-wishing they would show up and take him, too, Jed went to each of the dead soldiers around him and performed the same act of last rites. He set them into a pose of peace and calm, and whispered prayers for their salvation. He may not have been a priest and may not have done much in his life that could be called holy, but for these seven men, Jed felt it was his duty to help them to the next stop on the road.

As he knelt by the seventh body, he noticed the butt of an M4 underneath the car the soldier had been sheltered behind. He did a quick scan of the area, suddenly snapped from his sense of sacred duty. What if the monsters were out there and were just watching him? Or what if whoever had killed these men was still nearby?

He'd thought his courage had abandoned him ever since he washed out of the corps. And the past three weeks hadn't done much to change his mind. He'd run from the first battle and was ready to keep running until…

For her. For Meg, you gotta be a better man now, Jed Welch. You gotta do what's right instead of what's easy. You couldn't help her, and you couldn't help these men here, but you know there's people who need you in this city still. Somebody needs your help.

Jed performed the final prayer before snatching up the M4 from beneath the car. It still had a magazine in it, and from the weight Jed guessed it was about half full. He popped it out and confirmed he had close to ten rounds left. Jed went around to the other bodies, hoping to find more ammunition.

"Y'all don't need it where you're going. But I might."

None of the soldiers had anything on them. Their ammo pouches were empty, except for Pivowitch's. He still had one magazine. Jed took it, then the man's weapon sling, and his helmet. He strapped the brain bucket over his CBRN hood, and thought about putting

Pivowitch's tactical vest over the suit.

He looked at the dead soldier's face again. His unmasked face.

None of the men had any protective gear on. So whatever had turned the people of New York City into monsters, it wasn't happening any more.

That stuff the Air Force dropped must have killed the virus.

Jed set his M4 on the ground by Pivowitch's body, removed his helmet, and slowly lifted his hands to the CBRN hood. He took a deep breath and broke the seal, then removed the hood and let it fall to the ground. Letting his air out, Jed breathed in and nearly heaved up his guts. The city stank of death and ruin, and a sickly sweet stench of rotten fruit cut through everything. The reek of old hooch drifted from the liquor store, too. Jed took a minute to calm his gut and then, with rapid movements, he stripped out of the suit. He wadded it up and stuffed it under the car near Pivowitch's body. He looked at the dead man's vest again, but couldn't bring himself to take it off the body.

Strapping on his helmet, and taking up his M4, Jed set out in a crouch going up 99th Street. He followed the path of the heavy vehicle that had been there earlier. It was easy enough to spot the wide tracks of a dual-wheel truck in the broken glass and rubble. Whoever was in it had a few crimes to answer for, at least seven by Jed's count, and probably more than that.

At the end of the block, he found three more soldiers who had been shot in the back. They'd probably been part of Pivowitch's platoon, maybe the first to get taken down by the people with the truck. Jed performed a quicker version of his ceremony for the three men, pausing every few seconds to scan the area with his weapon at the ready. From this point on, he wasn't taking his finger away from the trigger guard. Not until the weapon was taken from his hands.

And they'll be cold and dead before that happens.

After finishing up the last of his prayers for the fallen men, Jed did a quick recon of the area. Another M4 was lying on the sidewalk, half under a car that had run over the curb and wrapped around a tree.

Jed wondered whose weapon he'd found. Nobody had been sheltering behind the car, at least nobody that had died there. Then he spotted streaks of blood, where someone had been dragged away. The stains abruptly ended at the sidewalk.

They're killing soldiers and taking prisoners? What the fuck is this all about?

Jed's mission changed in his mind then. He would find the people who had been taken, and whoever or whatever was responsible for these soldiers' deaths, Jed was going to call their asses to account.

***

The dual-wheel tracks led up 99th and around the next corner. Jed kept to his crouch and moved as quickly as he could. The monsters weren't around as far as he could tell. Their stink lingered in the air, but he hadn't seen or heard a sign of their presence. The truck tracks continued onto Lexington Avenue, but disappeared shortly after the intersection. Jed crossed Lexington and paused by the entrance to a bus depot. Two busses were turned on their sides in front of the building. They'd been knocked over as barricades. Their roofs were peppered with bullet holes and one had a hole that looked like a LAW rocket had been fired into it.

"The absolute fuck is happening?" Jed said to the empty street. He put his hand up to the hole in the bus roof, fingering the ribboned metal like it might help him unravel what had happened here. From what Pivowitch told him, he knew the monsters weren't the only threat he had to worry about. But why was this Tucker guy doing it?

Maybe the dude was a banger, just going back to his old roots since law and order didn't exist on the streets anymore. If that was the story, then Tucker had nothing to lose and everything to gain. All it would take is enough guys with guns and ammo and he could be the sheriff with his posse ruling the town.

Jed still couldn't accept that as the reason. Who would help what was left of the world die only to become kings of the aftermath?

Kings of what? Fucking monsters own this world even if they are hiding underground.

The roar of a heavy truck engine set Jed on alert. He dashed around the bus and into the shattered ruin of the depot, stepping through shattered glass and stains of dried blood. He had a good view of the street, but stayed as hidden as he could. One beat later, a black dual-wheeled truck raced by the front of the depot and peeled off down Lexington. Jed ducked down and stayed hidden until the sounds of the engine faded from his ears.

Creeping out of his hiding spot, he examined the depot, looking for anything that might help him survive. Ammunition, food, water.

Hell, some new drawers would be nice.

Desks and waiting room furniture had been shoved up against the windows of the depot, but the front door had been left clear, almost like whoever was in here had wanted to keep it that way. The service counter near the back of the room was smashed up and wouldn't provide much cover at all. At first Jed thought it had been destroyed by the monsters, but even from his position across the room he could tell it had been chopped up on purpose.

Everything else showed signs of the monsters having attacked before. Claw marks covered the floor and the chairs and couches. Even the ceiling tiles, what few remained, showed slash marks. Jed could picture the monsters hanging up there and dropping on people who were in the room below. He turned in a circle, curious about where the monsters came in from and why the front door had been left unblocked.

The floor was awash in sprays of blood and giant dried puddles, like a massacre had taken place.

Then Jed realized what he was seeing. The busses had been used to barricade the depot, but that barricade didn't hold. Whoever had wanted in had been armed for battle, so they'd gotten in.

And they'd let the monsters in after them.

He didn't want to believe it, but he couldn't ignore the signs everywhere he looked. Most of the blood was in the center of the room, except for where it had splashed onto the walls and ceiling. Somehow, for some crazy reason, this room had been used like a fighting ring. But why?

The barricade at the front door wasn't forgotten or ignored, it had been moved. Streaks and scratches on the floor showed where two heavy desks had been shoved aside. They were piled up with the furniture in front of the windows, but he could tell they'd been moved by a human. The monsters would push things aside, but only enough to make a gap for them to crawl through.

Jed turned in place again, trying to make sense of what he was seeing. He stopped mid-step when the shadow of a human figure darkened the windows. He could just make out a helmet before the figure disappeared from view, ducking down below the stacked furniture.

With his weapon at the ready, Jed paced back, deeper into the room, eyeballing the front door. His boots scuffed through debris as he moved and he winced, hoping whoever was outside hadn't heard him.

**

Gallegos watched the guy creeping around in the entryway. He'd tried to hide when the collaborator's truck went by, so maybe he wasn't with them.

Or maybe he was. Maybe he got kicked out or bailed out.

Whoever he was and whatever he was doing, Gallegos couldn't afford to let him discover her hiding place.

"That's far enough, chump," she said, leveling her M9 at the guy's back. He froze with his weapon at the ready.

She could tell he was eyeing the front door. He kept his weapon up, like he was ready to run for it or maybe try to spin around and take a shot at her. Gallegos pulled back the hammer on her pistol, hoping it would put the guy off his game.

If he's got any game. Dude looks ate up.

"Set down the weapon and turn around, hands in the

air where I can see 'em," she said.

Gallegos felt her heart settle when the guy's shoulders drooped and he let his M4 hang loose on its sling.

"I'm bending over to put it down," he said.

"Muzzle first. Keep it aimed at the ground, hand away from the trigger."

He repositioned his right hand to hold the weapon by the buttstock while he unclipped it from the sling and set it on the floor.

"Now turn around, hands up."

He slowly turned where he stood, lifting his hands level with his ears. He was a young white kid, but she had to look at him for a few beats to make sure. His skin was covered in dirt and probably blood.

Not much different from me. And the col-labs wash their faces. At least the ones I've seen so far.

"Who the fuck are you?" she demanded. She kept her weapon on him and stepped to her right until the remains of the service counter were between them.

"Welch, USMC. Who—"

"I ask, you answer," she said, tightening her grip on the gun in her left hand. She lifted her shoulder mic and told her team that it was okay to come in.

The sound of boots on glass and debris broke the tense air. Reeve and Mahton moved into the depot lobby, stepping past the new guy until the three of them had him in their sights. The other Marines trained their M4s on him. Gallegos kept her pistol leveled at his face.

"You with Tucker's crew?" the new guy asked, apparently no longer caring if Gallegos capped him. But he'd said a name, and it was one she hadn't heard before. Maybe this guy did know the col-labs and could give them some info before they dumped his dead ass back on the street.

"Who's Tucker?" Gallegos asked. She pinched her eyes into slits as she spoke, and kept her sidearm pointed right at the guy's face. He held her gaze for a second, like he was taking her measure. She gave it back to him, but he didn't flinch or open his mouth to answer her question.

"Hey, motherfucker," she said. "I asked you who Tucker was."

His face went slack, like he'd given up, but then his lips curled and he seemed ready to fight again.

"Tucker," he said. "You know, the guy who runs your little gang, killing soldiers and taking their gear. Why? I don't fucking know, but it's what you—"

"Hold up," she said. "You're with those guys? The ones in the truck?"

"No," the new guy said, shaking his head and then snapping it left and right to look at Reeve and Mahton. They were in full gear, too, and their faces were just as filthy as his. He couldn't possibly think Gallegos and her team were part of the col-lab shitshow.

But if he's not with them, where the hell did he come from?

— 4 —

"We're hunting the hunters," Gallegos said. "If you're trying to distract us, then you had better start praying. Collaborators are enemy number one. If you're with that bunch of assholes, we will rip you a new one and sew it back up so we can do it again."

"He's a deke. Gotta be," Reeve said.

"A deke?" the guy asked, twisting his head side to side and taking in Reeve and Mahton's stance. "I'm not with them. I'm not with those guys. I just—"

Before Gallegos could get a word in, Mahton lowered his weapon.

"I believe him. He's no deke. He might not be a Marine, but he's not a col-lab shitbag either."

"How do you know?" Gallegos asked. "And who told you to stand down?"

She was relieved when Mahton lifted his weapon again and held it at the ready. He wasn't drawing down on the guy anymore, but Reeve still had him dead to rights.

"Mahton," Gallegos said. "Why do you think he's legit?"

"He doesn't act like any of them. Look at his face; he's scared to death."

Gallegos stared into the new guy's face, searching his eyes for the truth. She kept her M9 out, but lifted the muzzle so it wasn't aiming at his forehead any more.

"You say your name is Welch, and you're USMC?"

The guy nodded, and his fear came through this time. His mouth shook around his words.

"Yeah—I'm Jed Welch. USMC."

"I don't see a name tab on your uniform, or any rank. You got three *real* Marines here cleared hot and with every reason to light your ass up. Prove we shouldn't."

Welch paused for a second before lowering his hands. Gallegos let him relax, but signaled Mahton with her eyes to keep his weapon up. Not surprisingly, Reeve just tucked the butt of his M4 a little tighter against his shoulder and maintained his aim on Welch's center mass.

"Bet he's a stolen valor shitbag," Reeve said.

"Could be, or he could be a col-lab. What's the story, Welch?"

"I'm not with them," he said, half choking on his words. "And you're right. I'm not really a Marine either. I used to—five years ago, I washed out for bad conduct. Then all this shit went down."

***

Jed told his whole story, about getting conscripted into the Civil Affairs unit, and finally teaming up with other Marines on the way into Manhattan. After that, the woman seemed like she trusted him, too. That got Jed on a roll. He told them everything he could remember, how the monsters attacked him and the Marines, and the other units converging on the fire station. Then how the firefighters had come out to rescue them all and it only ended up being Jed, Meg, and Rex who survived.

"Where are they? The firefighters?" the woman asked him.

Jed's throat seized up. He couldn't tell them what happened to Meg.

What I let happen.

He opened his mouth, and tried to get the words past his tongue, but the woman interrupted him.

"Never mind," she said. "How'd you get here? You said the fire station was in the Upper East. This is Spanish Harlem."

"We left the station this morning. After the Air Force did their last runs, it got kind of quiet. Whatever they dropped, it killed most of them things."

"But not all of them," she said.

"No. There's plenty left. Underground."

"We know," said the guy on Jed's left. He had a heavy beard along his jaw line, heavier even than Jed's, and it had been two weeks since his face had last seen a razor's edge. Jed let his eyes wander over the man's uniform until he spotted his name tab under the grime. He could only see a few letters.

M-A-H-T-

"You keep staring at me like that, I'll ask you for a cigarette when you're done."

Jed laughed, remembering all the trash talk from boot camp and his old unit. He stopped laughing just as fast, because nobody was laughing with him.

The guy on his right stepped a little closer, still holding his weapon aimed at Jed's chest. He narrowed his eyes at Jed and stayed coiled up like a serpent ready to strike.

"Hey," the woman said, snapping Jed's attention back to her. "What do you know about this Tucker asshole? He sounds like the guy who's been handing soldiers over to the sucker faces."

Jed staggered back a step and the guy on his right followed him with the muzzle of his weapon.

"I don't know who he is or why he's doing it," Jed said.

"Bullshit," said the guy aiming his M4 at Jed's heart.

"I ain't lying. Tucker killed a bunch of Army guys over on 99th below 3rd. I got there right after it happened. One of the guys was still alive. He told me it was a guy named Tucker doing it."

"Where's this *Army guy* now?" the woman asked.

"He's dead. He asked me to pray for him and I did. Him and the rest of his squad. That's where I got all this gear. But Tucker took almost everything else. All their weapons and ammo. He missed the one I have because it was under a car."

The others all stared back at him, like they were waiting for him to admit he'd been part of Tucker's crew.

"You gotta believe me. I ain't with Tucker. You've seen him handing prisoners over to the sucker faces. That's what you call the things, right?"

"Yeah, and how do we know you weren't one of the people helping him do it?" the woman asked.

"I don't know how to prove I'm not. I swear, though, I only know the guy's name because Pivowitch told me."

"Who's Pivowitch?"

"The guy I prayed for before he died."

Jed's heart had climbed into his throat and he knew he was about to fall to his knees and beg them to believe day's weakening light into the stairwell, casting gray shadows across everything. Debris from the ruined floor and walls filled the stairwell, but Jed could tell it had all been positioned to make a path up to where the landing used to be. Jed was about to suggest they move the debris to make a barricade.

Sergeant Gallegos changed his mind.

"They can climb just fine, and we know this won't keep us safe. But it's the best we can do. You're part of the Stable now, Welch," she said, looking up at the ruined landing.

"You're hiding out up there?" Jed gaped at the splintered wood and broken stone above them.

"It's what we got. Ain't worth a damn if the suckers get in here again. But if the col-labs show up, this'll give us more time than if we'd stayed on the ground. C'mon."

She kept her M9 in her left hand and used her right to steady herself on the stairs as she climbed over and around piles of splintered wood and crumbled cinder blocks. At the top of the stairs, she paused to holster her weapon and then grabbed at a pipe running up to the ceiling above the second floor. Jed hadn't noticed the pipe because it was painted the same color as the wall.

Finding supports with her feet, Sergeant Gallegos moved up the wall like it was second nature. Her movements were fluid and practiced, and Jed couldn't resist a smile as he watched her ascend. She used the restraining bands that held the pipe in place as hand holds and to push herself higher with her feet. When she was above the second floor, she stepped her foot to the window sill and leaned away from the wall to look outside.

"Clear," she said over her shoulder before she shifted her weight left and made a sudden swing back to the right. With a grunt, Sergeant Gallegos flung herself across the open space above the ruined landing. Jed held his breath, seeing her suspended in midair and knowing she was going to fall. But she didn't come crashing down. She went into a roll on the remains of the second floor, just beyond where the landing had been.

One by one, Reeve and Mahton followed their leader, until it was just Jed on the stairwell trying not to get sick from the reek of piss while he stared at the pipe on the wall. His M4 felt like a lead weight. The others threw some trash talk his way, but just for a second. Reeve and Sergeant Gallegos moved out of sight, weapons up and ready. Mahton stayed back, keeping watch out the window. He took a knee by a doorway and waved a hand for Jed to get on the pipe.

"It's clear now, but that doesn't mean we got all day, Welch. You don't haul ass, it's going to a long and lonely night downstairs smelling like piss. Until they come in and find you."

Jed looked at the pipe, then at Mahton. He let his M4 hang on its sling, stepped up to the wall, and reached for the first hand hold. As he put his foot on the lowest support, about knee height, an animal shriek sliced into the silence around the building. It was followed by another, and then a chorus of the cries came to Jed's ears.

— 5 —

"They always do that around this time of day," Mahton said as Jed repositioned his left foot, preparing for the jump.

The climb up the pipe hadn't been anything like he'd feared. By the time he got the rhythm of moving his hands and feet from support to support, he'd already reached the second floor. Mahton told him to go a bit higher before he jumped.

"You're too low. You'll just scrape your chin on the edge if you try it from there. Check the hash mark."

Jed had to lean back from the pipe before he could make out the mark. The others had scratched a line across the pipe and written GO HIGHER in black marker above the line.

"How'd you know?" Jed had asked.

"Gunny Pacau tried it from there."

Jed didn't miss how Mahton's voice went low and still as he spoke.

Putting his foot on a line of conduit, he pushed himself higher. The shrieks and cries continued outside, and Jed had to fight to stay focused. He was hanging off a pipe nearly forty feet above the floor now. If he missed

mound of metal office furniture crammed into the space, stacked floor to ceiling. It even went up into the empty space above the ceiling tiles. Mahton's head poked out from the bottom left corner.

"C'mon," he hissed.

Jed dropped to all fours and scrambled through the opening as Mahton retreated. The makeshift tunnel was tight, and Jed's gear seemed to hang up every second as he struggled to make it through. Then he was out and Reeve was yanking him forward with a grin on his face.

"FNG Deke made it. I figured I'd seen the last of you, but I guess you're more Marine than you look."

Jed mumbled his thanks, even though he could tell Reeve still didn't quite trust him. The scraping of metal on metal had Jed turning around onto his ass. Mahton and Sergeant Gallegos were muscling a heavy desk back into place in front of the tunnel. With a shove, they jammed it forward, sealing them all into the hallway space behind the barricade.

"That's high speed," Jed said.

"The fuck it is," Reeve shot back. "If that's high speed, then my name's—"

"Shut it," Sergeant Gallegos said. "Mahton, show Welch around. Don't forget the fire holes. Reeve, you got first guard in the art gallery. I'm in the gym doing my PT and then I'll rack out. Mahton, you and Welch got the long shift up top. I rotate with Reeve at 1900. He'll relieve you at 0100 until first light. Rah?"

"Rah, Sergeant," Reeve and Mahton said together. Reeve lifted his weapon and marched down the hall, disappearing into a room off to the left. Angled beams of light came into the hall from the open doorway Reeve walked through. Jed could just make out sheets of paper fluttering along the walls in the room.

"This way, Welch," Mahton said, motioning for him to follow.

Sergeant Gallegos gave him a half smile as he passed her. "Glad you made it," she said.

"Oorah, Sergeant," he said, feeling the words come naturally for the first time since he tried on a uniform.

He followed Mahton further down the hall. Splinters of wood lay scattered around every room or office they passed.

"What happened to the doors?"

"Kindling. We had a lot of bodies to burn on our first night here. This room here's the gym. You can use it when you're not on guard, but you'll probably be sleeping then."

Jed paused outside the room. Mahton held up a few paces ahead, but it was clear he wanted to keep moving. Jed took in the exercise equipment. The room had actually been a gym once, for the people who worked in the building. Free weights, a leg press and two treadmills filled the space. Jump ropes dangled from a rack on one wall, along with two sets of boxing gloves. A speed bag and heavy bag hung side by side against the far wall.

Sergeant Gallegos stepped by Jed and set her weapon and helmet on the floor just inside the door.

"Y'all got somewhere to be, rah?" she asked as she undid her vest.

"C'mon, Welch," Mahton said. "We're supposed to be on the roof, and I still gotta show you the layout."

They moved in silence the rest of the way down the hall until they reached a closed door. "This is the barracks," Mahton said as he opened the door. "Sergeant G has her own room down the hall. Me and Reeve bunk here. Guess you'll be joining us. You can have that corner."

He pointed to the near corner then waved a hand to take in the space. "Welcome to The Stable."

They'd laid out two exercise mats along the far walls. Each bunk had a couple pillows on it that looked like they'd been yanked from office furniture. At the end of the bunks they'd set up desk drawers to serve as foot lockers for whatever personal items they still claimed. Jed saw a couple photographs, some chewing gum and extra boot laces. In the far corner they had stacks of MREs, most of them still in the cases.

"Where you'd get all the chow?"

"This survivalist dude. He lived a few blocks away from here and had this all loaded up on his truck. He was driving through the city looking for survivors when we spotted him our first day here. Tucker and them took him prisoner."

"What happened?"

"His truck ran out of gas after we made the second supply run from his place. So we had to hump the last load. It was each of us carrying a case of MREs. The guy couldn't keep up with us. I hated him when we first met. Just—he was one of those people who would always need someone else to save him. But without him, we'd have starved and run out of ammo."

Mahton stepped further into the room, revealing a heavy desk and high back office chair just inside the doorway. A SAW mounted on a tripod filled the desk. It looked to be just right for someone sitting in the chair.

Three extra cans of ammo were stacked on a second chair. With a fourth in the weapon, they were set up to hold off almost anything.

"Fucking hell. That dude had all this in his attic?"

"He scavenged most of it. Before this world went to shit, he probably spent most of his time with a joystick in one hand and his dick in the other."

Jed and Mahton shared a short laugh, but quickly went silent. The survivalist guy may have been a lard ass who couldn't keep up, but he'd secured enough chow and ammo to keep Mahton's team alive for a good long while.

You never know who's gonna show up and be the blessing that you need.

Jed's mother used to tell him that all the time, back in Georgia. Before she threw him out of the house and sent him to New York to live with his grandma. He could still hear the cadence of her voice, the way she'd say everything like it was a warning.

Maybe that was why he ignored so much of what she'd told him back then. He'd let her down so many times and in so many ways.

Am I getting another chance here, to do what's right? Maybe I'm supposed to be the blessing these people need. Or they're the blessing for me.

"What happened downstairs?" Jed asked, remembering the way the lobby of the building had looked like an arena.

"They made people fight the things."

"Fight? How the hell—"

"I don't know, man. It's the big one. Fucking thing can still talk, and it gives orders. We saw it with some guys in digies. That must be the Tucker guy you were talking about."

"Wait a minute? What big one? Those things can't talk. They can't even—"

"It fucking talks!" Mahton's cheeks flared red behind the dirt and grime, and his eyes told Jed not to question him again. Not on this score.

"Okay, okay. It talks."

"It mostly spits and grunts," Mahton said, leaning against the desk for a beat. He stood up again and paced while he spoke. "I saw it, though, and heard it. The fucking thing gives orders. It can make words. The other ones listen to it, like the shit it says is the most important shit in the world. It made a deal with Tucker and them. They brought it the first prisoners and it let the other ones fight them, like it was teaching them how to survive by killing."

"Other ones? Like the other monsters?"

"Yeah, but some of them didn't seem to get it, you know? Like they were ate up. So the big one had the col-labs bring in prisoners and they got into the ring down there. We were all up here hiding out. We didn't know what they were doing until it was too late. By then—

"There were too many of them. We had wounded, and we were done, man. Just...fuck me, we were all done. I had nothing left that day.

"They set up the lobby for the fights. Fucking col-labs stood around and watched, and some of them—I swear, I ever see those motherfuckers, they'd better hope to hell they're fucking dead already."

Mahton paused to square himself away. Jed let him take his time, but he had so many questions eating him up inside.

"They cheered, like it was a fucking cage match. We could hear 'em, like—" Mahton stopped, and then turned away. Jed could tell the guy was holding in a mouthful of crying and then some.

"Hey, man. We'll get 'em back. The people Tucker took. If they're still alive out there, we're gonna get 'em back."

"I'm glad to hear you say that, Welch. But I'm not holding out for a win on this one. C'mon," he said, standing up and moving to the door. "Sergeant wanted me to show you the fireholes. And we're supposed to be on the roof. You need to see what we're up against."

— 6 —

Gallegos checked in with Reeve before she racked out. She'd done a few sets of curls. It hadn't been a full workout, but it warmed her muscles. That was enough.

Just get the blood moving, keep the mind alive.

She stood in the doorway to the art gallery now, debating whether or not she should take the first shift and let Reeve hit the rack ahead of her.

Mahton's drawings lined the walls. Reeve was staring hard at one of them in the opposite corner.

"Yo, Reeve. You good?"

"*Errr,*" he replied, turning on his heel and stepping into the room, where he had a better view of the window. She watched him walk and took in his stride. He moved like a robot, one foot in front of the other, eyes front, hands holding his weapon.

Finger on the trigger.

Gallegos pushed that thought away. It was a natural reflex for anyone standing guard in the gallery. The room only had one door and one window, which looked out over the street. If it came to it, and escape through the door wasn't possible, whoever was in this room had only one way out.

And they were three floors up.

The art gallery was probably an old conference room. It was long and narrow, with the window at one end and a drop down projector screen at the other. The screen was covered in Mahton's art now. Lines of charcoal and pencil formed what looked more like a child's scribbling than anything Gallegos would have called art, at least back before the MOMA was overrun with suckers and blood splatters became the only brushstrokes left for anyone to see.

Their platoon had nearly met their end in that building. Only she, Gunny Pacau, and a few of their men got out alive. That was where Mahton had grabbed his sketchpad and a few pencils.

"It'll keep me going," he'd said. And he was right. Even though his drawings were all pictures of the sucker faces, it had been enough to keep him from falling apart. She'd seen him near the breaking point so many times, and each time he picked up a pencil, it's like he went back to a time before monsters had eaten the world.

But Reeve doesn't have art or working out. All he has is that shit he stuffs under his lip. And it shows.

"Reeve, you need me to cover this shift?"

"I'm good," he said, spitting a wad of brown goo at the wall. It just missed one of Mahton's drawings.

"Don't bullshit me, Marine. You need down time, you gotta say something. Rah?"

"Rah. Oorah," he said, and looked at her over his shoulder. He'd stuck a pretty big wad of chew in his lip, making it bulge out. He looked like he'd been stung by some giant bee or wasp.

Reeve cracked a grin, the same one he always showed

her when he wanted to be left alone. His chew pushed his lip out even farther, making him look like a cartoon version of himself. Gallegos knew better than to push things with him, but she also knew that sooner or later, she'd run out of time to get him right.

We might be up one man with Welch joining us, but I'm still down half a man until Reeve gets squared away.

***

Mahton led the way out of the makeshift garrison and down more hallways full of empty offices and ruined furniture. Here and there he would point out a hole in the floor.

"Fireholes. They drop down into mop closets. If the suckers get in here, you make for the closest firehole. Bust out the door and haul ass."

"Where to?"

"Wherever the fuck you can. We have every hallway blocked from the entrances. You'll have to push your way through a barricade. The only easy way inside is from the roof. So if they're in here, somebody failed to hold our perimeter up top or in the guard rooms on the 3rd floor. That means we're short at least one of us and probably two."

Jed swallowed, thinking about what would happen if he was the guy who fucked up on guard duty. Would they decide he was working with Tucker and kill him?

Probably. If any of us are still alive.

Mahton pushed through a door into a stairwell and Jed followed. It took them up to the rooftop through an access door. Jed shielded his eyes from the glare as they stepped onto the tarred roof.

"Shit, it's bright," he said as he joined Mahton on the roof. "Guess that's good for us. They don't like the sunlight."

"Doesn't seem to bother 'em really. Not if there's food in their sight picture. C'mon."

They followed the edge of the roof toward the corner, pausing every few steps to listen and scan the city for any signs of the monsters. Mahton pulled Jed over to an air conditioning unit where they squatted down. A string of empty plastic water bottles dangled from a line of five-fifty cord. The cord was looped around the neck of each bottle in a quick-release knot. Jed was going to ask what they were for when he noticed the yellow liquid filling the last bottle.

"You guys save your piss?"

"Yeah, and it makes me sick to do it."

"Why?"

"Hygiene, motherfucker. It's fucking gross. You see any running water around you? Only water we got left is in a five gallon jug down in the barracks, and it ain't full. So taking a bath? Washing your hands? We got baby wipes, but they're about to run out, too. We gotta hold the piss bottle with one hand to make sure it doesn't spill."

Jed had to hold in his laughter. Mahton was killing him with this shit.

Dude's worried about getting a little piss on his hands when his face is covered in dirt and blood?

"You looked in a mirror lately, Mahton?"

"Fuck you, Welch. I'm dirty like you're dirty, because I

don't have a choice. I'd wash my hands every time if I could."

"So why don't you?"

"I said we're running out of wipes. We wash our hands once a day, after our last piss."

Mahton shrugged and shook his head like he wanted to forget the whole thing.

"What are you saving it for?" Jed asked.

"The suckers don't like it," he said. "It's a territory thing. When we get a bottle filled up, we take it down to the ground floor and pour it around the stairwell. That's why it's so stank down there."

Jed kicked himself for thinking Mahton was a candy-ass. He was doing what he could to survive. Just like Jed had always done.

Mahton nudged him to follow as he moved to the end of the cooling unit. They had a clear view of most of the city from there. And most of what Jed saw he wished he could forget. Destruction and ruin spread out like a stain in every direction. Seeing New York from this height, and in this state—it was like Iraq, all crumbling apartment blocks, and mounds of dust and debris everywhere he looked.

But it was so much worse. This had been home. These streets had been where Jed grew up, where he'd played, and where he'd had all the chances in the world to make something of himself.

And where he'd made all his biggest mistakes.

Now there was nothing left to remind him of the life he'd almost lost running with the bangers in high school. Or the life he couldn't save in the sewers down below the street.

Meg, I'm sorry. If I'm getting a second chance here with Mahton and them, I'ma make it right. I won't waste the life you gave me.

Jed sucked in a breath, swallowed his tears, and focused on the city again.

A path of bombs had leveled nearly every building around them except for two high rise apartments on the opposite side of the depot. The bombers had dropped their payloads in diagonals through the neighborhood, bringing down smaller apartment blocks, office towers, and every mom and pop pizza joint for as far as the eye could see. But they'd left the bus depot and nearby high rises untouched. Jed was stunned at how the depot seemed to stand above everything now, and it was just a four story building.

Mahton slid away from the air conditioning unit and waved Jed to follow. They moved together, duck-walking over to the low railing that ringed the rooftop, aiming for the corner that looked out over Lexington Avenue. Bits of the railing had fallen away in places. Jed froze when he saw claw marks and blood stains around one missing section.

"That's where they came up, huh?" he asked.

"Yeah, the suckers spotted the civilians hiding in the top floor offices. They had weapons and were pulling guard shifts when we got here. They were pretty good, I guess. Almost good enough."

Mahton waved Jed forward again as they made slow progress to the corner of the roof.

"Somebody fell asleep on guard?" Jed asked when they got in position.

"More or less. It was a guy who worked in this building. Dude was a fucking idiot. He knew all the hiding spots. Him and this girl he was banging forgot to keep one eye on the windows while they got busy."

"How'd you know?"

"We found them, still joined at the hip but missing their throats. The suckers took them out first, then ran through the halls eating up everything that didn't shoot back. And that was most of them."

"You, Sergeant G, and Reeve..." Jed let the rest of his question go unasked. Mahton ran a hand under his nose and told Jed to keep an eye on the street below.

"I gotta hit the head. Stay here, and stay low."

Jed nodded and went back to watching the quiet ruins. Nothing moved except the wind, blowing dust and debris across the shattered landscape. The city seemed to breathe around him again, a shaking and stuttering sort of inhale and exhale. New York looked ready to die any day, but it just wouldn't give up the ghost.

"Maybe you're waiting for someone to save you, huh?" Jed said to what was left of the skyline. He eyeballed every intersection and every still-standing building, but it was like watching sand dunes walk. If anything was alive out there in the city, he couldn't see it.

***

Gallegos laid down on her mat and stretched every muscle in turn, starting with her neck. Two days of living like animals and she still couldn't go to sleep without her little rituals. She flexed her forearms, then rotated her wrists. She spread her palms and stretched her fingers.

Then Alexandra Gallegos let out a deep breath as the weight of the day slid off her.

Half a beat passed and she rolled onto her side, scooped up her vest and shrugged into it. She sat up, strapped on her brain bucket, grabbed her M4 and clipped it onto its sling.

Reeve needs a break more than I do. My mission, my men, myself. Always in that order. Always until the end.

Jed felt Mahton come up beside him again. "Pretty fucked up, isn't it?" he said.

"Yeah, it is. Did the flyboys know you were here?"

"I don't know. Everywhere you look it's the same thing. Piles of shit on top of piles of shit. I think we got lucky."

"Maybe it wasn't luck. Maybe it was God looking out for you."

Jed continued scanning the city streets, what was left of them. Only Lexington Avenue was clear of damage in this area. All the cross streets were pockmarked, and in some places so badly blown apart that nothing would travel on them again. Even Park Avenue was full of rubble and shattered glass.

"I bet that's what it was," Jed said. "God spared this building."

"Maybe," Mahton said. "Whenever I look out there, I kinda think God gave up on us. Or maybe the bombers were told where to drop their payloads and this wasn't it. I don't really care. But it's that building you should be worried about."

Mahton pointed across the track of destruction left by

the bombs to where a low and also undamaged building hugged an intersection on the opposite corner of the next block.

"That used to be a fire department and police precinct," Mahton said. "Now it's the col-lab's stronghold."

The building was a lot like ones Jed had seen in Iraq, stout and thick, surrounded by destruction, and painted the color of sand. A parking lot behind it was mounded on all sides with debris and the ruins of cars and vans. Tangled pieces of chain link fence hung over the edge of the parking lot, like the claws of some demon rising out of the earth. And right in the middle of all that, in a cleared space, sat a black dual-wheeled pickup truck. Even from this distance, Jed knew it had to be the truck he'd seen earlier.

As he and Mahton watched the building, two figures exited a door, hopped down a short flight of steps, and walked over to the pickup. They stood near it talking for a bit. Jed wished he could hear them.

"Is that Tucker?" he asked.

"Shit, I don't know," Mahton said. "We don't have any binos, unless you've been hiding a set up your ass."

The figures by the truck finished whatever they were talking about and got into the vehicle. Another figure stepped out from behind a debris pile and moved to open a gate that was up against the building. It slid aside with a squeal, showing a clear path out of the parking lot, under a breezeway.

"So that's their hideout," Jed said.

"Yep," Mahton said. "We get lucky, someday we might be able to take them out and move into the place.

That building's a lot more secure than this one."

Jed focused on the truck. He didn't know who was driving it, and he didn't care. If it came close enough, he'd do what he should have done earlier.

Take 'em out. The driver first and then whoever survives the crash.

The truck wheeled away down Lexington, heading toward East Harlem. A few blocks up, the driver navigated a tight turn to avoid a crater that filled half the intersection. The rumble of the motor faded as the truck disappeared from view around the corner.

"They'll be back quick," Mahton said.

"How do you know?"

"All those craters in the road. There's only a few streets they can still use, so they don't have that much range. Besides, you try driving around a city run by monsters and see how fast you make for home."

"I thought you said they worked together."

"They work with one bunch, but there's more out there. More of the big ones giving orders and shit. We've seen at least two more, not counting Tucker's boss. It's like they got little gangs. This one made a deal with Tucker and his guys. Doesn't mean he can just hang out on the block. The other ones will tear his ass up."

Mahton went quiet and Jed figured he should let it drop. He'd learned enough about Tucker's operation in the short moments he'd spent on the roof. The mission was clear in his mind: Stop Tucker and save as many people as he could before they got turned into dummies for gladiator matches with the monsters.

Jed was about to ask Mahton if he'd ever seen other monsters attacking the truck when it appeared again, coming fast down Lexington, and this time from the same direction as it had when Jed was on the street. The truck pulled to a stop and idled half a block down from the depot building.

"How'd they get around behind us? Do you think they know we're up here?"

"Ran a circle around the neighborhood. That's what they usually do. Head out one direction and come back from the other. But they don't usually stop like that. Keep an eye on them. I'ma tell Sergeant G about this." Mahton duck-walked across the roof until he was at the air conditioning unit, then he ran in a crouch to the access door. Jed kept as still as he could, monitoring the truck and hoping against hope that he'd get a chance to end Tucker's operation right then and there.

— 8 —

Gallegos stepped into the ruins of another old conference room, on the Lexington side of the bus depot. She'd tried to convince Reeve to rack out for a while, but he was too wired from his dip. So she'd left him covering Park Avenue and came over to support Mahton and Welch watching Lexington.

Guess I'm too wired myself. Or maybe this is it. Maybe the collabs are about to make their move and my gut's telling me to stay on point.

She'd been worried that Tucker's people knew they were in the bus depot and were just waiting for the right moment to make an assault. She and her team could hold off a squad of men maybe, but more than that...

A rumbling engine echoed through the streets and Gallegos moved deeper into the room. She couldn't go too far forward because the windows at the end of the room were all blown out. She'd be spotted by anyone in the col-lab stronghold if they had binos.

With New York in a state of permanent sleep, even the slightest movement would be noticed. Her aunts used to talk about what could happen in a *New York Minute*, like it was a sight to behold, this huge city bustling and swarming with activity. They'd come over and drink with her mom and dad, laughing loud into the late night and telling stories about what they'd seen around the neighborhood.

Gallegos was still just *Little Alexa* back then. She envied her aunts for their life of freedom, the way they could come and go, walking up and down the streets with friends, going into clubs or bars.

They'd loved this city and never had a bad thing to say about it.

If you could just see it now.

The rumbling sounded again, and Gallegos crouched into the shadows of the far wall. The truck had to be idling nearby. She dropped to the prone and crawled herself forward through the debris, brushing aside pebbles of window glass as she moved.

She halted her movement just a foot from the window. A second truck engine growled through the dead streets. When it came to an idle outside, Gallegos slowly pushed herself forward with her feet and lifted her abdomen off the floor, straining so she wouldn't drag against the debris or snag her gear as she moved.

Weak voices came into her position from the street below. If it weren't for the silence of the dead city she wouldn't have heard a word being said. As it was, she had to strain to stay focused and ignore the urge to bring her weapon up and start shooting.

"Get 'em?"

"Yeah. *Four more feedbags. Said they were part of that Reaper bullshit.*"

"*Any ammo?*"

"*Not much. Couple mags' worth.*"

Gallegos had heard enough. She and her men had been assigned to Operation Reaper. They were supposed to take back the city. They'd come in hot with air support and armor. And they'd lost everything.

Now the col-labs had captured some of the survivors of that failed mission.

Gallegos shifted her weapon to the side and rotated it to aim the muzzle behind her. If she was about to see what she feared... She edged forward, keeping her head tilted to the side so she only had one eye on the street.

What she saw made her insides burn as she fought the urge to raise her weapon and open fire.

***

Jed kept low and tight against the railing. He could still see the truck below. It had stopped and was idling there next to the wrecked busses in front of the depot.

Had they seen him? What were they doing just sitting there in the street?

The monsters could show up any second and—The driver's side door opened and a man stepped out. Even from four floors up, Jed could identify his camouflage uniform, and the M4 he carried across his chest on a sling. Another man got out on the passenger side and took up a position behind the truck. He stood guard in a relaxed pose, like Jed used to do when he was keeping an eye out on quiet airfields.

Back before I fucked it all up and got shit-canned by the corps.

The guy on the street had the same casual attitude, just leaning up against the truck and putting his hands in his pockets like he was waiting for something and wasn't worried about any hostile contacts in the meantime. Quick as Jed could blink, the driver was beside the other man and slapping him hard on the shoulder. He stuck a finger in the man's face and gave him a dressing down.

"Get right, son. Weapon at the ready. Eyes on your AO."

How's it feel, buddy? Jed thought, remembering the times he'd been dropped into a front-leaning rest while he got lectured on the proper way to stand up.

Down on the street, the two men separated, with the driver going back around the tailgate to stand on his side of the vehicle. The other man held his weapon up now and paced a small circle beside the passenger door. The rumble of another engine echoed on top of the idling truck motor below. Jed scanned the area and spotted a second dual-wheeled truck coming their way down Lexington. Unlike Tucker's, the second truck was stained with dirt and blood and God knew what else. Jed could barely make out the white paint underneath the mess. He kept his eyes on the truck, hoping to get a better idea of who was driving it. Then he saw the people in the back. He didn't want to believe what his eyes were showing him, but it was plain to see.

They're prisoners! Shit!

Four people were piled in the truck bed, all bound and with hoods over their heads. And they all wore uniforms. The second truck came to a stop and the driver got out. The man posted behind the first truck went over with his weapon at the ready. They exchanged some words but a wind gusted over the rooftop and Jed couldn't hear what was said. The men shook hands, then stood still, like they were waiting for someone else to show up.

The next thing he knew, Jed was rubbing his eyes to

make sure he was really seeing what he thought he was seeing.

Can't be. Can't fucking be real. No way.

On the street below, while the men by the trucks stood guard, a small group of the monsters crawled from where they'd been hiding behind piles of rubble. The whole block had been leveled by bombs. Somewhere in that mess of ruins and destruction, the monsters had an entrance to their underground hive. Jed hadn't noticed them coming out because he'd been focused on the men in the trucks, hoping to identify Tucker.

Whoever the men were, they clearly weren't afraid of the monsters. They kept their distance, but they didn't shoot the things. From his high position, Jed couldn't see them as clearly as he had before, but he could make out their pasty white skin, and their joints clicked loudly in the quiet ruined street.

They're the kind that didn't die when the Air Force dropped those chemical bombs. They're the really bad ones. The ones that got Meg.

The monsters crawled across the roadway to the second truck where they clambered into the bed and grabbed the prisoners. One by one the people were yanked from the truck by clawed hands. Jed didn't hear any screams, and guessed the prisoners were gagged under their hoods.

Or just scared to death.

The monsters collected the prisoners and made their retreat, still not making a single move toward the men with the weapons. Jed wondered what it would take before the monsters would turn on the human collaborators. Would they have to be starving somehow?

Is that why the men were trading prisoners away like this?

They're keeping the monsters fed, so they'll leave Tucker and his crew alone.

Then Jed slapped a hand across his own mouth and held in a scream of terror, because he saw the big one. The one that Mahton had told him about. It lumbered out from the mess of rubble that used to be apartment buildings across Lexington Avenue. The smaller monsters crawled and skittered just like others Jed had seen. But this one walked upright, and it was huge. How the hell had it survived, and why was it so much bigger than the others?

The giant stepped out from the debris and crossed to the middle of Lexington Avenue while the smaller monsters carried the prisoners and ran across the street, disappearing into the rubble.

Jed caught sight of where they went only because one of the prisoners finally tried to fight back. The person was being carried on a monster's shoulder and tried to lash out with a foot at another monster nearby. That earned him a clawed hand across his throat. The prisoner relaxed instantly. Jed could still see the person moving. He cursed himself a coward. He should be taking out the col-labs and the monsters right now.

Before he knew he had even done it, Jed had lifted his weapon and sighted on the big fucker. It stood in the middle of the street with its arms out to the sides. It made scooping motions, like a wizard trying to cast a spell.

Then it grunted something and Jed ducked back down behind the railing. He'd heard it speak. He'd heard what it said.

"Eat… Hungry! More!"

Taking a breath and blowing it out, Jed spun back around and sighted onto the street again. The big monster was stomping back into its hiding place. The two men on the street stayed put, watching the thing leave. Jed drew a bead on the driver of the second truck, the one that had carried the prisoners.

You first, then the other guy. If you're Tucker, then this shit ends right here, right now.

Out of nowhere, Mahton's hand sliced swift and sharp, knocking Jed's hand away from the trigger. In a flash, Mahton had him down on his back and pinned against the roof.

"Do not, under any circumstances, fuck this up, Welch. You let those motherfuckers know we're here and any chance we have of getting our people back goes straight to hell. That's where you're going if you pull some shit like that again. You are not cleared hot. Not until Sergeant G gives the word."

Jed wrestled against Mahton's weight, but the other man was bigger and stronger, and he had the upper advantage. After one last try at getting his arms free to shove Mahton off him, Jed gave up.

"Fuck man, I wasn't going to fire. Just—if we can see those fuckers, why can't we take 'em out? That's gotta be Tucker down there."

"We don't know who it is," Mahton said. He slid aside and let Jed come to a crouch again in the shadow of the railing. "More importantly, we don't know their strength level yet. That could be half of what we're faced with."

"Or it could be all they got."

"Could be, but we don't know for sure. Until we do, we don't take a shot."

On the street below, the men were climbing back into their trucks. Jed fought the urge to snap his weapon up and lay into the departing vehicles. By the time he had himself squared away, the trucks were taking the corner at 102nd Street. He watched them crawl up the street, pull through the breezeway, and emerge into the lot behind the stronghold.

Did I just let them get away after they gave prisoners to the monsters?

Jed looked Mahton in the eye. "I saw it, man. The big one."

"Yeah? So you're a true believer now. Good for you. What was it doing? Did you hear it talk?"

Jed paused, afraid to say the words he heard in his mind. He went back to watching the stronghold.

"They gave it four prisoners. They were all wearing digies, man. All of them. We have to get down there. No way, no how, am I letting those fuckers get away with this."

Mahton's radio crackled and he moved aside to listen to the transmission. He grunted a reply and came back next to Jed in a crouch.

"Good timing, Welch," Mahton said.

"What do you mean?"

"I mean Sergeant G just told me the same thing. She was watching it go down from inside. We move on their stronghold tomorrow morning."

— 9 —

Jed stretched and yawned, shaking himself awake. He'd woken up every hour it seemed, but when he had slept, he'd dreamed about being safe and with his best friends from school.

Mahton and Reeve were already up, with Reeve pulling the last watch of the night. Mahton was cleaning his weapon on his bunk in the corner. Reeve stood by the doorway with his weapon at the ready, eyeing Jed but without the suspicion of the previous day. Instead, it was like he expected Jed to do something and was waiting for him to figure it out. When Jed didn't move except to stretch his neck, Reeve spoke up.

"Square away your bunk, Welch. And get your cover on. Sergeant G is on her way down."

Jed looked at Reeve and Mahton's bunks and saw they'd been straightened up. He shrugged into his vest, then set his helmet on his head before squaring away his AO.

When he was done, it didn't look much different from when he'd got up, but he had to admit the ritual made him feel a little better. He was more alert at least. Reeve nodded at him and lowered his muzzle another inch or two, almost relaxing his stance enough for Jed to think Reeve had finally decided to trust him.

Sergeant Gallegos stepped into the room and Reeve greeted her.

"Good morning, Sergeant," he said.

Mahton set his still disassembled weapon on the floor and stood up. Jed found his body moving on auto-pilot as he took up a position next to his bunk.

Back straight, eyes front. Hands at the small of my back, feet shoulder-width apart.

It had been a long damn time since Jed had moved that fast for anyone, but when Reeve greeted the sergeant, his words put Jed in a different head space. He snapped to without a second thought and waited for his orders.

***

Gallegos slung her M4 and checked she had a full magazine in her sidearm. Extra ammo, what little she had left, was stowed in the pouches on her vest. The weight of all the gear was familiar, and comforting.

Like a blanket you don't dare take off, no matter how hot it gets.

She would have traded some of her ammo for an IFAK, but her entire squad had used up what little first aid gear they'd had during the first two hours of Operation Reaper. Shrugging away the memories of that mission gone to hell, Gallegos stepped into the room and suppressed the urge to grin when Reeve said *Good morning.* Welch immediately stood at parade rest. She entered with a quiet step, just like Gunny Pacau would do when he inspected them. She scanned the room just like Gunny Pacau would do, and didn't miss noticing that Welch's bunk space was squared away, just like Reeve's and Mahton's were.

They're looking out for him. That's good. We might actually make it through this.

Gallegos went up to Reeve and gave him a once over. He was good to go. Same old Reeve. Cheeks all cut up from him dry shaving with his ka-bar, and probably enough funk under his fingernails to fill a fart sack. But he was good to go. Even though she'd had her doubts the day before, this morning Reeve was a US Marine, nose to toes.

She slapped his shoulder and nodded, then walked across the room to Mahton. She gave him the same quick inspection, noticing he'd tried to comb the wiry curls of his beard into shape. It almost worked. She gave him a nod and slapped him on the shoulder.

"Get your weapon squared away. Locked and loaded, ready to rock."

"*Errr*," he said and immediately dropped down to the mat he slept on. He scooped up the rifle, clicked the upper receiver into place, and reached for a magazine. Gallegos left him to it and walked back across the room to stand in front of Welch. She gave his bunk area a quick check, letting him sweat it before she met his eyes again.

"Looking good, Welch. You ready for this? You ready to be a Marine?"

"Oorah, Sergeant," he said, not missing a beat.

"I like to hear it louder, Welch."

"*Oorah, Sergeant!*"

"That's better." She thought about giving him a dose

71

of Gunny Pacau's best medicine, a little dressing down just to help the man stand up straighter, but Welch's voice and attitude said enough. He was good to go just like the rest of them.

"As you were, men."

Reeve was always relaxed, and Mahton was more or less the same. He stood a little straighter than Reeve, though, and with his weapon slung and ready. Welch, though…the dude just stuck at parade rest, like maybe he broke something because he moved too fast when she'd walked into the room.

"I said 'as you were', Welch. At ease."

Gallegos relaxed herself when Welch softened his stance and let his arms hang a little more loose. He seemed ready. But her doubts resurfaced. She still had to know for sure he could be trusted. If nothing else she did today went right, she had to at least start on a good foot. That meant knowing she could trust the men under her command, and knowing that they trusted each other as well. Gallegos didn't miss the shifty look Reeve kept throwing in Welch's direction.

He's still not convinced Welch is cool, and if I'm being honest, neither am I. Gotta get things right before we move out.

"You said you were Army before this, rah?"

"No, Sergeant. I—they picked me up, kinda drafted me I guess. When it all started, it was everybody on deck, you know?"

"Assholes and elbows, yeah. Was the same with us."

She paused for a beat, remembering what it had been like when they got to New York City in the early light of May 4th. The room stayed silent while she dragged herself out of her memories for the second time that morning.

"I'm from New York, you know? Grew up here. Like you. But we all used to be out of Camp Lejeune. Reeve and Mahton and me. Motor Transport 2/2. The Workhorse. Before that it was Afghanistan. We were on deck to deploy again when they called us up for Reaper."

"Reaper? What's that?"

"Just some shithead's idea of taking back a city that was already too far gone. We were supposed to clear the streets, make sure the suckers were all dead. Confirm what parts of New York were good for recapture. Joint forces would move in. Secure the city block by block. Except that didn't happen."

She let him take it in, watching to see if he flinched or showed any sign of being part of the clusterfuck that was Operation Reaper. Thousands died within the first few minutes of the effort to take back New York, and the few that remained either split off by platoon or squad, trying desperately to survive, or they turned tail and hid out somewhere, hoping it would all be over when they poked their chickenshit heads out again.

Was he one of them?

Welch met her gaze, but quickly moved his sight picture to a distant point in the room.

He's guilty about something. Was he a deserter?

She, Reeve, and Mahton found a guy playing possum, hiding in the bathrooms in the ruins of the art museum. His squad was wiped out in seconds, and he'd only survived by being the point man. Sucker faces had taken down the rest of his unit and were too busy eating to see him running full tilt into the MOMA.

Then he'd tried to run from us, and Reeve lit him up for being a coward. The gunfire drew the monsters to our location and we lost almost everyone we had left. Now we've been given this man to help us.

"We did what we could, Welch. But we lost our unit. We lost our mission. Then this Tucker asshole comes around and we have a mission again. We had each other before. And now we got you. Welcome aboard, Marine."

She extended a hand, and he grasped it, giving her a firm shake. She slapped a hand on his shoulder and looked him square in the eye before releasing him and stepping back.

"This is the game plan," she said, standing in front of them with her arms framing her slung M4. "We know the col-labs move out after first light to scout for hostages. We know they go out again in the early evening, before dusk, so they can avoid the other sucker crews in the area. We've seen them hunting during twilight mostly. Tucker's agreement with them must be to stay buttoned up until the hunt is over.

"His team is small, maybe a squad at best. They have two vehicles. My guess is it's Tucker who always drives the black truck. Whoever is in it, he takes a spotter with him when he goes out.

"It's the same with the other truck. Always a two-man team, at least as far as we've seen. That means our best chance will come when both trucks are gone. We missed our chance yesterday because we were busy saving Welch's ass and getting him up to speed. That's okay, though, because now we have two teams ourselves."

Gallegos relaxed and leaned back against the desk behind her, waiting for the men to ask their questions.

"Who's with who?" Reeve asked, giving Welch a look out the corner of his eye.

"You and Welch, me and Mahton," she answered. Reeve huffed once, blowing his breath out. Gallegos was in his face before he had time to blink.

"You and Welch. Me and Mahton. Those are the teams. Rah?"

"Rah. Oh, yeah," Reeve said, stepping back once to put space between them. She didn't close it up, and Reeve seemed to take that as permission to keep his mouth running.

"Oo-double-rah. Me and Private Fucking Schmuckatelli here. Been nice knowing you, Sergeant. You too, Mahton. Make me the fucking fall guy, I get it. Don't rush on my account, but when they finally get you, I'll be holding the door to hell wide open so you can come and join us."

Gallegos stepped forward like she might kick Reeve in his junk. Then she laughed, a short little bark that ended with her putting her hands on her hips and sending Reeve a shit-eating grin to end all shit-eating grins.

"That's why I like you, Reeve. You never back down from a fight. Maybe now you get why I want you with Welch? He doesn't know this building like you do, or those streets outside. I seen his kind before, back on the block. He's from Brooklyn or Queens. Ain't you, Welch?" she asked, turning to look him in the face.

"Yeah. Yes, Sergeant. I grew up in Corona and Elmhurst. Never saw Manhattan before all this really. Might have been here once."

"So, Reeve," Gallegos said. "I need Mahton at my six and Welch needs you at his."

"He's point man? Fuck, I'm toast. Ate up like—"

"Ain't nothing ate up except what Tucker'n them are doing," Welch said.

Mahton chuckled. "See, Reeve. Welch knows the score. He's ready to bring the pain to Tucker's operation."

"Okay," Reeve said, putting his hands up, palms out. "Fuck it. I give. What's the plan again?"

"Already covered that part," Gallegos said. "Need me to break it down Barney style?"

Reeve chuckled, licked a finger, and marked a '1' in the air. "Point goes to you, Sergeant. I've been voluntold."

Gallegos let him laugh it off, but she left room in the back of her mind to keep as close an eye on Reeve as she had on Welch. Before the day was through, she'd know if either of them were truly good to go.

But that's only if we all make it back alive.

Jed waited for Sergeant Gallegos to lay into Reeve, but she kept it cool. If she did have anything else she wanted to say to him, she did a good job of keeping it hidden. A beat after Reeve stopped talking, she pulled a map out of her pocket and spread it across the desk.

Jed and the others stepped up to flank her while she oriented the map and detailed her plans.

"We approach the stronghold from the northwest, here at the corner of Lexington and 102nd. That's where a gas station used to be. The fuel tanks underground made a crater when they went up. We have some rough terrain to navigate, but the apartments behind the gas station shielded Tucker's stronghold. And there's plenty of shit to hide behind over there. They shouldn't see us coming."

"I remember that place," Reeve said. "Last time we were on the street, we skirted the crater. That was before we knew Tucker was running his operation from the old police station."

"Lucky for us they were out on a run," Mahton said. "We'd be MREs otherwise. Marines Ready—"

"Enough shit, Mahton," Sergeant G said over her shoulder. A dark look swept across her face. Mahton must have caught it, too, because he shut his yap and even tucked his hands up at the small of his back.

Sergeant G picked up the thread and gave them the rest of her plan. "There's good cover for our approach, behind where the apartments used to be. We can use the alley there maybe. It lets out on the parking lot where they keep the trucks. Or we use the debris as cover to take out Tucker and his col-labs. They'll have maybe one or two people guarding the stronghold."

"How do you know?" Jed asked.

"We've been watching them. At first they just patrolled the immediate perimeter, taking out any of the monsters that came sniffing around. Then the big one showed up and started grunting at them. We didn't see the deal go down, but we know Tucker used to have a lot more people with him. Some Army. A few Marines. People from Operation Reaper that got wounded."

"Tucker made them fight the sucker faces. Right?" Jed asked.

She nodded. "They stopped hunting this neighborhood since then, or they all moved off somewhere else. It's like they've drawn territory lines. We've seen Tucker's crew patrolling the parking lot where they keep the trucks, and sometimes the street outside. They haven't been hassled by the monsters, so that makes me think we don't have a lot of them to worry about. It's just us against whatever's left of Tucker's army."

"I thought you said they only had a few guys, like maybe a squad. So I could have lit 'em up yesterday," he said, staring at Mahton.

"That's our best guess of their strength, Welch," Sergeant G said. "We've only seen a few pairs of boots walking around the stronghold since they made their deal with the monsters. It's possible they have more people inside that we've never seen, or maybe they're down to just the two teams you and Mahton saw earlier today. Maybe the other monsters out there got to 'em. But we don't know, and I'm not risking the last Marines alive in this city on a gamble. We go in careful and sure, assessing their strength every step of the way. When we learn something new, we adapt. We improvise. We come out on top by being smart, not rushing to shoot the first enemy we see."

Jed mumbled an *Errr*, and stood at rest again.

"What's priority one, Sergeant?" Reeve asked.

"Commo. From what we've seen, they always post one man on the breezeway gate with a radio. That dude is priority one."

Mahton sniffed. "None of them were ever Marines. Any fool knows one is none."

"Welch, you and Reeve hold position at the parking lot after we take down the gate guard. Mahton and I go inside and clean house. If the truck comes back, there'll be nobody to open the gate, so they'll be ready for something to go down. Light 'em up before they get inside, rah?"

"Rah, Sergeant," Reeve said.

"Welch?"

"Oorah!" Jed said, feeling the buzz of adrenaline burning in his arms and legs.

Mission first, everything else second. Tucker, your days are numbered.

— 11 —

Sergeant G gave Jed a handheld radio of his own. It was a beat up piece of green gear, but it worked. Mahton told him they'd collected as many as they could when they were retreating during Operation Reaper.

"We knew we'd need commo. As long as we got batteries, we got commo."

Jed went down the hallway and did a radio check with each of the others, confirming he could hear them clearly when they were out of earshot.

"Batteries are in short supply, Welch," Reeve said over the channel. "That one should last until we're done, or until you're done, whichever comes first."

Jed mumbled to himself as he stepped back down the hall. "Man, I hope that motherfucker can find a new attitude and fast."

Back in the barracks room, he double checked the fit on the tactical vest they'd given him. Then he squared off in front of Reeve and stared the man in the eyes. He'd had enough shit and wanted to clear the air before they moved out. Sergeant G saved him the trouble.

"Reeve, one is none, rah?"

"Rah. And two is one," he said, staring back at Jed like

he was daring him to make a move.

"So how about you and your other half get right, and get right fast. We're moving out. Now."

Sergeant G and Mahton checked their commo one more time and left. Jed kept eyeballing Reeve. A few beats passed and Reeve cracked a grin, shook his head, and broke the staring contest. He waved a hand in the air like he was swatting a fly before he went to the desk and hefted two of the ammo boxes for the SAW.

"That's your boom stick, Welch. Leave the M4 here. Grab the other two cans and make sure you got a full one locked and loaded in the weapon. And here," Reeve said as he reached into a pouch slung over his shoulder. He took out two small tubes with pull rings at one end.

"Flash-bangs. We got 'em from that survivalist dude. More shit he'd scrounged up."

"Good thing you found him first instead of Tucker."

"Yeah, no shit. Sergeant G wants us all to have a couple in case of hostages in the stronghold. Mahton has our last frag, but we're going with just bangers unless we have no choice."

Jed took the grenades and tucked them into a pouch on his vest. "Okay, man. Now what about that attitude adjustment?"

For a second Jed thought he'd pushed too hard, too fast. Reeve got a twitch across his cheek and he looked ready to throw the ammo cans at Jed's face. Then he chuckled and dropped his eyes to the floor.

"You're a candy-ass if I ever saw one, Welch. But you got balls. We'll be jake out there."

"What about in here?"

Reeve looked up at him and Jed saw nothing but fire

in the other man's eyes. Then his gaze softened. He reached into a pocket and took out a tin of dip. He opened it and held it out, like some kind of peace offering. Jed shook his head.

"We good, Reeve?"

"Rah," he said, after he'd packed a wad under his lip and stowed the tin again. "Sorry I've been a dick, Welch. I lost a lot of friends when all this shit happened. Sergeant G and Mahton are all that's left. Don't fuck things up for us."

"I feel you, man. I lost people same as you. I'm good to go."

Reeve turned his head and spat into the hall. He looked back to Jed with a goofy grin before he moved out. Jed went to the SAW and unhooked the pins holding it to the tripod. He slung it and hoisted the spare ammo cans in their bag. All the gear made him feel like a damn donkey at first. And Reeve's attitude still didn't sit right. Then Jed remembered where they were going and what they were doing.

We're coming after you, Tucker. For Pivowitch and his squad. For Reeve and Mahton and Sergeant Gallegos, and all the people you took from them. And for Meg. We're coming for you.

Jed caught up with Reeve and followed him through the warren of hallways and ruined offices. Jed stayed back about three yards and checked their six at every turn. Finally, they got to a firehole that Mahton had shown him the day before. Reeve held out a hand for the extra ammo cans.

"We go down here. Sergeant G and Mahton are already on the street. You first."

The firehole dropped them into a mop closet on the

first floor, which let out into a service hallway at the back of the building. They stepped outside into a dark covered drive that extended from the street down to berths holding busses that would never be used again. The busses sat behind metal screens that dropped from the ceiling.

Their headlights stared back at Jed like dead eyes.

Smoke stained the ceiling in front of the berths. Jed wrenched his gaze away from the blackened mounds of bone and cloth piled there. Trash and debris filled the middle of the three deep drives. Across the space, a low railing bordered a raised walkway. A string of windows lined the wall above the walkway. Yellow safety pylons stood at the far end, nearest the street.

Reeve went fast through the debris field in the driveway until he got to the yellow pylons. He waved for Jed to follow as he moved into the street. Jed emerged from the covered drive into a hazy morning with mist sprinkling through the air and nothing but silence in every direction.

The street was a mass of craters and rubble in every direction. Park Avenue sloped down from the bus depot in the direction they were headed. The tracks that ran alongside the avenue went from being level with their position to sitting on top of a brick trestle in an elevated run that stretched away for blocks. The brick was stained with smoke where it was still whole, but had been broken up by explosions every few yards. The tracks splayed out at these points like the rib bones of some dead giant.

"This is Park Avenue?" Jed asked. "Damn."

Reeve put a finger to his lips and paced along the depot's back wall, heading toward the next corner. When he got there, he signaled for Jed to take point. Keeping the SAW ready, Jed moved around Reeve to the front. They kept to Park Avenue, leap-frogging across open spaces, and made to the next block. Reeve had told him that Sergeant G and Mahton would be waiting for them two blocks ahead.

Jed stepped fast but carefully, sweeping the street and eyeballing every shadow like it held the threat of instant death. The tracks beside him reminded him of his entrance to Manhattan with the Civil Affairs unit. He shook those memories away and concentrated on his mission now.

Stay on point, stay on mission. Eyes out and weapon up.

Mounds of dead monsters littered the street. Some lay sprawled and alone in the middle of the road. Others were heaped together against the remains of buildings or the elevated tracks. Even with so many dead ones, Jed didn't dare let his guard slip.

I know you ain't all dead. You got plenty left underground.

Most of the buildings near the bus depot had been leveled or turned into skeletal ruins by the bombing runs. An entire block of apartments along 100th Street had tumbled like matchsticks into a tangled mess of splinters and concrete dust. Here and there Jed thought he saw a human body in the mess, but he never let himself look for too long. He could only pray they'd gone somewhere better.

As they neared 101st, Reeve tapped his mic and blew twice. That was their agreed signal to hold position, so Jed set down on one knee and rested the SAW on a mound of broken earth and concrete. He scanned the area, trusting Reeve to be doing the same at their six. In front of them was an open area that used to be a tree-lined alley between apartment blocks. Now it was just a mess of dirt, tree limbs, and rubble, with nothing but the frames of buildings to show where the apartments had once stood.

A crackling in Jed's left ear startled him so bad he nearly raced back to the depot. Then Mahton's voice came through his earpiece.

"Got eyes on you. Close it up so we can move."

Jed shifted to look back at Reeve. He made eye contact and signaled he was moving. One at a time, they sped through the open space and took up positions at the end of the block. Cars were scattered around like toys thrown by a giant child. The street was pockmarked in places, but most of the pavement was clear of obstacles.

Except for the stains and blood and wrecked cars. And bodies.

Like he'd seen when he was with Rex and Meg, the monsters that had died in the Air Force's chemical attack lay all over the place, filling the city with the stench of rotten fruit and death. They'd all succumbed instantly it seemed, with most of them just lying in piles in the middle of the street or on sidewalks. A few had tried to hide under cars. Their scabby, pale white legs jutted out with the clawed feet curled up in a clutch of pain.

Like I care what those things felt when they died…or do I?

Jed shook his head to clear his thoughts. He and Reeve continued their movement to the corner of 102nd Street where they connected with Mahton in a little hollow of debris.

Sergeant Gallegos wasn't there.

"She's scouting ahead. Said she'd be back in two."

Sure enough, Jed spotted the sergeant crawling over a

debris pile that loomed at the opposite end of the block. At first he thought she was a monster coming for them, until he saw the weapon in her hands.

***

Gallegos flashed a hand signal, clicked her mic, and blew twice to confirm it was her and not some col-lab shitbag. She breathed a slow sigh of relief when Mahton clicked his mic and flashed the matching hand signal. When she got down to street level again, she raced over and sheltered with her men.

"Tucker's about to move out. They're at the truck Four of them out there."

"Plan?" Reeve asked.

"Same as before. Take out their commo; get inside and clean house."

"What about after?" Welch asked.

"Make a run for it back to the hide."

Welch didn't say anything else. Neither did Mahton or Reeve. Gallegos put her hand out and one by one the men stacked theirs on top, like every committed team had done probably going back to ancient times. They'd all signed on for the mission and would complete it without any more questions being asked.

Or we'll die trying.

Gallegos led the men forward along 102nd Street. As Lexington came into view, she spied the crater left by the exploding gasoline tanks. It filled the opposite corner, like a great black pit in the middle of a city covered in concrete dust and rubble and ash.

A truck motor revved once and then rumbled steadily. In the thick silence, the doors slammed shut and the motor revved again. A scraping of metal on stone pierced the dead calm.

That's the gate. They'll be coming out soon.

Inch by inch, the black truck appeared from the breezeway. Gallegos held back the urge to race forward and open up on the col-labs as they exited their stronghold and turned to drive away. She felt Reeve and Mahton behind her and glanced back to see them glaring at the truck's tailgate, just as she had been doing.

"We're going to get them," she said. "This shit ends today."

"*Errr*," Reeve said. He shouldered his weapon and motioned for Welch to move out ahead of him. Gallegos waited while the men dashed across Lexington and into the crater. No sniper fire cracked the air, and no sucker faces came tearing out of the shadows.

Gallegos checked left and right, listening to the truck motor disappear into the neighborhoods up ahead. The street was clear, and she didn't see any signs of the monsters. Still, something kept nagging at her like an itch. What was she missing?

A bank of clouds rolled across the sky, partially obscuring the sun for a moment. Did she hear the suckers' joints clicking? Was that scraping?

No time to waste. Go! Go!

Gallegos nudged Mahton and raced across Lexington, listening to her teammate's steady footfalls behind her. She nearly stumbled at the edge of the crater, but hopped over the rim, dropping to a crouch and moving fast across the blackened pit. Shards of metal and bits of stone stuck out from the earth where the fuel tanks had once been. Gallegos skirted the obstacles and came up alongside Reeve and Welch on the other side. Mahton joined them moments later. Together, the four of them held position, scanning the rooftops and ruins.

Immediately in front of them were the remains of two apartment blocks on either side of an alley. Trees that used to fill the space were nothing more than blackened sticks poking out of the ground. Mounds of ash covered everything in the area.

Checking her men one by one, Gallegos caught Welch's stricken face. The dude looked ready to crumble just like the buildings around him. She tapped his helmet and signaled for him to keep his eyes out. He gave her a sharp nod and *Errr* in return, then went back to scanning his zone.

I hope to hell you don't lose it, Welch. Time to find out if I was wrong about you.

"Reeve, you and Welch will move out through the alley. Climb up to a vantage point there," she said, pointing at the mounded debris.

"Me and Mahton will come from this direction. I'll signal you when we're in position. Get eyes on us to confirm. You take out the gate guard first, then anyone who comes out to investigate. We'll move in and make sure the gate is secure. Then we go inside. Throw a flash-bang and clean house."

"What about the noise, Sergeant?" Reeve asked. "If Tucker's still nearby, he'll hear the gunfire and probably the grenade. And if it ain't him, the sucker-faces will hear it. They'll be on us like flies on shit."

"We deal with that if it happens. We've all seen how

the suckers are timing their hunts. They aren't just roaming around like before. They've got Tucker feeding them prisoners. Game plan right now is you and Welch secure the parking lot. Mahton and I go inside with a flash-bang. If they got hostages inside, we want to greet them with a smile, not a bunch of shrapnel in the grill. You stay ready to come in hot on our six, rah?"

"Rah," Reeve and Welch said together.

"Move out, Marines," she said.

Reeve and Welch peeled off and moved toward the alley. Mahton picked up beside her and they were scrambling over the ruins, making their way up the debris pile in front of them. The climb was a struggle with so much ash and dust. Every step could be a one-way ticket to a broken ankle or knee if the debris shifted under their weight. Scrapes and squeals of metal on concrete came from the parking lot.

He's closing the gate. Good. That'll give us more time in case Tucker comes back.

As they climbed, they found their footing on the remains of people's homes. Gallegos dodged around a splintered headboard and ignored the people's faces staring at her from behind shattered picture frames.

At the top of the pile, Mahton set down against a mound of earth and ash, sighting on the gate guard in the parking lot below. Gallegos set down beside him and scanned the lot for additional targets. The guard was closing the gate the final few inches. Gallegos thought about taking him out herself, but she'd told Reeve he could have the first kill. He needed it and she knew it.

I just hope it's enough for him to get focused. If that man goes rogue…

She spotted Welch and Reeve in the alley. They had made their own ascent and were in position. Gallegos clicked her mic and blew twice. Reeve and Welch both flashed a signal in reply.

She was about to give the command to move when she saw the white truck still sitting in the parking lot.

***

Jed scanned the parking lot from his position. The guard was struggling with the gate and almost had it closed. It was just like the shit Jed had seen insurgents use in Iraq, a heavy makeshift fence built of chain link and barbed wire. Tucker's version was all strapped together with plates of metal, tied with cables, and thick as hell. The guy on the ground gave a tug and scraped the metal across the pavement, finally bringing the gate closed. He leaned up against the stronghold when he was finished and put his hands on his knees as he breathed heavy and loud.

Man, if they didn't have a deal with the sucker faces, those things would be all over his ass in a heartbeat. He's making more noise than this city has heard in weeks.

Sergeant G and Mahton were in position a few feet away. She was shaking her head and looking grim. Jed scanned the area and spotted what was up. Tucker had taken the black dual-wheel, but the second truck was still in the lot. It was parked up against the debris pile Jed and Reeve had climbed.

Maybe she'll have us wait 'em out. See if the other truck takes off in a bit. But why did the guy close the gate? Shit.

Reeve nudged Jed in the ribs. Sergeant G was giving the *Go* the signal.

I guess we ain't waiting.

Reeve sighted on the gate guard. Jed held the SAW ready to light up the breezeway in case Tucker came back fast. He had just wheeled away down 102nd and was at least three blocks over by now. The gate guard was almost done having his little heart attack. He leaned back against the wall and fished a pack of smokes out of a pocket. A sharp crack from Reeve's rifle split the sky and the guard went down in a heap, hanging up on the barbed wire of the gate.

Sergeant G and Mahton were on the ground in a flash. They double checked the gate while Jed and Reeve kept watch over the area. Jed swept his muzzle from the door of the stronghold and back to the breezeway while Reeve watched the roof and other high ground for movement. Most of the buildings around the stronghold were no more than skeletons, but they still had plenty of places to hide.

A truck motor roared from somewhere in the ruins. Jed couldn't place it, and he prayed it wasn't a sign that Tucker was on his way home.

Please don't come back. Please don't come back.

If Tucker showed up before they'd secured the interior—

Sergeant G and Mahton dashed across the lot, moving past the white truck to the steps leading inside. They climbed the steps and breached the door. Mahton threw in the flash-bang and it clapped loud in the silent city, sending a ball of smoke out the stronghold door. Sergeant G and Mahton darted inside, with weapons up and at the ready.

A second later Reeve was on the ground and racing forward.

"What are you—?" Jed called after Reeve. They were supposed to stay put and keep an eye on the lot until Sergeant G gave the word.

Reeve roved the lot, quickly poking into every dark corner. Finally, he circled the white truck and signaled back to Jed that the lot was clear. Jed stayed put, still waiting on Sergeant G's command. Reeve posted at the tailgate of the truck.

Jed scanned and listened, willing the sound of a truck motor to stay distant. It rumbled somewhere out in the ruins, but even in the empty quiet of the city, he couldn't place which direction the sound was coming from.

Just stay away. Stay gone long enough for us to do this. And then come back home and get what you deserve.

Small arms fire rattled from inside the stronghold and Jed snapped his attention back to the door. Reeve was already moving, running toward the steps.

A hiss and shriek from behind spun Jed around. He flopped over on his back and sent a burst into the sucker face that was crawling up the debris pile to his position. It flailed and fell to the ground. Two more hung onto the ruins of the apartment block that loomed above him. Their mouths popped open, dripping with saliva, and their sickly pale flesh glowed in the early morning light. They sprang forward as Jed fired.

The suckers landed in the loose debris and scrambled to get a foothold. Jed fired at them, but they raced in opposite directions. He focused on one and sent a burst into its chest. The other was on him a second later. It tried to get its mouth onto his arm, but he got the hot muzzle of the SAW against its cheek. The monster reeled away only to whip its head around and under Jed's guard. It slashed at his vest, ripping at the material. Its claws snagged and jerked, making Jed's ribs ache as it thrashed him from side to side. Jed screamed at it and wrestled against its hands, twisting his torso and slamming the muzzle of his weapon into its face.

A rifle cracked loud behind him. Blood spattered across his chest and the monster went limp.

Jed felt an arm slip under his, gabbing onto his vest and tugging him out from under the dead thing. Ringing in Jed's ears muffled Reeve's voice as he shouted "Tell me you're good, Welch! Tell me you're good!"

"I'm good, man! I'm good!" Jed hollered and struggled out of Reeve's grip to a kneeling position. He scanned the area with the SAW up and ready. No more sucker faces were crawling toward them or lurking in the jagged ruins waiting to leap. At least none that he could see. It was quiet inside the stronghold. Jed sent a look at Reeve and gave him what he'd been holding in ever since they met.

"What the fuck, Reeve? I could've been a plate of fucking hamburger helper. Thanks for coming back to save my ass, but why the fuck did you take off like that? Sergeant G didn't give the word, did she?"

Reeve may have outranked him, but he was still just a PFC, and Jed was done with the guy and his shit anyway. Even if Reeve had NCO rank, it only mattered so much when the world was at an end. If you were just going to wear the rank and not live it…

Reeve still had a hand on Jed's shoulder. He dropped his eyes for a beat. When he looked back up, Jed saw the man was holding himself back. He had a war to wage, and Jed was getting in the way. "Let's get inside, Welch."

Jed shrugged off Reeve's hand and moved up to where he'd been before. The parking lot was empty and the stronghold door stood open like the mouth of a grave. Reeve told Jed to monitor the lot and said that he'd keep an eye on their six.

After a few minutes of not much changing, Jed finally broke the ice between them. "What do you think's going on? Are they still in there?"

"Yeah. They should be. Just keep an eye out. I'ma try the radio."

Jed caught the note of fear in Reeve's voice as he took a breath and thumbed his mic. "Golf-Mike, Romeo-Whiskey. Come in."

A beat passed and Jed knew they were done. Whoever was inside, they'd taken out Sergeant G and Mahton, and now they knew another team was out here. Like it was on cue, Tucker's truck engine rumbled through the empty city, and even though he couldn't place it, Jed knew it was closer than the last time he'd heard the heavy motor.

He's coming back. Sonofabitch!

Jed nearly sent a burst into the parking lot when his radio crackled with Mahton's voice. *"Whiskey-Romeo, go ahead."*

Reeve replied first. "Hostile contacts our side. Three suckers. Shitbirds may be incoming. You good?"

"Affirmative. Actual says Charlie-Mike. Cover our six from inside."

"Good copy. We're moving."

Reeve slapped a hand onto Jed's shoulder.

"Got a job to do, Welch. Let's go do it."

"Rah. No time to give each other a handy. But you're going first once the mission's done."

Reeve spit his tobacco into the dust beside Jed's elbow. It just missed him.

"We'll get right when we've got time to get right. And I don't do handjobs unless they're reach arounds."

"Guess that means I'm point man," Jed said with a grin.

"See, you know what's up," Reeve said and jerked his chin up, signaling Jed to move out.

He scrambled over the top of the debris pile, scanning left and right, up and down, always expecting another monster to leap at him in his peripheral. But he felt Reeve at his back and knew the other man was scoping the area as they moved. If anything came their way, one of them would see it before it got too close.

They reached the parking lot, dodged around the white truck, and moved fast to the steps. The growl of Tucker's truck sounded closer now. He had to be coming down Lexington, which meant he'd be at the breezeway in under a minute.

At the door, Reeve tapped Jed on the shoulder and they switched places. The SAW weighed heavy in Jed's arms as he took over monitoring their six. He swept the muzzle side to side and tried to focus on the shadows.

That's where you're hiding. I know it.

His vision blurred and he shook himself to stay alert. The shock of having the sucker on top of him only now settled in. His muscles twitched with fatigue and he nearly stumbled as he edged backwards into the doorway behind Reeve.

Reeve stayed with him for a beat and then moved out

fast through the stronghold. The room they'd entered was a narrow space. A blast mark on the floor showed where Mahton's flash-bang had landed. Across the room an old microwave filled a countertop near a sink. It was like a smaller version of the day room back in Meg's fire station. For a split second Jed expected to see her coming around the corner. Then he remembered the last time he'd heard her voice, screaming at him for help from the sewers. He nearly fell over on his ass with guilt.

Tucker's truck rumbled outside on the street, pulling Jed out of his pain. The engine revved once and then idled.

A radio crackled from a loudspeaker somewhere inside the building.

***

Gallegos and Mahton squared up in front of the prisoners. They'd found the group inside the fire station bays, all tied up on cots, except for a couple that sat alone against the wall. They'd been just inside when she and Mahton burst in after the flash-bang went off and were still pissed off about having the grenade thrown in so close to them. Gallegos didn't tell them it could have been worse.

No sense letting them know we have a frag. Not unless they make us use it.

The couple looked like husband and wife, and could have been people Tucker was going to give to the sucker faces. But she didn't get a clean vibe from them. Something about their eyes, and that neither of them were tied up when they'd come in.

The guy had one arm in a sling, and Gallegos just realized she couldn't see where his other hand was.

"Move your hand out in the open," she said. He stared her down and didn't move either arm. She wanted to call Reeve and Welch in, but if Tucker was coming back, she needed them at her six.

The guy with the sling shifted his weight from side to side.

"Why don't you just leave?" he said, earning him a look of death from both her and Mahton.

"You don't give the orders. You don't do or say shit unless I give the word. Clear?"

"You sound just like your partner. Fine."

"Partner?" She was ready to pop the guy, and maybe the woman, too.

But she's covered in bandages. And the others are tied up. Who's the threat here? Shit!

Mahton had already sprayed a couple bursts over their heads to get them to sit down and shut up. His face was twisted with anger, like he might do it again and might aim lower this time. The people on the cots stayed still and silent, but she knew they couldn't be with Tucker's crew. They all wore dark blue uniforms except for one young man in dirty scrubs. They were nurses and firefighters.

They can't be col-labs. Unless they're the team from the second truck and they're playing possum.

Before she could ask who was who, the crackle of a radio broke the tense air in the open bay.

"Homebase, this is Truck Daddy. Where the hell are you?!"

Despite the ache in her chest and arms from holding her M4 up, Gallegos nearly doubled over with laughter at what Reeve said in reply. His voice echoed through the stronghold and into the bay.

"Truck Daddy—are you for real with that call sign? That's ate up like a damn football bat. Anyway, this here is Bag o' Dicks. How about you open wide? Over."

Tucker came back with a string of curses. He went on for a solid minute just letting loose, and he didn't leave anything to the imagination. Some of it even had Gallegos wincing in disgust. Then an engine roared outside and the screech of metal on stone threatened to bring their operation to a fast and bloody end. She grabbed her mic.

"Romeo-Whiskey, on me, now!"

***

Jed wished he could get a line of sight on his people, but he had to watch the breezeway. Tucker was out there, and Jed was the only line of defense they had against him.

A voice cracked over a radio channel inside the stronghold. It was Tucker. It had to be. Nobody else could be *Truck Daddy*.

Nobody but that douche.

Jed held in a chuckle, but couldn't help barking out a laugh when he heard Reeve's reply. Seconds later, the roar of a revving truck engine filled the parking lot and a crashing and squealing of metal on stone split the stillness outside. Sergeant G's voice hollered at him over the radio.

The gate flew forward and the tailgate of Tucker's black truck shot through the breezeway. Jed lit it up with a burst. The truck shuddered then flew forward, bouncing over a speed bump in the breezeway and out to the street.

Jed sent another burst at them, peppering the fender and truck bed.

Tucker's voice crackled over the loudspeaker again.

"Whoever the fuck thinks he can walk into my house and play games is about to get a point five-oh sized wake up call. Let's see what kind of jokes you want to tell with my Barrett jammed down your throat! We got eyes on every exit. Go on and leave whenever you like, but don't run, boy. Don't you dare run. You'll just die real tired."

The loudspeaker crackled again and went silent.

"This guy's a fucking joke," Reeve said from deeper inside the building.

The rumble of the truck motor faded into the neighborhoods and Jed felt the emptiness of the city around them once more. All around the parking lot, the mounds of debris seemed to crawl with slinking monsters moving from shadow to shadow. But Jed knew it was just his eyes playing tricks on him. The city was dead and silent as far as he could see. The debris was the same as it was before.

Nothing but dust and ruins. And us, stuck here in this building until we decide to go outside and let Tucker shoot us from five hundred yards.

Sergeant G shouted over their radio net again.

"Romeo-Whiskey, move it!"

Jed backed down the narrow room until he couldn't see the parking lot through the door anymore. He heard footsteps clattering down stairs from somewhere behind him.

"Welch, let's go," Reeve called to him.

Jed turned to see Reeve coming down a flight of steps and going down a hallway that ended in a corner. With a measured pace, and still expecting a sucker face to come in the parking lot door at any moment, Jed moved past the stairs Reeve had been on. A faint glow like filtered sunlight came from around the landing, and he heard the hiss of a radio signal.

He checked back the way he'd come, through the little day room. The air around the doorway seemed to shake, but nothing moved into his sight picture. No monsters came flying through full of spittle and blood and scrabbling claws.

Jed finally let himself relax and moved around the corner to join Reeve and the others.

Jed followed the sound of Sergeant G's voice around the corner in the hall and into the open space of the apparatus floor. Thick pillars supported the roof, forming three separate places for the firetrucks to park. Heavy hoses hung from the ceiling, dangling like guts. Everywhere he looked, Jed saw signs of the ruin that New York had become. He couldn't help it.

Nothing looks alive anymore. Nothing should be. I'm amazed any of us are still standing.

"You made it," Sergeant G said over her shoulder. "Make it faster next time."

"Rah, Sergeant."

"Post at the end there." She pointed with her right hand toward the last pillar in a line that supported the high ceiling of the bay.

Jed moved to where she wanted him and did a quick scan of the apparatus floor, remembering how Meg had shown him where they'd kept protective gear and first aid in her station. The same lockers and cabinets lined the walls of this room, only the doors were all open and most of the equipment was gone. Only a single trauma bag and one case of bottled water were left.

Jed reminded himself to stay focused and on mission. He kept his weapon up and roved the muzzle across the line of people they'd found on the apparatus floor.

Seven people, a mix of men and women of different races, sat on the floor or on cots over in a corner. An injured man and woman, both white, were a little apart from the other five. They all sat on the cots and wore hospital scrubs or dark blue uniforms. Jed could just make out a shoulder patch on one of them showing the number 53.

A line of bullet holes decorated the wall above the couple's heads. Sergeant G stood at the left end of the group with Mahton and Reeve standing to her right. Jed glanced at Mahton and saw him twitching. His face was pinched, and he had a hollow look in his eyes.

Dude's out for blood, just like Reeve. Somebody's gonna get theirs.

"We *want* to think you're all good guys," Sergeant G said. "Most of you look legit, except for you two…"

She pointed at the couple, who sat by themselves. The man sat closest to the others, with the woman on his right. Her eyes darted side to side, stopping on each of the Marines for half a second. Jed guessed they were married from the way they stayed close together, and especially now that the woman put her arm onto the man's leg, resting her palm there like he was a life raft on the open sea. Not that he or the woman could do much in their condition. He had his left arm in a sling and the woman's legs were both wrapped in bandages, along with the right side of her face.

The man stared at Sergeant G, Mahton, Reeve, and Jed in turn, like he was taking their measure or something. It wasn't the eye-balling that Jed was used to on the block, but he knew when he was being sized up. The guy didn't even try to hide it. Jed gave it back to him, but kept his attention open, watching for any movement among the group of people in the corner.

Something about the way they were sitting caught his eye. They were much better off than the couple, with no injuries he could see. But they still didn't look that great. They were all hunched over. The men sat with their hands between their knees, like they were scared to even speak. Jed didn't see any visible wounds on them, and was about to ask why they were on the cots. Then he saw they were zip-tied, wrists to ankles, and had more ties holding them to the cots.

"What the—They're prisoners!"

***

"We're first responders," one of the men said. He wore a set of pale green scrubs and looked young, maybe twenty years old if that. He had a narrow face, pale brown skin, and a strong Spanish accent. Back in school, he could have been one of Gallegos' friends.

"You're all firefighters?" she asked.

"*Sí, chica*. This was our house until these *pinche culeros* and their friends showed up and started giving orders." He whipped his head in the direction of the couple sitting off to the side. "I sure hope you a different bunch of gun-crazies."

"Cool it, Luce," said another young man in the group. He wore a firefighter's uniform. His skin was darker, and his English wasn't accented. He sat in a relaxed pose, even with his hands tied to his ankles. "We're EMTs, except for Luce," he said, nodding at the man next to him. "He's a phlebotomist."

The young man looked back at him and pinched up his face. The other man half-whispered, "She's not with them. I think we're good here."

"You think, Dom? You *think*? I *know* this girl is pointing a fucking gun at my face *and* yours. So—"

"Where are the others?" Gallegos demanded. She had to cut Luce off before he got on a roll. Mahton and Reeve both had their weapons back at the ready, but as soon as Luce started hollering, the men lifted their muzzles a bit, like they were going to draw a bead on his ass.

"Which others do you mean?" asked the firefighter named Dom.

"We know Tucker has at least two teams in here. One for each truck. The other truck is still outside," she said, then motioned with her weapon at the injured couple. "These two have been laid up for a while, unless that sling is a fake. So where the fuck is the other team?"

"They all left," said a woman at the back of the group.

"Jo, don't say nothin," Luce told her. "We don't know who they're with. Maybe they're just—"

"You don't give the orders, Luce," Jo shot back. She and the other woman in the corner were older than the two Latinos. They were both white or mixed, Gallegos didn't really care. What she needed to know was who could be trusted, and right now it was looking like the people on the cots really were prisoners, not col-labs playing possum, and that they weren't lying when they said Tucker and his people had all left.

The two women in the corner were bound just like the men. The last man in their group was black. He sat up against the wall with his head drooped down over his chest. Gallegos thought he was dead at first, but she could see his chest rise and fall evenly, like he was asleep.

"They all left?" Reeve asked, letting out just enough of his frustration that Gallegos knew she had to get control of the situation and fast.

"Yeah, they left. All of them," Jo said. "They do that sometimes, when they need supplies. We're running low on food and water."

"It was a chow run," Reeve said. "Good thing they don't know—"

"Shut it!" Gallegos ordered.

Over on the cots, the black man's head jerked up and he took in the Marines with wide eyes. Reeve swallowed whatever he was planning to say, but Gallegos could see the damage was already done.

The old Reeve would never make a pog mistake like that. Dios, we're all slipping. We're all so beat down.

The wounded couple had their eyes locked on Reeve, and the man had shifted his injured arm to the side. Gallegos still didn't see a weapon anywhere, but that didn't mean he wasn't holding. When the man shifted again, she trained her weapon on him.

"Mahton, back me up. Reeve, you watch the others."

Mahton shifted his aim to cover the injured pair. Reeve brought his weapon up and ready to cover the people on the cots.

"What the fuck? We're on your side you dumbshit," said the woman next to Jo.

"How do we know that?" Gallegos asked, still sighting on the couple. "Maybe that sling *is* just a cover for a gat."

"It's not," said the black man, as he leaned away from the wall. "His arm was broken in two places when they came in here. We set it as best we could and bandaged up the other wounds they had. She was the worst of them. I tried to convince them we should go to the hospital. It's only a few blocks away. Tucker didn't want to leave, and neither did they." He tilted his head in the direction of the couple but kept his eyes on Gallegos.

She felt the M4's weight dragging on her neck. The sling rubbed against her collar and pressed her vest tight against her shoulder.

Something doesn't break soon, everybody here is getting capped.

The man with the busted arm shifted on his hip and made a jerking movement with his good arm. Mahton's weapon cracked loud, echoing in the open bay.

— 13 —

Jed had the SAW up, but didn't know where he should aim it. Mahton fired into the wall and the bandaged woman screamed. The man rolled away from her to his left, cradling his injured arm with his good one and turning to show his flank to the Marines. Mahton had only fired a warning shot, but it had done the trick. The guy with the bad arm whimpered and started sobbing.

"My ass is going numb on this floor. I had to move. I won't move again. I promise."

Jed roved his weapon back and forth, covering the couple as best he could. If either one of them made a fast move—

"Who's in charge?" Sergeant G demanded.

"That's me, *chica*," Luce said.

"The hell you are," Jo said to him. The other woman, Dom, and the black guy all shook their heads and eyed Luce like he was an idiot.

"Yo, Luce, is it?" Sergeant G asked him, bringing her muzzle around to aim at his chest. "You don't call me *chica* because you don't fucking know me, *cabrón.*"

"And you don't fucking know me, so you don't call

me Luce. The name is Luciano, like my cousins who went to be with God on 9/11."

For a little guy, Luce had plenty of fight packed inside. He stared down Sergeant G and Jed's finger hovered over the trigger guard, ready to snap back. The room buzzed around him, and the tension threatened to drop him where he stood. Mahton and Reeve kept switching their aim from the couple to the group in the corner. Jed was sure he was about to witness another bloodbath until Sergeant G lowered the muzzle of her weapon, still holding it ready but no longer aiming right into anyone's grill.

"Okay. Luciano. You like to talk, so talk. Tell me what's up. I'm not an idiot. You're not in charge, but who is? And are these two with Tucker, or were they hauled in as hostages?"

"We're not *with* Nat Tucker or any of his people," the bandaged woman said. "My husband and I were living upstairs from him when it all happened. He said he'd look out for us because we—"

She flicked a look at the firefighters on the cots and Jed caught her lingering on the black guy. Sergeant G must have noticed as well.

"So he's that kind of *pendejo*?" Sergeant G asked.

"Uh-huh," the black guy said. "If you wouldn't mind cutting us loose, we could get the hell out of here. Or we could wait for them to come back and kill everyone they don't need."

"Need?" Mahton asked. "The fuck's that supposed to mean?"

Luciano answered him. "Means he's only keeping us alive because he doesn't know shit about first aid. Matty here knows how to set bones better than any of us. Tucker would have shot his black ass otherwise."

Matty didn't even flinch at Luciano's words, except to crack a grin.

"It isn't my black ass I'd be worried about, Luce," he said. "You know that man has a hard-on for killing anyone in this city that doesn't look like him. Dominic here is about as dark as it gets around the Barrio."

Jed caught a flash of anger in Luce's eyes. A wave of fear crossed Dominic's face, but it passed just as fast and he was back to his casual self.

"Just cut us loose, please," the woman named Jo said. "We're on your side."

The other woman added her voice, and pretty soon the whole group was hassling Sergeant G to cut them all loose. The injured couple stayed huddled close together, and quiet as church mice. Finally, Mahton lowered his weapon and reached for his bayonet. Sergeant G nodded at him and came over to Jed while Mahton went to cut the firefighters free.

"Welch, you and Reeve secure the hallway back there."

"Rah, Sergeant," he said and moved out. He posted at an oblique to the entrance, so he could catch anyone coming down the hall before they got close enough to shoot into the room. Reeve joined him a few seconds later, taking up position to watch the opposite side of the hallway.

Back in the corner, Sergeant G was talking to everyone, getting their names and asking what they were trained for. Jed heard things that made him feel better about their chances. They didn't have Meg with them, but they did have a team of professional medics.

"We all have a common enemy," Sergeant G finally said aloud to the group. "So who wants to show him what happens when you make an enemy out of people with friends?"

For the first time in a long time, Jed felt something he hadn't known he was missing. The sense of having a mission again helped him get his legs, find a place to stand even if it was at the bottom of the totem pole. But Sergeant G's words about having friends gave him something else.

He had a crew around him again, people who would look out for him just as he looked out for them.

And together they were going to put Tucker where he belonged: *six-feet-the-fuck-underground.*

While the firefighters rubbed circulation back into their limbs, and the injured couple took their places on the cots, Sergeant G made the introductions.

"Dominic Cardeñas, Emmanuel Luciano, meet Private Mahton. I'm Staff Sergeant Gallegos. Over there watching the door is PFC Reeve. Private Welch has the machine gun. Who else is with your crew?"

"I'm Matty Washington," the black guy answered. "Technically I guess I'm highest rank. Jo King and Dom here drove an ambulance, but didn't work in the station. Leigh Barton was here with us when the shit started. When'd you all get here?"

"We came in two days ago. You said your name was Washington? You're highest rank?"

"That's right, and call me Matty."

"Matty then. Why'd Luce say he was in charge?"

"He likes to be on top," Matty said with a chuckle.

Jed had to resist the urge to keep looking back at the group as they continued to chat and talk shit together. Sergeant G even laughed once, but Jed had to keep his eyes front and on mission. He hadn't heard any echoes of a truck motor outside since they'd come into the building. Still, he knew better than to turn away from his post again. That'd be when the hit would come.

You never hear the one that gets you.

He remembered his platoon sergeant saying that once. That was the day they went out on patrol and Jed saw his first and last firefight. The day his platoon sergeant died.

"Yo, Welch," Reeve said from his position opposite Jed.

"Yeah."

"You're spacing out, man. Back to earth."

Jed focused again, eyes front, monitoring the hallway back to the corner.

"That's enough bullshitting for now, rah?" Sergeant G said behind him. "We're taking the second truck back to our location. Reeve found the keys hanging on a hook when he was upstairs."

Reeve held them up and laughed. "*Oh, dah-ling, the Lexus is a mess. I suppose we'll take the Toyot-ah.*"

"I said cut the shit, Reeve. Watch that hallway."

"*Errr,*" he said, pocketing the keys again.

Jed refocused on his zone of fire. Weak light glowed from back down the hallway to the parking lot entrance. If anything came around that corner—

He sent a burst down the hallway when a heavy shadow broke the light.

"The fuck?" Reeve asked, tensing up. "What'd you see, Welch?"

"Something down there. There's something around the corner."

Sergeant G was ordering the firefighters to find shelter behind anything they could. Most of them crammed together around the pillars behind Jed and Reeve.

"Welch," Sergeant G said. "What's up?"

"Just a shadow, Sergeant," he said. "But something's moving in the hallway. Around the corner."

She stepped up next to him. "Move to contact. Flash-bang in case it's friendly. Be ready to light it up if it's not."

"Rah," he said, already letting the SAW rest on its sling while he reached into his vest pouch for one of the grenades. He had it in his hand and was two steps from the hallway when another shadow split the light.

"Sergeant?"

"Throw the banger, Welch, then we move in with a purpose. We're clearing rooms, just like in boot."

Jed cupped the safety lever in his palm and yanked the pin, then shuffled toward the hallway entrance. He heard Sergeant G behind him, directing Reeve to keep an eye on their approach.

"You cover us, rah? The rest of us will—"

A loud shriek cut her off, and was followed by the sound of countless claws scraping across stone and brick. Hisses and howls filled the hallway as a mass of greasy pale white flesh poured along the ceiling, racing into the apparatus floor. Needle teeth and claws flooded Jed's vision as the suckers dropped to the floor in front of him. A few smaller ones spread onto the walls.

The first few went down to shots from Reeve and Sergeant G. Jed fumbled the grenade and it rolled off to his left. He had the SAW in his hands and was ready to fire when the grenade exploded in a blinding glare and deafening thunderclap. Jed's head swam with confusion. He couldn't hear a fucking thing, and his eyes didn't work. All he could see was a ball of white light that seemed to surround him as he felt his feet go out from under him. His ass hit the floor hard, sending a jolt up his spine.

Someone yanked on his neck and he felt a tapping or clicking that vibrated through his shoulders. Hot metal bounced against his face and seared his cheek over and over again. He screamed and felt the roar in his voice, but all he could hear was that constant tapping and clicking.

Jed blinked his eyes. The white light faded around the edges of his vision. An endless line of clawed hands and feet sat tangled in front of him, like he was looking into a mass grave and the dead were reaching out to him for release.

The yanking on his neck settled down. The clicking and tapping sound got louder then cut out suddenly. Jed blinked his eyes again. He could see better. The hands and feet in front of him were connected to arms and legs and mangled bodies peppered with holes that leaked blood. Angry monstrous faces stared at him from the pile of corpses. He reached a hand up to rub his eyes and felt another hand grab his collar.

A muffled shout from somewhere nearby made Jed worried that people were dying because he'd dropped the grenade. Then he remembered it was a banger, not a frag.

The monsters got in. But if I'm not dead, then…

Someone grabbed his hand, and another pair of hands lifted under his arms, hauling him up on his feet.

"You dropped the banger, Welch, but that saved us, man."

"Who'd I save?" Jed asked. His vision cleared, and he finally blinked away the last of the shock from the grenade. Mahton was holding him up. Sergeant G and Reeve stood near the hallway entrance with their weapons up. A mass of dead monsters crowded the floor in front of the hallway, and a few more lay in the hall itself. They'd all been shot to pieces. Brass and belt links were scattered around Jed's feet.

Smoke drifted away from the muzzle of his SAW.

Somebody went cyclic. Was it me?

"Mahton, get Welch squared away," Sergeant G said over her shoulder. Jed lifted the SAW and spun around to take in the rest of the room. He wobbled on his feet and only got a hand out in time to stop himself from eating the floor. He rolled onto his back and felt a sharp pain in his hip. With a grunt, he got to his feet and steadied himself with a hand on the nearest pillar.

The firefighters and Luce were standing together around the back of the pillar. Over in the far corner, the injured man and woman were lying in a puddle of blood and gore, with three dead sucker faces nearby.

"Reeve and me got them, but not before they had dinner," Mahton said.

Jed turned back to listen for Sergeant G's command and nearly stumbled over his own feet as he shifted his weight.

"Yo, lay off the hard stuff this early in the morning, Welch," Mahton said from nearby. Jed stayed still and just turned his head this time, looking for Mahton. The Marine stood a few feet away to Jed's right, laughing to himself.

"What the fuck happened?" Jed asked.

"You dropped the banger, man. Sergeant G saw it coming. She turned away and covered her ears when it went off, so she was first to react. The sucker faces, man… You should have seen them. Like cockroaches on a cold morning. Sergeant G grabbed the SAW and sprayed them fuckers like bugs. Good ol' M249. Best damn can of RAID you can find these days."

"What about you and Reeve?"

"We've all been around bangers before. You get used to it. I closed my eyes and backed up as soon as you dropped it."

"And them?" Jed asked, sticking a thumb in the firefighters' direction.

"Ate up like you, I guess. But they were farther away. Same as the sucker faces that got behind us. They were up on the ceiling."

"Mahton, Welch," Sergeant G said from where she stood by the door. "Eyes on our six in case those things found a place to hide. We know they like to ambush when they can. Matty, keep your people tight. You're in the middle. Grab whatever supplies and weapons you can as we move."

The firefighters each grabbed something from the cabinets on the edge of the apparatus floor. Matty had a trauma bag slung across his chest, but the others just had a few bottles of water between them stuffed into pockets.

"All right, people," Sergeant G said. "Let's move out."

"What about Tucker?" Jed asked, remembering what the man had said over the radio.

"What about him, Welch?"

"He said he's got snipers out there. With a Barrett."

"That's bullshit," Leigh said.

Sergeant G went over to her. "Why do you say that? You know something, you need to tell us. What do they have and how much?"

"I don't know what a Barrett is, but he doesn't have any snipers out there unless they've been out there the whole time. He has everyone with him, like we told you before. All four of them. His son and another two guys. They all have guns, like you do. The same kind and a lot more. Shotguns and pistols. I don't know how much ammunition they have. They never let us see the arms room."

"*Arms room?*" Reeve asked.

"Watch the hall, Reeve," Sergeant G said. To Leigh and the other firefighters, she demanded: "Show me."

"It's on the police side," Luce said. "Upstairs. We was gonna tell you—"

Sergeant G cut him off with a sharp hiss. She moved up beside Reeve at the hallway entrance and waved Welch to the rear with Mahton. The firefighters took their place next in the middle.

"Everybody top off," Sergeant G said. Jed joined the other two Marines in a chorus of *Errr*. He dropped the empty box in his weapon and grabbed a fresh one from the bags Reeve was carrying. Mahton and Reeve took turns replacing their magazines. When they'd all finished, Sergeant G did the same. With a wave of her hand, she directed them all to move out.

When they reached the stairs Reeve had come down earlier, Jed took point again. He rounded the landing so he could cover the upper floor until Reeve joined him. Moving in tandem, they ascended the stairwell to the landing, which opened into a hallway in both directions. A heavy black radio sat against the wall there, with a long-whip antenna sticking out a broken window. Sergeant G called Reeve to switch positions with her. She climbed the stairs and told Jed to move down one side of the hall opposite the windows.

"Go right. They say that's the police station side."

Jed moved out, sweeping his muzzle into every open door he passed. The building was a mix of small offices, a gym, a day room, and a small, square kitchen, not much different from Meg's fire station or the bus depot where Sergeant G and the others had set up their hide. Every room in the stronghold showed signs of being occupied, just like the makeshift barracks Reeve and Mahton had set up. Except each of these rooms was being used like a separate bunk space.

Jed kept his eyes and ears ready to catch any sign of movement as they moved down the hall. A darkened doorway up ahead on the left got his attention, and he roved the muzzle of his weapon in that direction.

"You got something, Welch?" Reeve asked from behind him.

"Negative, just getting ready in case I do."

"Rah. Keep on keeping on then."

"Rah," Jed said as they stepped slow and sure down the hall.

If anything comes out of that door…

Gallegos kept pace with Mahton as they tailed the firefighters down the hall from the stairwell. Without weapons, they were all easy targets. Even worse, she knew, they'd become liabilities if they got between the Marines and any of the suckers. She'd seen how the monsters changed their attack patterns when they had unarmed civilians in their sights. They'd swarm those people first, because the people who were armed would be reluctant to shoot into a group of those they were trying to protect.

It was like the sucker faces could read human behavior perfectly well, even though every last trace of humanity had been wiped away by the virus that made monsters of men and women.

If they figure out that we need the first aid they're are carrying…

Gallegos shook those thoughts from her mind and focused on the mission at hand.

Get to the arms room, get back to the hide, then get the hell out of town.

"They keep the food in here," Leigh said as the group stopped outside the kitchen door. "There's not much left, but we should take it anyway."

Gallegos nodded and signaled Welch and Mahton to watch their six. He posted by the kitchen door, facing back the way they'd come. Mahton took a position on the opposite side of the hall and aimed back at the stairs. Reeve posted with his back to him, watching the hall ahead of them. Gallegos joined him on the opposite wall, across the kitchen doorway from Welch.

The firefighters went in to scavenge the last bits of food. When they didn't come back out right away, Gallegos backed up so she could see inside the room.

"They took all the damn cereal," Jo said staring at empty cabinets. "They eat it like it's candy."

"Who are they?" Reeve asked. Gallegos turned to hush him up on instinct, but she stopped herself when Luce spit on the floor and said, "Punks. They just a bunch of fucking punks. Come in here all macho and shit with their stolen guns, talking about *cleaning off the scum*, and shit like that."

"Yeah, I'm looking forward to seeing them guns," Reeve said. "I'ma clean out that *arms room* like it's fucking Christmas. And that radio back down the hall. We should grab it, Sergeant. Monitor their commo."

"It's too heavy. And they'll switch frequencies anyway," Mahton said. "Probably already did."

"Maybe, but what if they don't? They sound ate up as shit."

"If we have room and can carry it, we take the radio," Gallegos said, stepping into the kitchen and waving for the firefighters to hurry it up. "Whatever we can't carry, we destroy before we leave, including any weapons we have to leave behind. Either way their commo and strength gets compromised."

"You pretty hard for a lady soldier," Luce said.

***

Jed's heart skipped a beat when he heard a slamming sound and a grunt from behind him. He took his eyes off the hallway for a second to look into the kitchen. Sergeant G had Luce pinned against the table with the butt of her weapon pressing his face to the side. The guy struggled for a second and then started breathing heavy through his nose.

Jed smiled and got his head back on mission, watching the hall back to the stairs. But he spared a little attention to listen to what was going on behind him.

"Let me *go*," Luce said through gritted teeth.

"I will, but first you get one thing fucking straight. I am a Marine, and I am saving your ass. That is all you need to know about me. Rah?"

"*Rah?* The fuck does that mean?" Luce asked. Jed had to look back again. Luce was still breathing heavy and trying to get Sergeant G's weapon off his jaw. But she had him bent over backwards and with a knee up against his junk.

That guy ain't going anywhere until she says so.

"It means you don't call me *lady soldier*."

"*Fine!* You a Marine. I fucking get it."

Sergeant G backed off and Luce sprang upright. He shook off the fight in his eyes and went to help the others with the food. They had a few small boxes, a bag of oranges, and some jars of pasta sauce.

"Welch," Sergeant G said, motioning with her chin for him to lead the way farther down the hall.

Jed turned back to the hall and spotted a flash of movement on the stairs they'd come up. In a rush of screeches and howls, monsters erupted from the stairwell and swarmed onto the walls, floor, and ceiling. Mahton's muzzle flashed hot. Jed added his own to the task, but there were so many of the things all he could see was their greasy flesh and snarling mouths.

They snuck up on us. Fucking hell, they snuck up on us!

— 15 —

Jed squeezed off a few sustained bursts before going cyclic. He sprayed left and up the wall, then back across the ceiling. Most of the sucker faces were hit and flailed backwards or dropped on top of the others. But the ones that he missed came rushing forward, screeching and hissing, baring their spiked teeth in a wave of glistening pale white skin.

Mahton picked the first two off. Reeve and Sergeant G stood side by side next to Jed, firing into the others that got through. Jed kept his aim on the stairwell, forcing the suckers to spread out as they emerged and making easier targets for the other Marines to take down.

"Down the hall! Move!" Sergeant G shouted.

Stomping feet and shouts came to Jed's ears from behind him. The firefighters were racing away down the hall. More of the beasts poured from the stairwell and Jed mowed through them with a constant stream of fire. Sergeant G slapped his shoulder and yelled for him to fall back. He kept firing into the swarm, stepping back as quickly as he could without stumbling over his own feet.

Reeve and Mahton moved in Jed's peripheral vision,

back pedaling and firing high and low. Gunshots muffled Sergeant G's shouted orders and the suckers' screeching, and through it all Jed felt the steady thunder of the SAW in his hands, spitting death into their enemy.

To his left, the other Marines swapped out magazines as they moved. Reeve changed his first, then Mahton. Jed felt the SAW lock up just as Sergeant G went to change hers.

"Fall back!" she shouted. "Fall back!"

Reeve and Mahton continued to knock down the monsters that raced toward them. Jed cleared his weapon, and lifted the muzzle just in time to spray a burst into a monster's face as it dropped from the ceiling to land in front of him.

Three more suckers sped forward, skittering up the opposite wall and around the Marines in a blur of pasty white skin and spittle. Reeve tracked them, but couldn't keep his aim on their movement. Mahton and Sergeant G stayed on those coming down the hall, picking them off one by one as they scrambled left or right, trying to dodge around their shots.

Sergeant G yelled again for them to fall back.

Jed stepped back, keeping in a line with the others. The tide of sucker faces slowed down until only a handful remained in the hallway, darting up and down the walls. Jed picked off the closest of them. Then the SAW ran dry. He dropped the empty box and had a hand in his bag for a new one when Mahton roared and charged forward.

***

Gallegos knew they'd make it. They weren't going down

in this hallway. Not here, not today. The firefighters were behind them somewhere and out of the way. Reeve took down the three suckers that scrambled around them. Now they only had a handful or so left to deal with. She dropped one on the ceiling and Reeve got another. Welch had dialed back to sustained fire and got a sucker face that was slinking along the wall.

Mahton was grabbing at his vest and Gallegos took her eyes off the hall to see what he was doing.

Then she felt the SAW pump out its final shot. Mahton gave a war cry and raced forward with a frag in his right hand. Gallegos shouted for him to come back, but it was too late. He reached the stairwell just as a new mob of suckers exploded from it and filled the hallway. They surrounded Mahton and he vanished into their swarm. But the sucker faces stayed put, skittering back and forth across the hallway, sometimes up onto the walls like spiders running from a broom.

How did we not hear them coming? They're timing their attacks, moving slow so we don't hear their joints or claws. These fucking things are learning how to beat us at our own game!

Reeve was shaking next to her, weapon up and ready. She closed the space between them.

"You frosty, Reeve?"

"Rah, Sergeant. But they got Mahton. They're down there dick dancing instead of attacking us. And we didn't hear them coming. What the fuck? What the *absolute fuck?*"

The sucker faces kept squirming around in the hallway. She took a risk and fired at a lone one that had scrambled up a wall. It dropped and the others all surrounded it, forming a tighter clutch.

With Mahton right in the middle.

They weren't eating him, but they kept him hidden from view except for a glimpse of his boot or helmet. To her right, Welch had his weapon open and a fresh ammo box in his hand. He slid it into the SAW, but it wouldn't seat.

"Welch, get that SAW up!"

His hands shook as he struggled with the ammo box. The belt was curled up over the top. Gallegos reached over and flopped the loose end out of the way. Welch slid the box into place.

Reeve screamed something and fired. Gallegos turned back in time to see a sucker face drop from the ceiling ahead of five others that raced along the floor in a group. Two more peeled away from the swarm and clambered up the wall to the ceiling. The rest of the swarm kept Mahton covered from view.

Reeve fired again, dropped his magazine, and slapped a hand on his vest.

"I'm out!"

The five sucker faces tore forward over the mounds of their own dead and the ones up above followed.

They're timing their attack. They know when we're vulnerable. Shit!

Gallegos fired at the ones up top, but they moved so fast she only hit one and didn't even kill it. The SAW barked a steady beat again and the five on the floor took hits from Welch's fire. He dropped two of them. Gallegos took another down as the ones on the ceiling dropped onto Reeve. Gallegos shouted his name and tried to slam the suckers aside by ramming them with her shoulder. Reeve was doing the same with the butt of his weapon.

125

He still had his feet under him, and Gallegos was about to fire on the one closest to her when a shout broke everyone's concentration. Even the sucker faces stopped what they were doing and backed away, leaving Reeve scraped up but still alive. The shout came again.

"Stop!"

Gallegos froze and felt everyone around her do the same. The voice came from the office back down the hall, just beyond the kitchen. And Gallegos recognized it immediately.

***

Jed didn't know who was next to him anymore, and the monsters' shrieks mixed with gunfire kept echoing in his ears. Someone screamed behind him, and then right next to him. He looked at the hall again and he stared into the eyes of the biggest monster he had ever seen. It was the one from the street earlier. And now it stood there, not ten feet from him, holding Mahton by the throat. It's other hand clenched Mahton's arm in a death grip. Jed felt his own arm aching and burning as blood dripped from between the big monster's fingers and Mahton twisted his face in pain.

The sucker face's skin was just as greasy looking as the smaller ones. But its muscles had to be twice as thick, and it stood a head taller than anything Jed had seen so far.

Its mouth was shaped differently, too, like it still had a jaw almost instead of a sucker full of needle sharp teeth. It grunted at them and shook Mahton like he was bait and they were all supposed to jump for him. Jed saw the trap right away. The smaller monsters gathered around the big one. Most of them were poised to leap, but a few reached around the floor like they were hunting for something. When Jed saw one come up with an empty magazine in its hands, he felt his stomach flip flop.

The sucker face used its claws to crack the magazine open, splitting it down the side. The other monsters each stood up with a magazine or two and did the same thing.

They know we need those to fight. They've figured us out and are making us weaker.

Reeve and Sergeant G were still next to Jed. He could see them out of his peripheral. Sergeant G had her weapon up. Reeve's hung on his sling.

He's empty. Shit!

"Bring more...*more*," the big sucker grunted while the smaller ones kept searching through the bodies on the floor for more magazines. Jed met the big one's gaze. It was eyeballing him. He stared at it in shock and it stared back, locking its dark yellow bloodshot eyes onto his. Its mouth pulled in on the sides, curling its puffy upper lip away from the little needle teeth that filled its mouth.

Is it smiling? Did it just fucking smile at me?

He was too shocked to even blink. The sucker face grunted at him twice and held Mahton up by his collar. Jed could feel the sucker's claws digging into his own flesh again. Blood flowed out between the beast's fingers and down Mahton's vest. He squirmed, choking out a cry of pain. The monster opened its mouth wide and made a sound like it was laughing, except to Jed it was like ice picks in his ears.

"You...*want him*... Bring more," the monster said in between its sharp laughs.

***

Gallegos kept her left hand close to her chest and moved slowly, reaching into her vest pocket for a flash-bang grenade. She had it pinched between her fingers and was lifting it out when the big sucker face stepped backwards down the hallway, holding Mahton like a rag doll.

He's still holding the frag. If it lets him go... Does it know what will happen? They're destroying our magazines. They know how to weaken us.

All it would take is a head shot and that thing goes down. But then so does Mahton, and probably so do we.

As if they sensed her thoughts, the smaller suckers stopped digging through the remains of their own dead and crowded around the bigger one. They formed a screen so that all she could see in her sight picture was the big fucker's slimy white hand grabbing Mahton's throat.

"Reeve, tell me you got some ideas."

"Got nothing, Sergeant. Nothing the fuck at all."

"Welch?"

"I—I can see it, Sergeant. But—"

"We can all see it, Welch. I'm asking what you're thinking right now."

"No talk...you talk, he die."

Gallegos stiffened as the sucker face lifted Mahton high, grabbing him tighter around the neck. Mahton's face reddened, but the monster relaxed its grip.

It wants him alive. They like living meat, not dead. How the hell do we get out of this?

The smaller ones scrambled around now, shifting the

screen they made so none of the Marines had a clear shot at the big fucker.

Not without risking Mahton's life. Either we hit him or it crushes his neck, or we all go down when the frag drops.

When Welch had dropped the flash-bang in the fire station, the monsters had been neutralized instantly. Only one of them actually recovered in time to be a threat. Mahton had taken it down as soon as it moved. The others had all frozen up, covering their eyes and ears and scurrying for shelter like a bunch of frightened bugs.

She'd given them no more mercy than they'd deserved, and she would do the same this time.

But how do I do that without risking the frag going off?

Mahton struggled and twisted his head to the side. His arm was still held in the sucker face's iron grip. He locked eyes with Gallegos and flicked his gaze toward his right hand.

She didn't want to accept it, but she knew what he was saying. She blew out three short breaths and winced when Mahton matched it with three fast blinks.

Mahton, you were a damn good Marine. Semper fi.

***

Jed couldn't take his eyes off the big thing. He wanted to kill it, and knew he should. But how could he fire with Mahton held in front of it like that?

Before he could make a decision, Sergeant G told him in a hushed voice to stand down.

"Be ready to fall back. Fast."

Jed flicked his eyes at Sergeant G. She was tapping her vest pouch where she kept her flash bangs. He looked back at Mahton and could tell from his face that he was ready for what came next.

Damn. We can't just do him like that. Even if we knock the suckers back with the banger, they'll tear him apart before we can get all of them.

"Sergeant—"

She hissed him quiet and he stayed that way. Whatever she had decided, he couldn't change her mind. And it looked like Mahton was in on the idea. He was ready to die so they could live.

Like Meg would have done.

Jed let his finger rest against the trigger guard of his weapon, but he kept the muzzle on the big sucker, waiting for Sergeant G to throw her grenade. She hadn't pulled it out of her vest yet.

The monster acted like it was smiling again. It lifted Mahton higher still, so he was held up like a trophy. Then it grunted at them.

"This mine... Bring more. You live."

Sergeant G began counting.

"One," she said.

Jed focused on the enemy as best he could, wondering what she was counting for.

Is she trying to fake it out? Why doesn't she pull her banger?

The smaller ones kept shifting around the big sucker face. This left Mahton out in front of the whole mass sometimes, so he'd be the first one hit if Jed opened fire.

"Two," Sergeant G said.

Jed had the SAW angled away from Mahton, aiming at the door to the kitchen. He still couldn't accept the idea of sacrificing one of their own to the sucker faces. Even if Mahton was okay with it himself, Jed had to do something. He'd fire a burst to take out any suckers in his zone, and then move up and left to catch the big one in the chest or head.

All he needed was a clear shot. Like they were listening to his thoughts, two smaller suckers crept aside, giving him a clear view of the big fucker's left flank.

He was ready to risk it. If he got one head shot, the monster would drop Mahton, and then Jed could spray the rest of them without hitting his buddy.

That's how it'll go. Sergeant G isn't going to throw a flash bang. She doesn't even have it in her hand. She's trying a fake out.

Jed let his finger slide onto the trigger. He angled the muzzle up just enough that he knew he'd miss Mahton with his first burst. The big sucker face shifted its grip on Mahton and Jed saw the dark green ball in the Marine's hand.

Oh shit.

"Three!"

— 16 —

Gallegos called the last count and reached to her left and right, grabbing her men and lurching backwards. She spun on her heels and came face to face with the firefighters, still carrying all their food and first aid gear. They stood there like they expected to be needed.

"Grenade!" Gallegos yelled as she ran forward, pushing Jo and Matty out of her way. Luce and Dom fell in beside her. She felt someone else turn and run behind her and the others.

"Bring more!" the big one shouted from behind them.

Gallegos looked over her left shoulder. Welch was right there with Jo trailing him. Behind them a group of three sucker faces clung to the wall, scraping at the air. Mahton cried out behind her and then screamed.

The *thud* of the frag hitting the floor put her heart into her throat and she threw herself forward into a prone position.

I hope you all know what to do—

The explosion clapped loud and sudden, sending Gallegos' stomach into her mouth. Her ears rang and she heaved a mouthful of spit onto the floor. As she rolled onto her back and brought her weapon up, a burst from the SAW clattered against the humming in her ears.

On her right, Welch had stopped firing. He roved the SAW back and forth across the floor. A spray of blood and bone coated the walls. None of the smaller sucker faces were moving except for one right in front of Welch. Its chest was a constellation of holes leaking blood. It shook once and went still.

Down the hall, the big one lay on its back with Mahton off to the side. Another body lay in the middle of the floor, next to a pile of the smaller monsters.

The bag of oranges Leigh had been carrying was a mess of pulp and juice mixed into the mess around them. Reeve stirred at Gallegos' left. He got to his feet and she watched him walk down the hall to Mahton's body. The food the firefighters had collected was scattered around them, with crackers and dry pasta spilling out of split packages or crushed boxes.

Matty and Luce came from behind her and followed Reeve. Together, they squatted on the floor next to the body in the middle of the hall. Dom and Jo crouched against the wall behind Welch. Blood marked Dom's arm where some shrapnel had caught him. Jo moved over to help him with some bandages and water she'd been carrying.

Welch stayed by them and monitored the hall while Jo treated Dom's wound.

"It's too deep to extract easily. We'll need more than we have in the trauma bag."

"Just wrap it for now," Dom said. "I'll be fine."

Gallegos stood and went forward to join Matty and Luce, so she could get a look at who was on the ground.

Leigh had jumped toward the grenade and shielded

everyone else from the blast.

The sucker faces were dead, even the big one.

Leigh and Mahton were gone with them. His weapon was on the floor where the big fucker had been standing. It was peppered with shrapnel and the butt stock was a jagged shard of blackened metal. Gallegos swept it up and threw it down the hallway, screaming her rage and agony.

***

Jed waited until Sergeant G was cool again. She hollered long enough that he was worried more of the suckers would show up. But nothing came tearing out of the stairwell. The last ghosts of the grenade drifted down the hallway and Jed let his shoulders relax.

Sergeant G went to Luce and Matty and put a hand on their shoulders. The two men stood and they all shared a quiet second together around Leigh's body. Reeve stayed back with Dom and Jo, and said something about getting gone. Sergeant G nodded.

Jed stayed focused on the stairwell, but shot a look out the nearest window every few breaths.

Just what we need. One more place those things can sneak in from. How the fuck did they get so close without us hearing them?

Sergeant G's voice broke into his thoughts.

"People, we need to go. We're down by two now, but we still outnumber Tucker. Let's get into that arms room and get the rest of you saddled up."

She marched forward with Reeve at her side. The firefighters gave one more look at Leigh's body before joining her. Jed stayed at their six, watching the hall, the window, and the stairwell.

Don't you fucking dare come after us. You got lucky today. Next time will be different.

***

Gallegos turned the corner at the end of the hall and came face to face with a solid door. It had a coded lock on it.

"How the hell did they get in?"

Jo stepped forward and turned the handle. The lock clicked and she pushed the door open.

"Before the cops left, they gave the code to a few of us. In case we needed to be armed, but then the power went out so it didn't matter."

Jo stepped back, making space for Gallegos to push into the arms room with Reeve trailing her. The firefighters all followed them inside.

"Welch," Gallegos called over her shoulder.

"Rah, Sergeant."

"You got our six until I say otherwise."

"*Errr*," he said without missing a beat. She didn't need to check him. She'd seen how shaken up he was after the attack, and the grenade, but his voice told her he was good.

Whatever strength she took from trusting Welch quickly waned when she saw the empty shelves, racks, and lockers in the arms room. The cops' guns were all gone, along with almost every round of ammo. Empty green cans lay around the floor.

"So much for an arms rooms," she said.

"I don't know, Sergeant," Reeve said. "You think that contraband might be worth taking with us?"

Gallegos shifted her position to look past Reeve. He was pointing into the corner behind the door.

Sport shotguns, a few M9s, and an old Vietnam-era grenade launcher were piled up together behind two ammo cans. The pistols had likely been stolen from people Tucker had killed or taken prisoner.

And that's as good as having killed them, with what he's been doing.

"He had a goddamned thump gun," Reeve said.

"They had a lot more than this," Jo said as she came deeper into the room.

"That's the truth," Matty said from behind Gallegos.

"How much more?" she asked.

"When they got here, they had stacks of those," Jo said, pointing at the ammo cans. "At least a dozen. Plus guns like you have. Assault rifles." She turned to leave. Dom put a hand on her shoulder but she pushed past him. Gallegos eyeballed Dom, signaling he should let her go. Jo had just lost a partner. The storm would pass and she'd be good to go.

Right now, she needs that space. I hope Welch knows to give it to her.

"Let's see what they left us," Gallegos said to Reeve, moving to the stash in the corner.

The first ammo can was unmarked, and even though it looked like it would hold .50 cal rounds, it was pretty light. She popped it open and found a full magazine of 5.56, two bandoliers of ammo, and an old metal speed loader. She handed the magazine and one bandolier to Reeve.

He reloaded his weapon, dropped his pack, and stuffed the bandolier into it. Gallegos pocketed the speed loader and slung her bandolier on her shoulder. She'd top off her magazine before they moved out. The one in her weapon was her last, and it only had three rounds in it.

The other ammo can wasn't marked, but she recognized its slim size. It was for 7.62 rounds.

Just our luck they leave us ammo we can't use.

She lifted it. "Feels about half full," she said.

"Be nicer if we had the right weapon," Reeve said.

"We still take it. Weaken him any way we can. We might find a weapon for it."

"Rah," Reeve said as he accepted the can from her. He handed it off to Dom while Gallegos checked out the new weapons they did have. She counted five Remington 11-87s. Tucker had probably looted them from a sporting goods store. She lifted one and spotted a bundle of OD green fabric hidden behind the others. When she realized what it was, she almost let out a shout of joy.

Stuffed into the corner behind the guns were two bags holding M18 mines with their blasting caps and detonators. Next to the bags was a belt with six rounds of forty mike-mike for the thump gun.

"Hell yeah!"

Reeve came back to her side in a hurry.

"Sergeant? What's—"

Gallegos handed him the M79 and the belt of rounds.

"Ammo was behind the shotguns. Give it to Jo. The shottys go to the men, and we take the shells from the ones we don't need. Everybody gets a sidearm, and now we got these," she said, holding up the M18s in their bags.

"Claymores? Oh, we are in. The. Business."

"You only got two of those?" Luce asked.

"What do you mean 'only'?" Reeve asked.

"They had a lot more than two when they got here. Just like them ammo cans. I seen way more of them bags."

"So they have two less," Gallegos said.

"Hey," Dom said. "This can's got more of those bandoliers in it."

He was kneeling next to the 7.62 can they'd found, but he was holding up a bandolier of 5.56.

"Merry Christmas to us," Reeve said. "Who's humping the extra ammo, Sergeant?"

"I'll carry it," Dom said, closing up the box.

Gallegos gave him a thumbs up. "Way to take charge, Dom. Reeve, get the thumper to Jo, and reload another mag if you can find a good one out there. Give that last SAW box to Welch."

Reeve gave her an *Err* as he stepped past Luce to leave the room.

Gallegos handed out the pistols to Matty, Luce, and Dom. "We have five, so everybody who needs it has a sidearm. Luce, give this one to Jo when you get out there. And I want her carrying the thumper. Welch is gonna stay on the SAW. Y'all get the shotguns. Me and Reeve are good to go with these," she said, patting her M4.

"I'd rather stick to iodine and gauze," Dom said.

"I need you armed, Dominic," Gallegos said, handing him a shotgun. "We're all targets for the sucker faces. They don't care what you did before they showed up. And if you're not armed, you're probably their first target."

"Why would they go after him if he doesn't have a gun?" Luce asked.

"Because they've learned our strengths and weaknesses. They know our weapons can kill them. You saw them destroying the magazines out there, right?"

"Yeah, I did. But—"

Gallegos passed the second shotgun to him. As she put it in his hands, she looked him in the eye and said, "I've seen the sucker faces tear into a crowd of unarmed civilians, forcing the Marines that were shooting at them to kill the people along with the monsters in order to save themselves."

"Why did—"

"If they hadn't, the sucker faces would have taken the Marines down one by one, using the civilians as cover. I saw one platoon make that mistake. We all did, and after that, none of us made the same mistake."

That shook Luce up, and she was glad to see it. He took the shotgun and held it in the crook of his arm like a hunter.

She needed every one of them to understand that their roles were changing. They'd been rescuers before the world ended. Now they still needed to use those skills to survive, but they would be doing so as warfighters.

Dom and Matty weren't happy with what she'd told them either. Matty hugged his trauma bag close against his hip as he accepted the shotgun she handed him. Dom rested his weapon on one shoulder and slung the bandoliers of 5.56 over the other.

"We should move out, yeah?" he asked.

"Rah," Gallegos said. "Let's go."

Outside the arms room, Reeve and Jo were standing near the door. Welch was up at the corner watching the hall.

Gallegos handed Reeve one of the Claymore bags. He dropped his pack again and stowed the mine. Gallegos waited until he was finished before she did the same. Then she dropped her magazine and started reloading from her bandolier. The other men all moved up closer to Welch in a huddle.

Reeve shifted so they were all at his back. "Sergeant, we should grab Mahton's tags."

"Good call, Reeve. Oorah," she said and continued loading her magazine.

When Gallegos finished, she stood up and Reeve asked her in a hushed voice, "You sure they'll be good to go out there?"

"Yeah, I'm sure."

"They're lifesavers, Sergeant. Not life takers. You saw how that Dom guy was acting. He's not—"

"They'll be good, Reeve. We aren't taking lives. We're avenging them. One of theirs, and one of ours."

— 17 —

Jed stayed at their six, watching the hallway and forcing himself not to fixate on Leigh and Mahton lying amidst all the dead monsters.

Why'd we have to lose them? Why now?

He stepped back a pace, rounding the corner so it was harder to see his fallen comrades. He was closer to the firefighters now. They stood apart from Reeve and Sergeant G, in a cluster just behind him.

"Hey, y'all," he said over his shoulder. "I'm sorry about Leigh. She saved us."

"Yeah, she did," Matty said. "Sorry about your man, too. Even if he did almost shoot me in the head when he first saw me."

Jed held in an awkward chuckle. The instinct to laugh made him feel like an asshole and it seemed like Matty felt the same way. A smile faltered on his face and drooped into a grimace in a heartbeat.

Sergeant G moved away from the arms room to stand by Jo. The firefighter had an old-as-hell grenade launcher and a belt with a few rounds on it. Jo slung the belt over a shoulder and held the thump gun at the ready. Jed could tell something was eating her up, and he had a pretty good idea what it was. He was feeling the same pain working on his insides about two people.

First Meg and now Mahton. Doesn't matter what I do…

He turned to Jo again and saw her eyes twitching with tears she was only just holding in.

"You couldn't have saved her. None of us could."

"It's not that. I'm not sad about it. I'm pissed off."

"Huh?"

"All she needed was an opportunity," Jo said.

Dom turned where he stood and clapped a hand on Jo's shoulder. "Leigh wasn't like that, Jo, and you know it. She didn't go out just to go out. She was always thinking about other people, even if it meant forgetting herself."

"I know," Jo said. "But she could have let us know first. We didn't even get a chance to change her mind."

Jed simply nodded and put his eyes back on their six.

Didn't have more than two seconds to change her mind. Or Mahton's. We'd be down one more at least if we'd tried. We might all be dead if it wasn't for them.

Silence filled the hallway between Jed and the firefighters. As much as Jed wanted to say something else, offer some sympathy or show he understood what they were feeling, he knew that his words would just made it worse. He wasn't sure they'd hear him anyway. They were all carrying shotguns and pistols now, and it looked like the first time any of them had ever held a gun. Except for Jo, who had the funky grenade launcher and an M9 tucked into her belt. She might have been torn up inside, but she held the thump gun like it was second nature.

Sergeant G and Reeve came forward, next to Jed's position. Sergeant G turned back and faced the group.

"We've lost people, but we still have our mission. We move out to the hide. Regroup, resupply, and get everybody some chow. Then we go after the ones who did this to us."

"I'm all for stopping them," Matty said. "But wouldn't it be better to wait until they show up again? I mean we could get back to wherever you're holed up, but then just wait it out. See if they come around?"

"We don't have that kind of time because the people Tucker gave to the monsters don't have that kind of time. Everybody pick up empty magazines on the way out. We need to reload and be ready for what's outside. Welch, you got point."

"*Errr*, Sergeant," he said and stepped forward, clearing the corner and going back into the remains of the battle that took Leigh and Mahton.

***

Gallegos held in the anger and pain as they passed Mahton's body. Reeve stooped down and lifted the slim chain off his neck. He held it in his closed fist for a moment before standing and putting it in his pocket.

On the way to the stairwell, they picked up close to a dozen empty magazines. She had the team hold at the top of the stairs, with Welch and Reeve watching both directions for any signs of the sucker faces.

Only five of the magazines were serviceable. The others were damaged by shrapnel from the grenade, or the sucker faces' claws. Gallegos showed the firefighters how to use the speed loader, and they did two mags for now.

"We top off completely at the hide. Right now Reeve and I have a full magazine each, plus one spare. Welch, you have a full box in the SAW plus two in the bags, oorah?"

"Rah, Sergeant."

"Good. We're saddled up. Let's move out."

Welch led them away from the scene of the battle and down the stairwell. Even with the new equipment they'd scavenged, Gallegos had to fight to hold in the shakes and screams that kept tearing at her inside. Her adrenaline drained away, leaving the shock of battle to settle over her, pushing her down. She fought against it, holding her head up proudly, just like she had in the sandbox. She'd done everything she could to make sure they all got away. The monsters found a way to be one step ahead.

And they took two of ours with them.

Beside her, Reeve was his old self again, weapon up and watching the path ahead.

"They snuck up on us," he said. "They always made noise before. Always."

"They changed," Luciano said from behind Gallegos. "Fucking things changed. It ain't the first time."

Gallegos signaled them all to keep quiet and move out with a purpose.

We knew they might change. Command told us to watch for 'new variants' right before they launched Reaper. Sure enough, they changed, and Luce says it ain't the first time.

I bet it won't be the last.

— 18 —

Downstairs, Jed crossed the entrance to the parking lot. He scanned the shadows outside for any movement. He didn't see anything, but had only given himself a second to be in the open. Before he waved the others to follow him, he slid back along the wall of the little dayroom and took in as much of the parking lot as he could.

After two weeks of staying quiet so the monsters wouldn't hear them at Meg's fire station, it was weird to suddenly feel such a heavy silence all around him. It should have made him feel safer, happier, he thought. Every street they'd been on out there had the scattered remains of monsters killed by the chemical bombs. And getting into the stronghold had been almost like going home for Jed. It was another fire station, and that was the closest to home he could imagine now.

But the sucker faces got in, and now Mahton's gone. And Leigh.

"Welch, I want you to post at the truck. Watch for enemy. Reeve will come out and drive the truck back here to the steps. Stay tight with him. We'll load in from here. Keep exposure to a minimum."

"Oorah," Jed said.

Thinking about being outside on his own, he felt the silence of the city put him on edge even more. He scanned the parking lot one more time, and every high point he could see from his position. He said a quick prayer for his squad's safety and moved outside.

At the bottom of the short steps, Jed cut left and posted by the hood of the dirty white truck. He inspected the grill first. When he didn't see any wires or obvious signs of a bomb, he moved around the truck to the left, checking it as best he could. Reeve had done a quick check of it when they'd arrived, but Jed wasn't going to have them all taken out because of that cowboy's mistake.

If Tucker had left a trap on the vehicle, Jed wanted to make sure he saw it before anyone else came close.

None of the side windows were whole anymore. Pebbles of safety glass lined the frames. The windshield was intact except for a crack that started in the passenger side corner and went up to the top. Shorter cracks split off like veins from the main line. Jed checked the interior, gave a quick look into the bed, and went down on his knees to check underneath. He didn't see anything suspicious, so he stood and moved back to the steps.

"Looks clear, Sergeant."

She waited just inside the stronghold with Reeve on the opposite side of the door.

"Good lookin' out, Welch. Stay by the truck."

Jed grunted a *Rah* and went back to the truck, posting by the hood and monitoring their perimeter again.

Reeve came out behind him and jumped into the driver's seat. He fired up the engine and flashed a thumbs up. Jed peeled away from the hood to stand by the passenger door, weapon up and scanning their perimeter. Reeve called over to him.

"I'm gonna back it up to the door. Stay with me and stay frosty. Rah?"

"*Errr.*"

Jed stepped away from the truck. Reeve wheeled it around to aim the tailgate at the steps. Jed kept pace with the vehicle, using it as cover on one side.

If the hit is gonna come, it's gonna come. Can't stay covered from every direction. Just gotta stay sharp. Stay frosty.

Splintered wood and shattered stone filled his view wherever he looked. Rubble and mounds of earth surrounded the parking lot. And all of it carried the threat of another ambush, or one of Tucker's snipers. Even though Leigh had told them Tucker was bluffing, Jed couldn't shake the sensation of being watched every second he was outside.

Reeve crawled the truck back to the steps, letting Jed move at an easy pace while he watched out for the enemy.

Tucker. The monsters. They're all the same now.

The truck stopped and Jed stayed by the passenger door. Reeve jumped out and ran inside. A beat later, he and Sergeant G came out. They posted at the bottom of the steps flanking the firefighters as they came out.

Dom and Luce had their shotguns up and moved to the rear cab of the truck. Matty came next carrying the trauma bag against his hip and his shotgun held tucked against his side. Jo came out last with the grenade launcher up and ready. The firefighters all moved fast, but with every passing second, Jed felt like an hour passed as the dead city surrounded them and threatened to add them to the body count.

One by one the squad climbed into the extra cab, until only Jo was left outside.

***

"In the truck," Gallegos said, waving the firefighter on. But Jo shook her head and went to the tailgate. She hopped onto the bumper and into the truck bed in a single movement.

That's all right. She needs to be out in the action. And if that thump gun does work, we need her out back with it, not stuffed in the cab.

Gallegos watched the others all crouch low in the rear cab, staying out of sight as best they could. She moved around the truck and directed Welch to move up to the front. He did and rested the SAW on the hood, roving the muzzle around their perimeter and the roof of the stronghold. Gallegos did the same, watching the debris around the parking lot for any signs of Tucker or the sucker faces.

The ruins around them stared back, empty, lifeless, and silent except for a howling wind that snuck through the cracks and found its way under Gallegos' collar.

"Reeve, let's move."

He stepped forward and climbed into the driver's seat again. Gallegos moved up to the passenger door.

"Let's go, Welch," she said. "Hop in back with Jo. If Tucker shows his ass, I want to finish it quick so we can get on with the mission."

Welch moved out and Gallegos climbed into the truck.

"Back home?" Reeve asked.

"Rah. Back to the hide. Secure our position, resupply. Then we patrol underground. Find the hive and get our people back. With the big one dead, the sucker faces around here should be easier to take down."

"Oorah on that," Reeve said. "I hope you're right."

Gallegos grunted an *Errr*.

Mission first, everything else second.

Right now, her mission included keeping her people alive, saving anybody trapped underground, and killing the motherfuckers responsible for making them prisoners in the first place. They might be dead, or they might be alive. Whatever condition they were in, she wanted their captors in her sight picture, and from the looks on everyone else's faces, she knew the rest of her squad, new members and old, felt the same way.

***

Jed hopped onto the tailgate and scooted into the bed. Jo sat against the cab with the grenade launcher held across her chest. Jed sat to her right with the SAW resting on his knees.

The motor started up and Jed watched the dead city spin around him as Reeve positioned the truck to reverse through the breezeway. For a second, he thought Jo would be blowing them a hole through the gate, but he felt Reeve put the truck into neutral. Sergeant G jumped out and headed for the gate.

"Eyes out," she said as she ran by the bed.

"Rah, Sergeant."

"Why do you all say that?" Jo asked.

"Rah? It's just what we say. It's easy, you know? You

149

could say a whole sentence, or a whole paragraph. Or you could say *Rah*."

"I think I get it."

"Rah?"

She let out a quick laugh and said, "Rah."

Jed grinned and dared Tucker to reveal himself. If the guy was telling the truth about having snipers, then he and Jo were sitting ducks. Even though that scared him to think about, he was part of a squad again. He had brothers and sisters around him, bearing the burden. The way Jo looked at the city around them, holding the grenade launcher, Jed figured she was ready for whatever came next. Then he noticed her white knuckle grip on the weapon.

"Hey, Jo," he said. She looked him in the eye. Her shoulders were tight, and she blinked fast as she stared back at him. Jed had never been here before, facing off against another person's fear and knowing it was up to him to help.

"Hey, it's just the shakes, Jo. You'll be good. Keep your eyes cool and easy, you know? Stay frosty. Try to see as much as you can, and don't forget to breathe."

Jo let out a breath and coughed. "I didn't even—," she said.

"I know. That's why I reminded you."

Sergeant G was at the gate and yanking it open. Jed clapped a hand on Jo's shoulder. She was still a little tense, but she'd fought back the flight response. He gave her a nod and a grin, and went back to monitoring their perimeter.

If you're out there looking at us, Tucker, just take the shot. Show us where you're hiding and it'll be the last thing you do.

***

Gallegos motioned for Welch and Jo to watch through the breezeway. At the gate, she paused to listen for another truck motor. The city was still and quiet, and that made every sound echo all the more. Fearing what that meant for their escape, Gallegos grabbed the gate and took three breaths before she pulled. The tangle of metal plates and wire squealed against the pavement, and it only moved a few inches before snagging on the ground. She, breathed in and yanked on it again, moving it a little more. With each screech of metal on stone, she expected Tucker's black truck to slam into her, or for a swarm of suckers to flood the parking lot.

Inch by inch, Gallegos cleared them a path. When the breezeway was open, she got her weapon up and back pedaled to the truck, slapping the wheel well as she passed the bed. "Move out!" she shouted. The truck rocked as she leaped into the passenger seat and Reeve put it in gear. Gallegos said a silent prayer that Welch or Jo would see the enemy first and that their aim would be true.

Reeve reversed them through the breezeway and they left the ruins of the stronghold behind. The street outside was empty and quiet, and no sniper fire came slamming into the truck.

We're out. We're going to make it!

Reeve cranked them around to face toward 3rd Avenue. The truck pitched forward. For a brief second, Gallegos wanted to smile. Then she pictured Leigh's and Mahton's bodies in the hallway upstairs, and imagined other people from Operation Reaper trapped underground with the monsters. Her half-grin faded to a scowl and she felt the burn of rage in her chest.

We're coming to get you. Hold on, Marines. We are coming.

***

They turned the corner toward where Jed had come across Pivowitch and his squad, and where Tucker's partner showed up with the prisoners later that afternoon.

Please don't be there. Please just be somewhere else, hiding like the fucking rat you are.

Yesterday was Jed's first real effort at prayer in as long as he could remember. He'd never spent much time in churches except to say goodbye to one of his friends who got taken out by some punk on the block. When Reeve took them onto Lexington, he turned right, bringing them up beside the buses lying on their sides in front of the depot. The street was quiet and Jed thought for once his prayers were being answered.

We made it back to the hide. We're good.

Jed let himself relax, but the calm only lasted a second. He spotted Tucker's black truck sitting silent two blocks behind them.

"That's them," Jo said. She had the grenade launcher up, but didn't have the sight raised. Jed reached over and flicked it up. He opened his mouth to tell her how to aim when Tucker's headlights flashed and small arms fire popped and rattled through the neighborhood. Jed spotted muzzle flashes in the high rise apartments next to the depot. Rounds zipped in, pinging into the truck bed. Their truck roared forward, away from the kill zone, and

Jed forgot about helping Jo with the launcher. He lifted the SAW and squeezed the trigger, filling the dead streets with the heavy chop of the weapon as Tucker came racing after them.

— 19 —

Jed's view shifted as Reeve swerved them around craters, dead monsters, and debris in the road. The tires barked against the ragged pavement. Jo slammed up against the wall of the truck bed and Jed grabbed for her arm to make sure she didn't go over the side. Then they were up on the sidewalk and back on the road just as fast. Tucker kept coming. Jed lifted the SAW and spit a trail of bullets behind them, but none of his shots hit home. With the shifting range and constant swerving, he couldn't get a good bead on the black truck.

Tucker's passenger leaned out with a weapon and fired. Jo dropped down and slid toward the tailgate. She grabbed hold of Jed's left boot and held the grenade launcher tucked up tight against her. Jed let himself slide down in the truck bed next to Jo. Cracks of gunfire came from behind them. A few rounds impacted on the tailgate, but most of the enemy's shots went wide or overhead.

Good. They can't aim any better'n me with all this juking and shit. Still, they can get lucky just like anybody else.

"We gotta stay against the sides of the bed," he said to Jo.

She nodded, pushed away from him, and grabbed one of the tie down hooks inside the bed. Jed scooted backwards and did the same. It wasn't much to hold onto, but it would help.

More rounds pinged against the truck. Jed let go of his handhold so he could lift the SAW to send back a burst over the tailgate. Reeve had them swerving too much though. Everything Jed sent back at Tucker just disappeared into the ruins on the side of the road.

"I can't hit him! Reeve, get us around a corner and hold up!"

The truck took a hard left and Jed and Jo reached for the bed walls to steady themselves. She put a foot out and braced against his hip, holding him against the hump of the wheel well.

"Can you aim better if I hold you steady?" she shouted.

"I'll try."

Tucker's spotter popped off a few more shots as the black truck rounded the corner they'd just turned. Jed lifted up on his elbow and took aim. He fired one burst and then another. Some of the shots hit the truck, but Tucker still raced after them. They were only about fifty yards behind Jed and the others now, and closing fast.

***

Gallegos fought to keep her eyes on the sideview mirror while she slammed around in the front seat. The firefighters behind her stayed as low as they could with three of them stuffed into the extra cab. Now and then they would shout or grunt as they were rocked into each other.

"Keep loading those magazines!" she yelled back to them while Reeve whipped them side to side down the road. Welch kept a steady beat of sustained fire going out the back. But either Reeve's driving made it so Welch couldn't aim for shit, or Tucker had the protection of angels. Gallegos checked her mirror again. The black truck was still coming after them.

Reeve slid them around a corner, bouncing the truck bed and throwing Gallegos into the passenger door.

"The fuck, Reeve! This isn't a hockey rink!"

"Fucking holes in the road. I had to turn here."

Gallegos flashed a look at her mirror. Sure enough the intersection they just passed was a mess of craters and debris.

"Just get us steady so Welch can—"

Gunfire sounded from behind them and bullets pinged off the truck body. The firefighters crouched down lower, almost putting their heads between their knees. Still the steady clicking of rounds being loaded into magazines made Gallegos feel better about their chances. She turned back to give them a thumbs up and came eye to eye with Luciano. He was tucked down lower than Dom and Matty.

"I seen a lot of shit, but I ain't never been shot at," Luce said, his voice shaking around every word as he reloaded a magazine.

Dom reassured him. "Stay cool, Luce. Stay cool."

Matty added his voice to the effort.

"Get us somewhere we can hold up. We'll send some

lead back their way. Fire their shit up."

"Just hold tight, people," Gallegos said. She shifted onto her hip so she could bring her weapon around to return fire.

***

Jed and Jo braced their backs together and held onto the truck for support as Reeve brought them around another corner. They'd turned onto Park Avenue. Jed risked looking up. The street behind them was empty, but he could still hear Tucker's engine. The black truck was coming their way.

Jed picked up the SAW and told Jo to get ready with the thump gun.

"They come around the corner, you let one go, rah?"

"Rah," she said and pushed herself up to a sitting position with the grenade launcher at her shoulder. Tucker's truck was still out of sight, but it had to be near the corner.

What's he waiting for?

Jed flinched when they passed through the narrow space between two smashed up minivans.

Those weren't in the road before. Were they?

He stayed up, SAW ready to rock, and waiting for Tucker to appear. The steady beat of an engine told Jed the black truck was idling around the corner.

Why aren't they following us?

He looked at the minivans again, now receding behind them. Debris and the bodies of monsters lined a path in the street and on the sidewalk, showing where the vans used to sit before they were pushed into the street to form a gateway.

Or the door of a trap.

Tucker's truck appeared at the corner, and slowly nosed into view, staying mostly hidden behind the minivans. Jed sent a burst at them anyway, but all he did was take out one of Tucker's headlights. Reeve was putting more distance between them with every second. After three blocks, he began to slow down, and then finally came to a sharp halt, throwing Jed and Jo up against the back of the cab.

"What the—?"

Jo was up first with the grenade launcher. But she didn't fire. "Shit. He's penned us, and now I know what he did with the extra mines."

"He's what?" Jed asked, pushing himself up on his elbow to look over the tailgate. Sure enough, Tucker's black truck filled the space between the minivans. They could always back up with Jed firing, but moving in reverse would make it hard for Reeve to change course.

Then Jed spotted the Claymores lining the street. They faced into Park Avenue a few blocks behind their truck. If they wanted to get back to the hide, they just had to keep going forward. Unless Reeve stopped because they were blocked in up front, too.

Jed moved to look over the cab and froze. To his left, the blackened brick walls supporting the elevated tracks led down Park Avenue. Even with a few broken spots where bombs had ruined the tracks, the wall loomed like a curtain Jed expected to be swept aside, revealing a horde of the sucker faces. He looked back down their route at each block they'd passed. Arched tunnels passed beneath the tracks, but most of them were clogged with wrecked cars and debris. Some of it looked purposefully shoved into place.

The more he looked, the darker the tracks grew and the more threatening the shadows became until Jed couldn't take it anymore.

He shifted his position and lifted the SAW to aim at the tracks. If anything moved over there, he'd light it up. He sent his focus into every dark corner, and was happy to see Jo doing the same. She kept the thump gun tucked against her shoulder and ready to fire.

"Do you see any of them?" Jo asked.

"No. Not yet. But they gotta be there."

The ruins of the el-tracks reminded Jed of his escape from Queens with the Civil Affairs unit. They'd taken the Queensboro Bridge and were ambushed from the tracks that ran overhead. The monsters had raced ahead of their convoy and dropped onto them, taking out almost everyone in Jed's truck.

God, don't let that happen now. Not now.

Jed wanted to shout for Sergeant G, tell her they had to move, but he didn't dare take his focus off the tracks, not with so many shadows haunting him from every direction.

***

Gallegos gripped the dashboard tight and rested her M4 on the door. Tucker's truck had vanished from her mirror.

They stopped. Or they're going in reverse. What the hell are they doing?

"Are they gone?" Reeve asked. "Shit, I should've

flipped us around back there. If they're just a bunch of candy-asses—"

"Eyes on the road ahead. We don't know if we're clear yet, and there's no easy way off this street. Not anymore."

Park Avenue was crossed by three streets along their path, but almost every road beneath the el-tracks was filled with smashed cars, like a barricade.

And some of those cars were just pushed into position.

Gallegos felt the world slow down until everything seemed to move in half time. The brick wall beside her was broken up ahead, with ash, rubble, and jagged steel spilling into the roadway. Reeve swerved around the mess and braked suddenly, sending everyone in the cab forward in their seats. Luce nearly tumbled into the front of the cab.

"What the fuck are you doing, Reeve?" Gallegos demanded, pushing off the dashboard. She'd only just put her hands out in time to avoid slamming into the windshield. "We need to get to the hide."

"With respect, Sergeant, the hide ain't an option anymore." Reeve gestured ahead. Gallegos followed his finger, but he started ranting before she could pick out what he'd aimed at.

"That little race around town was a fucking dangle. Check the mirrors."

She did, and what she saw put a ball of rage into her throat.

The road behind them was lined with the familiar mix of holes and bodies and debris. But something new had been added since they'd left the hide in the bus depot. Three blocks behind them, a pair of minivans had been pushed together, forming a gateway. She hadn't noticed it before because she was too busy watching her mirror for Tucker's truck. And now there it was, filling the space between the vans like a drawbridge being slammed shut.

"If that ain't bad enough, take a look up front."

Two blocks ahead of their position, at the back corner of the bus depot, a line of cars had been moved to fill the roadway, and even from this distance, Gallegos could see the small green rectangles spaced across the cars.

"Guess we found the rest of them mines," she said.

If they wanted to continue, and stay far enough away from those mines, they'd be forced to turn around and deal with Tucker first. The tunnels below the elevated tracks were jammed with cars and debris, but the crossing one block back had looked clear. They'd been moving fast when they passed it, so Gallegos couldn't be sure.

But going under the tracks wasn't exactly the most desirable option. Even if they could find a clear tunnel, they'd probably be driving into a dead end. Adding insult to injury, the crack of an M4 sounded from behind them. A few more shots were fired, and two of them hit the truck.

Tucker's no idiot. He's penned us like cattle and now he's trying to herd us into the mines.

"What now, Sergeant?" Reeve asked, breaking her from her thoughts.

"Use the thump gun and blow that truck out of the way."

"Won't he set off the mines?" Luce asked. "He's got us in a cage. We shoot, he blows the mines, and then we're all dead."

Matty and Dom said as much themselves, and Reeve turned back to answer the firefighters.

"We're far enough they won't hit us, at least not that bad. That's why he's shooting at us. He wants us to get closer so he can use the mines to finish us off. That means he's a punk ass, just like I thought. Motherfucker knows he can't take us out man to man."

"Everybody stay really low," Gallegos said. "Reeve, put it in reverse and get ready to floor it. Somebody open the window and tell Welch to wipe that piece of shit off our ass."

Her order was met with a knock on the back window. Matty slid it open and Welch's voice came into the cab.

"Sergeant G, why're we stopped? We got four Claymores on the street back here—"

"Shit! They mined the street up ahead, too."

Another round impacted on the truck.

"Get us out of here!" Welch shouted.

"Use the thumper, Welch! Clear him off our ass!"

More rounds came in and Welch shouted back, "We gotta get away from these tracks. The sucker faces hide in 'em."

"Negative on that, Marine! Clear us a hole! Now!"

The rounds kept coming from Tucker's spotter, but they were only hitting the fenders.

Reeve slammed the steering wheel. "We let him do this. We goddamned let him do this."

"What do you mean?" Dom asked.

"He means we should have seen it coming. We underestimated Tucker, and now we're fucked," Gallegos said. She resisted the urge to shout for Welch to take action and scanned the area, looking for a place they could hold up and make a stand. She spotted a mound of debris a little way back and on their left. Keeping her voice low, she said, "Reeve, turn us around over there, behind that shit pile. Tucker and his spotter won't have a clear shot at us."

"You're thinking we ditch the ride and try to fight on the ground?"

"No. I'm thinking we blow that roadblock up there. Make a hole and move out," she said.

"Welch said he saw four Claymores behind us, right? That's gotta be two on either side of the road. Tucker's no dummy. I don't know, Sergeant; those mines are closer than the ones up ahead. He might blow 'em. I don't like our chances."

"I don't like our chances either way, Reeve. I like sitting here in the street even less. Turn us around. Over there," she said, aiming a finger at the debris behind the remains of an apartment block.

Reeve spun the wheel. "So they blow the roadblock. Then what?" he asked as he moved them off the main roadway. No explosions rocked the street, but more rounds impacted on the truck, still just hitting the fenders. Gallegos waited until Reeve had them positioned before answering his question.

"First, we deal with Tucker. Then we get back to the hide. The sucker faces are quiet now, but I doubt they'll stay that way for long."

— 20 —

The truck jerked and Jed again watched the city spin around him as Reeve took them in an arc that aimed the rear of the truck at the roadblock. They took a few more rounds from Tucker's spotter, but nothing that came close enough to be a threat. And the Claymores didn't go off either.

Jed checked their position. Reeve had brought them up behind a mountain of wood and concrete that spilled out of the apartment block beside them.

Another round came in and pinged off the truck.

"It's like he's missing on purpose," Jo said. "I swear he's hit the same fender every time. He obviously knows how to aim, but he's not aiming at us."

"Probably hoping we'll move closer to the mines," Jed said. Another few rounds came their way, but they all missed. He worried a lip between his teeth and kept glancing between the roadblock and the el-tracks. Even with the roadway between them now, the sucker faces could still leap out of anywhere.

Beside him, Jo held onto the side of truck bed with one hand and kept the thump gun snug against her side with the other.

Since they were turned around, Jed took a good look at the blockade Tucker had put together. About a hundred yards away a line of cars had been pushed into position, probably by Tucker's truck. The cars snarled the road from the sidewalk to the el-tracks.

"If the mines go off, will we get hit?" Jo asked.

"Shouldn't. Not from this far, but you never know. We gotta put a round out there and drop down fast. Even then we might get hit."

Behind them, the cab window slid open again. Sergeant G shouted back to him.

"Welch, make a hole!"

"Oorah, Sergeant!" he said and reached for the grenade launcher. Jo still held it tight.

"Waiting on you, Christmas!" Sergeant G yelled out the window. "Let's go!"

"Let me take the shot," he said to Jo. She held the thumper like it was a life line. Her eyes met his and for a split second he thought he could see the girl she used to be. She looked like a kid, like a girl he used to know in school, scared and alone and not knowing what the hell was going to happen next. Then she was Jo again, the firefighter who wasn't afraid to take action. Just like another woman he'd known once.

Now she's in the sewers with the sucker faces and me and Jo are sitting in the middle of a battlefield with nobody but ourselves to say it's going to be all right.

Jed reached for the grenade launcher again and Jo finally let him lift it out of her hands.

"Get down and stay down. I'll cover you, just in case. If anything comes our way, it should be me that gets one in my fourth point of contact."

Jo's face softened. "I hope nothing comes our way," she said. "But thanks, and rah."

She slid down to lie flat in the truck bed. Jed checked he had the right grenade loaded. They'd come away with five high explosive rounds, and one Willie Pete. "Gotta save that one for crowd control," he said, showing the WP round to Jo.

"What's it do?"

"Makes a smoke screen, but the shit burns forever. If we get swarmed, this'll give us something to hide in, and if you land it in the middle of them, it'll take out sucker faces quicker'n shit. These," he said, holding up an HE round, "are what you use when you need to make a hole in a wall. Stay down now."

He lifted the thumper and had the sight flipped up. He aimed and was about to squeeze the trigger when Sergeant G shouted from the cab. The crack of an M4 drowned her out, then Jo screamed next to him and a pair of clawed hands clamped onto the truck bed just above her face.

***

Gallegos gave up waiting for Welch. She put her eyes back on the ruins around them, and especially the mound of rubble they were using as cover from Tucker's spotter. They hadn't taken any more fire since they'd moved into this position.

"He's taking long enough," Reeve said. "Fucking deke."

"Chill, Reeve," Gallegos said. "Eyes out. That goes for everybody."

Reeve spit out his window but brought his weapon up and scoped the area for movement. The firefighters shifted in the rear cab. Gallegos turned around and checked out their version of keeping an eye on things. An easy smile spread across her face. Luce was tucked down in the middle with a handful of shotgun shells in his lap. He nodded at her and she gave him a thumbs up. Dom and Matty sat on either side of Luce, weapons up and watching the area outside the truck.

The rear cab window was still open, and she could see Welch and Jo moving around back there. It looked like he was loading the thumper. She turned back to watch her zone of fire.

If she'd still been watching out the back, she wouldn't have seen the three sucker faces that low-crawled toward the truck from around the back of the debris pile.

"Enemy at three o'clock!" she yelled and fired off a shot at the first of the monsters. It went down and the others scrambled off to either side, disappearing in Gallegos' peripheral. Then Jo's scream had her turning in her seat to watch out Reeve's window.

A trio of sucker faces darted forward from a broken section of the el-tracks. Reeve fired, taking down the lead of the three. A single shot from his weapon put another down. The third launched sideways and was instantly knocked back by a burst from the SAW.

The street was quiet for a second. A truck motor rumbled down the block, followed by the squealing of tires and explosions sending a cloud of dust and debris through the already ruined street.

In a flash, Reeve had them backing up and into the roadway.

"Now's our chance," he said. "Welch! Make a hole in that roadblock!"

Gallegos let him take the lead and focused on watching their flank for any of the sucker faces. As Reeve got them back into the roadway, she knew why Tucker had bailed out.

The street one block ahead was a mess of blood and the shredded remains of sucker faces.

A swarm of the monsters filled the street beyond the carnage, pouring out of the ruins and down from the el-tracks. Where the two streams met in the middle of the roadway, they crashed together in a frenzy of claws and blood. The sucker faces from the tracks were faster and worked in teams, taking down their enemies by joining up in twos and threes. The ones from the ruins were like a herd. They all moved as a unit, but individuals were always left off on the side, and these were taken down quickly by the stronger and faster monsters racing into the street from the el-tracks.

Behind the melee, Tucker's truck flew backwards and nearly rolled up on two tires as the driver whipped them around the corner in reverse.

"Must be the other gangs," Gallegos said. "We killed the leader that Tucker made a deal with. The others are coming in to claim territory, and the ones from the tracks are winning."

"Tucker knows it," Reeve said. "He's bugging out and leaving us here in between his minefield and this fucking cage match."

A roar cascaded around them. Gallegos looked left and right, trying to spot the leader that she knew had to be nearby.

"There," Reeve said. "On top of the tracks."

"Damn," Matty said from behind her. "It's bigger than the one Tucker was fucking."

He was right. The sucker face standing on top of the elevated tracks was a lot bigger than the one that took Mahton. It easily stood seven feet tall and wore a shirt of what looked like bones all strung together.

It's collecting trophies.

A clutch of at least a dozen smaller ones scrambled around the tracks near the big fucker. Several of them held onto the bigger one's legs or hands, almost like children. The smaller ones were all wiry and covered in cuts and scrapes.

As she stared at the grotesque sight, the big one grunted something, then turned to face the smallest of the group. It was leaping around to the left of the giant. The other small ones immediately snapped their heads around and locked onto the smallest one. In a flash, they swarmed it, and with slashing claws ripped it to pieces so they could eat.

They're starving and eating each other to survive.

The big one stomped further down the tracks, and the smaller ones followed. They moved closer to the fighting by the mini-vans. Shrieks and screams split the air as the monsters clashed. The big one gave another roar and waved a hand. The small ones around it charged forward, racing into the swarm of others that were fighting.

Gallegos nudged Reeve to raise his weapon.

"Take it out, Reeve. Then we get back to the hide."

"Rah, Sergeant."

Reeve lifted his M4. Gallegos said a silent prayer for his aim to be true. She leaned forward as the giant on the el-tracks turned around. It waved a hand behind it, like it was calling forward reinforcements. While Reeve lined up his shot, Gallegos strained her neck to see around him. She quickly fell back into her seat when a swarm of sucker faces rose up from the el-tracks and poured over the side.

Reeve dropped his weapon on its sling and had them in gear. He stomped on the gas and tore away from the flood of monsters descending from the el-tracks. Their claws scraped against brick, concrete, and pavement, adding to the horror of their howls and screeches of rage.

Gallegos had to turn her attention to the road beside her. Sucker faces raced toward the truck up ahead, trying to take their flanks. Reeve dodged them around a clutch of the monsters that dropped down from the tracks and landed in the middle of the street. Gallegos picked one off when it latched onto the hood with its claws. Another leaped up from the street to replace the one she'd just killed. This one held on and got a foot onto the passenger door.

One of the firefighters had a shotgun out the window behind her. A blast from the weapon ended the sucker's attempt at climbing inside. Gallegos fired at two more that sped out of the ruins, putting them down. She checked her mirror and saw smaller groups drafting behind the truck as Reeve drove them ever closer to the melee. Welch was firing sustained bursts at suckers that followed them, but he wasn't hitting consistently.

He'll run out of ammo before he gets them all.

Gallegos put her attention back on the road ahead, firing at the onrushing sucker faces. "There's a tunnel at the next block, Reeve! I think it's clear!"

"I hope to fuck it's clear!" he shouted back.

In the rear cab, Matty blasted at the suckers as they raced alongside the truck. Dom did the same on his side. The thunderclaps of the shotguns pressed in on Gallegos' ears, adding to the constant chop of the SAW from the bed.

A sucker face leaped onto the top of the cab and reached down to the window where Matty was firing from. The monster grabbed the barrel of his shotgun and yanked it out, almost pulling him out the window with it. He let go just in time as another clawed hand came stabbing down at the space in front of the window. Luce handed him the spare shotgun, but as soon as the barrel cleared the window, the sucker face up top slashed a hand down and yanked it away.

Gallegos drew her sidearm and fired through the top of the truck. All she got for her trouble was a louder ringing in her ears.

The monster came down to Matty's window and reached in to grab his shirt. Its arms were still wrapped in sickly pale flesh and ropy muscles, but they were spindle-thin and ragged from cuts and scrapes. Matty swatted the grasping hands aside with his pistol. Gallegos turned in her seat and tried to get a bead on the monster.

Dom had the last shotgun and rotated in his seat. He pushed the barrel into the sucker face's eye socket, knocking the thing's head back. It grabbed onto the door post with one hand and tried to yank the shotgun away with the other.

"You want it?" Dom yelled as he fired.

The blast filled the truck cab and a spray of gore coated the back of Gallegos' seat. Matty had his arms up in time to catch most of the mess on his clothing.

The sucker face slid off the top of the cab and fell to the street. Reeve gunned the motor, launching them up and over a debris mound and back onto the roadway of Park Avenue. In the back of the truck, Welch fired sustained bursts at the horde that spilled from the el-tracks like a tidal wave.

"Keep up the fire!" Gallegos shouted, grabbing for a loaded magazine from the pile they'd made in the back. Luce was funneling shotgun ammo to Dom in between loading the last of the magazines they'd collected.

The swarm from the tracks had to be at least three hundred strong or more. Even though they were concentrating on taking out the ones coming from the ruins, it wouldn't be long before the truck was completely surrounded.

We have only two boxes left for the SAW and maybe three hundred rounds up here, if that. Salve nos Dios.

— 21 —

Jed sprayed down the sucker face that latched onto the truck. He got the first wave that rushed off the el-tracks, but then his sight picture was a blur of pale flesh and ropy muscles, bulging lips, spiny teeth, and claws. Every round hit something, but Jed couldn't be sure his shots were effective. Blood sprayed and then vanished as the monsters clambered over their own fallen to race behind the fleeing truck.

Jo fired at them with her pistol. She hit two of them square in the chest and they dropped, but the weapon was empty after a few more shots. Jed saw her throw it out of the truck in anger.

"Willie Pete! Use the Willie Pete!" he shouted, still firing sustained bursts into the swarm. He knocked them back again and again, but every wave he took down was quickly replaced by another.

The truck swerved sharply and crashed against a small car in the road, knocking it aside. Jo rolled away from him and slammed against bed wall. Jed reached for her as a dark shadow covered the truck. Black walls surrounded them and Jed felt the world closing in from all sides.

"Shit, where's he taking us? Shit!"

Next to him, Jo was steady again and scrambling to load the thump gun. Then they were out in daylight and leaning up as Reeve took them over something in the street. Jo lost her grip on the weapon when she reached for the bed wall to steady herself. The truck angled away from a ruined building and Jed feared they would go over onto the side, but they leveled out just as fast and raced on.

Reeve cornered hard and Jed pitched over onto his side. He slid into the bed wall and just grabbed a hand hold before they were swerving sideways again. The wheels barked and squealed against the pavement, but Jed could still hear the scraping of the monsters' claws. Their snarls and hisses grew louder as they came, hungry for the squad's blood.

A pair of claws grabbed the tailgate, and then another. Two suckers rose up, flicking thick tongues and drooling spit. Jo brought her foot up and slammed her heel into one's face, knocking it off the truck. The other grabbed hold of her leg and yanked, but Jed had his hands under her arms and pulled back, tugging the sucker face into the truck bed. Jo kicked at it and Jed did the same as let her go and tried to get the SAW around. It bit at his feet. He kicked once more before he had the muzzle against the monster's cheek and squeezed the trigger, feeling a single round spit out before the weapon locked up.

The sucker face fell dead against his boots. Jo kicked at it until it was at the rear of the bed.

"Fuck! Jammed up again!" Jed screamed as he went to clear the weapon. He held it aside and covered Jo with his body as he lifted the feed tray cover.

She pushed away and raised the grenade launcher, firing it over the tailgate. The explosion made the truck lurch to the side and Jed lost his grip on the SAW as the street filled with a cloud of smoke.

"That was HE! Where's the Willie Pete?" he yelled, searching the truck bed for the belt of grenade rounds. It had slid down to the back, and was under the body of the dead monster. Before he could move, Jo had jumped forward. She grabbed the belt just as another sucker face latched onto the tailgate and raised its clawed hand to swipe down at her.

***

Gallegos picked off as many as she could from inside the truck cab. She had to stay back from the window or risk getting grabbed and yanked out. Reeve swerved them left and right through the bloodied remains of the sucker faces taken out by the mines.

"I'm going for the tunnel," he said as they raced away from the horde that kept coming from the elevated tracks. Gallegos gave a quick glance at the road ahead of them. A burned up Volkswagen Beetle had been shoved into place in front of the tunnel.

"Reeve—"

"Hold onto your asses!" he yelled as he aimed them at the little car's fender. They swerved hard and smashed the car aside, sending the truck rocking as they shot into the tunnel. Gallegos whispered a prayer as they flew under the tracks and burst out again. She turned and fired behind them at the swarm of sucker faces pouring down from above and joining the others in the chase. Gallegos kept firing, one shot at a time, picking her targets and dropping them.

Aim, squeeze, aim again. Aim, squeeze—

She put a hand out to brace herself when Reeve took them over a mound of debris to avoid a horde that sped at them from the left. They cleared most of the suckers, but a trio launched into the air and landed on the hood. Gallegos finally risked it and leaned out with her pistol, cracking two of the sucker faces with head shots. The third lost its grip and was ground under the truck tires as Reeve stomped the gas and they sped forward. On the other side of the truck, Dom had the shotgun out the window and was taking the monsters down as quick as he could fire.

The shotgun blasts were nothing more than thumps in her ears now. And then they stopped.

"Out! We're out of ammo!" Dom yelled.

***

Jed recovered his grip on the SAW as more clawed hands grabbed onto the tailgate above Jo. She'd rolled to the right and dodged the monster's claws, but now she had three of them looming over her and reaching for her legs.

"Help!" Jo screamed.

The truck spun to the side and Jed frantically swiped at the feed tray, clearing belt links and an empty brass casing from the weapon. He slapped the cover down and charged the SAW as the truck slid up against a ruined wall, scraping the fender against the shattered stone. The sucker faces caught flecks of concrete and sparks until Jed sent a burst at them. Two went down with holes in their heads. The third caught a round in its throat and still it came forward, leaning over the tailgate to swipe at Jo's retreating boots. Jed fired again and it fell backwards with its limbs flailing.

Jed kept a watch in every direction, scanning around them to watch for any monsters that had closed the distance from the main pack to the truck. Next to him, Jo was reloading the thump gun.

"Willie Pete this time?" he asked.

"Rah."

The truck took a hard bank and lifted up as they came over a debris mound again.

Jo lifted up onto her hip and sighted. Jed raised up and covered her with burst after burst, but he knew he'd have to swap boxes soon.

"Take the shot!" he yelled. "I'm almost out on this box!"

Reeve swerved them in an arc across the street, sending Jo back on her heels against the bed wall. She kept the thump gun tucked in and put a hand out to steady herself.

Jed fired his last burst at the sucker faces that were coming in a wide wave, aiming for the cab and truck bed.

"Changing ammo! Take the shot!"

Jo looked back at him, then turned to face the onrushing swarm. She aimed and fired the thump gun.

***

Dom used his empty weapon to jab at any sucker faces that came close. Gallegos sat back into her seat, holding her M4 ready at her window. She turned to look out the windshield in time to see the barricade ahead. She braced herself with her legs while Reeve spun another tight circle, bringing them around to straddle the road. A fresh swarm raced at them from the direction of the el-tracks, and it stretched across the road, filling her sight picture no matter where she aimed. Others poured over the barricade and out of the ruins of the neighborhood behind them.

We're surrounded. And we're almost out of ammo.

"What do we have left?"

"Nothing," Matty said. "Just pistols. Y'all?"

"On magazine, half gone," Reeve said.

"Less than that in my weapon, plus one full," Gallegos added. "Make every shot count. If this is our time, then this is our time. We make it hurt, for Mahton and Leigh and everyone we couldn't save."

The squad replied as one. Gallegos lifted her M4 and sighted on the sucker faces running toward them from the el-tracks. A loud *thump* sounded from behind the cab. Gallegos counted the seconds until the horde vanished in a cloud of flaming smoke.

***

Jo fired and Jed pulled her back down. The grenade impacted and the air around them filled with the stench of garlic and burnt meat. Jed slotted a fresh box home in the SAW and set the belt into the feed tray. Closing the cover, he shifted and leaned up to see spears of smoke spiraling out from the mass of sucker faces. The monsters shrieked, and not for the first time Jed felt a hint of mercy for them. The street was filled with their crawling and flailing bodies as the phosphorous ate into their skin. Jo had fired into the center of the group, and most of the pack there had been hit.

The ones that weren't seemed to dance around the main group, looking for the weakest ones. A sucker face shrieked behind Jed and he spun around to see another swarm racing for the truck. They streamed out of the neighborhood ruins, over crumbled walls, out of the wreckage, and around splintered tree trunks. Jed sent a burst at them and they split apart, into smaller groups that raced around the street, dodging and juking so fast that he couldn't aim if he tried.

Like they'd done back on Park Avenue, the two tribes of suckers charged into each other in the street, ripping and slashing at each other in a frenzy of blood and howling. The ones from the neighborhood sped by the truck, like they didn't even notice Jo and Jed sitting in the back.

"They're not even looking at us," Jo said.

Jed wanted to believe her, but he knew different. "They see us," he said, "but they got bigger problems. At least for now."

The swarms clashed and fought, with screeches and roars filling the street and echoing in the dead air of the city.

"They could just swarm us right now," Jo said.

"They could, but they aren't. They'd rather figure out who gets to be on top. Then they'll come after us."

"They're fighting for the *privilege* of killing us? That's so disgusting, I can't—"

"Fucking animals," Jed said through a chuckle. Then he spotted one that had its eyes locked on him. It danced around behind larger ones that were plowing forward into the battle with the sucker faces from the el-tracks.

"That one knows better," Jed said, lining it up in his sight picture.

A roar of rage filled the air around them just as Jed fired. He hit the one that had been staring at him. It dropped in a heap as the others charged forward. Another big one came stomping out from the neighborhood ruins. The smaller ones in the street raced ahead of it with a tiny, fast one out front, like it was leading the pack. A blast from the truck cab put it down. The swarm drew together, slowing their progress, but still closing in around the truck.

The big one picked up the broken body of a dead sucker face and flung it at the truck. It impacted against the front fender and slid across the hood. The small ones formed a circle around the truck while others still sped onward to join the battle up ahead.

Jed sent a burst at the big monster. It didn't flinch, even as two of the rounds struck it in the chest. Instead, it reached for another of its fallen children and hurled it toward the truck. Jed had to duck to avoid getting hit. The body bounced off the cab and landed in the street. Jed and Jo stayed tucked down as low as they could, but he kept firing sustained bursts toward the giant.

***

Gallegos stared at the big fucker outside as she slapped her final magazine into the receiver and released the bolt. The monster reached for another body and hoisted it over its head. It threw it at the truck and roared. The

Willie Pete round tore up the swarm from the tracks. Most of them had crawled away to lick their wounds. Gallegos spotted some being eaten by the stronger ones from the neighborhood, which were rapidly closing in and forming a melee that filled the roadway and spilled over into the ruins on either side.

Gallegos lifted her M4, locating the big sucker face in her sight picture.

I could go for a head shot, but these are my last thirty rounds. Every single one has to count and count good.

The monster dodged one way, then the other, before it leaned down and hurled a severed limb at the truck. The arm bounced off the door to the rear cab and Dom ducked away from the window. A second later, something threw the arm back toward the big monster, and it was followed by rocks and other bits of debris from the battlefield.

The monsters from the el-tracks were hurling anything they could find at the big fucker and its minions. Then their leader appeared from behind a wrecked semi-trailer. It had a bench seat hefted in its hands and raised it overhead as it ran forward. With a growl that seemed to shake the city itself, the giant sucker face heaved the bench seat into the melee, scattering the smaller ones.

The groups from the neighborhood moved off to the sides of the street and climbed onto ruined walls and into the remains of trees. Those from the el-tracks stayed in formation around their leader, grouping up in twos and threes again like they had on Park Avenue, when Gallegos had first witnessed their tactics.

They're down on numbers, but I still think this is their fight. The ones from the neighborhoods don't have the same combat sense.

And they're all ignoring us now, like we're just bystanders to their feud.

The el-track tribe paced around their leader, still clad in its shirt of bones and, Gallegos now noticed, sheets of skin that it wore like a cape. It roared at the other leader, which strode into the street behind a pack of five smaller ones. Those were immediately met by a dozen of the el-track sucker faces and taken down quickly. Then the neighborhood's leader roared and waved its hands. As Gallegos stared, dumbfounded, the two tribes flooded the roadway in a roiling mass of claws and teeth. Shrieks and howls filled the air, and through it all the big ones continued to throw whatever they could find at hand. Bodies launched through the air to rebound off the truck, or to collide with small groups of the monsters.

Soon enough the tide clearly turned, with the el-track sucker faces beating back their enemy from the neighborhood. The path behind the truck was clear now, with the monsters grouping along the sides of the road as the neighborhood tribe was chased away or torn to pieces on the sidewalks.

"Get us out of here, Reeve."

He wheeled the truck around, away from the melee. Behind them, the street was a bloodbath of dead sucker faces. Clutches of the monsters scampered away from the road to hide in the ruins while gangs of now three and four gave chase. Finally the big one wearing the bone shirt held up the broken body of the neighborhood leader.

It roared and flung the body at the ground where it landed in a heap. Then it pointed at the neighborhoods. The hordes around it moved as one, grouping up and scrambling over debris and corpses to disappear into the ruins.

Gallegos couldn't believe their luck. They'd escaped only because they'd been a less important target. That wouldn't last, though, and she knew it. A new leader ruled the streets now, and it would send its minions after them as soon as it was done cleaning out the remains of the enemy tribes.

Howls and pain and shrieks of rage followed them as Reeve pushed the truck farther from the chaos. He floored it, taking them back beneath the el-tracks and onto Park Avenue again.

Jed snapped his attention away from watching the big monster stomp around the battlefield, throwing bodies and rubble in every direction. It had ordered the others off to fight the ones from the neighborhoods.

"Guess he really wants a clean house for his grand opening tomorrow."

"What?" Jo asked. Jed wasn't surprised she missed his warped attempt at humor.

"You know, when he puts a sandwich board out and opens his deli? I figure that's gotta be why he's so pissed off. He's just an honest businessman trying to earn a dollar for his family, put food on the table. You know, like ya' do. Street all shitted up like this, he can't expect customers want to eat at his place."

Jo let a smirk crease her mouth, but that was about it. "I'm glad you can laugh about it. One of us probably should."

The truck bucked and wobbled as Reeve took them over the corpses of dead sucker faces. Jed put his head back in the game and scanned the street, checking every shadow and possible hiding spot for suckers that might jump out.

Or for Tucker to come racing out. Motherfucker got off easy. Not next time.

Off on the side of the road, two sucker faces were taking bites out of a third. They quickly left their meal and came charging after the truck. Reeve had them moving fast enough that the two suckers couldn't keep up, but they didn't leave off the chase.

Jed kept his eyes on them, watching them peel off the road and into the maze of ruins around them.

"They're stalking us. Keep your eyes open," he said to Jo.

"How do you know they're not just going to find the quickest meal they can? Maybe we're too much trouble, you know?"

"Maybe."

"I almost feel sorry for them. But not really."

Jed nodded his agreement.

Just like wild animals. Eat to survive. Fight to be better. Lock horns. Come out on top and get the prize.

The truck lurched and they both slid around the bed as Reeve took them back down Lexington at a steady pace. He wasn't moving fast enough for Jed's peace of mind, but right now wasn't the time to be arguing about their rate of travel. Sergeant G was in the cab. If she was cool with their pace, then Jed would suck it up and get cool with it himself.

He sat back against the truck cab, holding the SAW against his chest and mentally counting the ammo he had for it.

One in the bags, and half a box ready to rock.

They had three rounds of HE left for the thump gun.

If they hit another swarm like the last one, they wouldn't get very far.

***

Gallegos' tracked the pair of sucker faces in her mirror. Reeve had them moving fast enough that the monsters couldn't keep up. After following for a block, they darted away from the road and disappeared into the ruins.

"Keep going, Reeve. We have to get inside and regroup. Pick out every last round of ammo we have stashed in there."

Reeve put the pedal to the floor and the truck raced forward, closing the distance to Lexington in half a breath. At the corner, he slowed down to a crawl before making the turn. Gallegos watched the dead streets like they would come back to life at any minute, full of hungry sucker faces out for blood.

"Eyes out, men. Watch high and low."

A chorus of grunts and *Rahs* filled the cab, and Gallegos felt the calm of leadership again. Her men were willing and able. They didn't have much ammo, but they still had fight left to bring and bring it they would. Whatever came at them, it wouldn't be leaving in the same condition, if it left at all.

Reeve took them around the corner and accelerated down Lexington. The firefighters struggled to stay upright in the rear cab, holding themselves steady on the headrests of the front seat. Gallegos kept her eyes to the front, holding her M4 out the window and ready to light up anything that moved into her sight picture.

No such thing as friendlies out there. Not anymore.

They were still four blocks from the hide when she saw Tucker's truck come around a corner two blocks up. She leaned out her window, took aim, and fired. She hit the hood and the truck swung down another street and out of sight.

"Fuck this hide and seek bullshit," Reeve said and stepped on the gas.

***

Jed whipped around and checked their path. They were on Lexington and coming up on the bus depot fast. Reeve had punched it hard and the truck surged forward. Jed ducked back down into the bed. Jo was holding herself steady with her feet on the wheel well.

The dead sucker face kept rolling side to side as the truck swerved along the road.

"Can't we get rid of that thing?" Jo asked.

"Maybe. I'm starting to like him."

She gave him a look that said *What the fuck?*

"No shit," Jed said, chuckling. "I think I'll name him Tucky Two. Bet they look alike."

Jo seemed ready to laugh, but slid down the truck bed and grabbed the dead monster under its arms. With a heave she lifted up and set it tumbling out of the tailgate.

"Sorry, Tucky," she said, scooting back up near the cab again. "There's only room for two back here."

"See, you can laugh about it, too. That's good—"

A rattle of small arms fire and the pinging of metal on metal startled Jed out of his skin. He whipped to the left and right, scanning the shattered buildings for muzzle flashes. Another volley came in from somewhere he couldn't see, impacting on the tailgate and rear of the truck bed.

"Gotta be the shooter they had up top. In the high rises."

"We're sitting ducks back here. Can I hit him with this?" Jo asked, lifting the grenade launcher.

"Maybe, but—"

A string of rounds impacted against the fender from above and Jed rolled to the side. Reeve swerved them as another burst rained in, peppering the truck bed and missing Jed and Jo by inches.

"Shooter's in the high rises! Sergeant G, we're taking fire from the high rises!"

Jed and Jo swung around in the truck bed as Reeve swerved a serpentine trail down Lexington. A steady rattling beat told Jed they were still in someone's sight picture. Heavy *thunks* sounded up front.

Shooter switched his aim. He's going for the engine.

Reeve cranked them to the side again, and Jed slid up against the wall of the truck bed. Jo crashed into him as more rounds came in from above. The truck jerked right, coming up closer to the ruins near the bus depot. The shooter sent another volley their way, hitting the pavement beside them. The truck bounced hard and Jo slammed into Jed, driving a shock of pain up his back. The truck pitched toward the street and Jo slid away from him again. He held tight to the bed wall with one hand and reached for her with the other.

Their hands met and they both tensed up their arms to maintain space between them. A series of shots came from up top and Matty screamed inside the cab. Jed did his best to get eyes on the shooter's position, but with all the jerking he could hardly focus for more than a second before he had to put his mind back to staying steady in the truck bed.

**

Gallegos hated being on the run. It was her job and her mission to make other people turn tail.

Or die where they stand.

"Anybody got eyes on their shooter? Welch said the high rises. I don't see *anything* up there!"

"They're up top somewhere," Matty said from behind her. "Shots are coming dow— *Shit!*" he screamed.

Gallegos spun around to see Luce slumped with blood pouring down his shirt front. His head lolled to the side. Dom reached for him and held him up.

"C'mon, Luce. Stay with us. I got you, *hermano*. I got you. I got you…"

"He's gone, Dom," Gallegos said.

She didn't need to check a pulse to know it. The bullet went through Luce's head and out his neck.

"Goddamit," Dom said between barely held in sobs. He wrapped his arms around Luce. "Goddamit, goddamit…"

Gallegos let the anger and fury burn hot inside her. The day had now taken three of her own.

The truck roared down Lexington, sliding left and right as Reeve wove them through the kill zone. Sniper fire kept coming. The hide was just a block ahead now. All they had to do was get inside.

And then we find these culeros and put them down.

Reeve had their truck on the sidewalk down the block

from the bus depot. The sniper stopped firing.

"Welch was right. Shooter is in the high rise next to the hide. Gotta be."

"The hide's blocking his view now," Reeve added.

"Since he's not firing anymore, that's where he is."

Reeve slowed them down, slotting the truck in behind the wrecked busses in front of the hide. The front end was just behind the wheels of the bus. Reeve edged them forward, but the space was too narrow to continue.

"Shut if off. Let's get inside."

The engine idled a ragged beat until Reeve turned it off.

"Eyes out. Reeve, you got point," Gallegos said, opening her door. She had both feet on the ground when the rumble of Tucker's truck echoed through the street. It was close by and getting closer.

***

Jed struggled to his knees behind the cab of their truck as they came to a stop behind the busses. Jo sat in a crouch beside him, keeping her head down and shifting her weight from one foot to the other.

"I'll go out first," Jed told her. "Stay behind me."

Sergeant G's door opened and she got out.

"Let's go," she said and moved out to a position against the depot wall. Reeve came out next, sliding from the cab. He moved out around the hood to post behind the bus. Matty and Dom followed from the back seat. They moved into position behind Sergeant G.

"Where's Luce?" Jo asked.

Jed leaned around the cab and checked in the backseat.

He nearly slipped out of the bed but caught himself against the door. He pushed off and spun back to sit against the cab.

"Luce ain't coming," he told Jo. "C'mon. We gotta get under cover."

She didn't move and the heavy growl of Tucker's motor came closer still.

"Jo, c'mon now," he said, climbing onto the bed wall. "We—"

She stood up and lifted the thump gun, sighted, and fired.

The street shook with the explosion and Jed fell back into the truck bed. Jo came down beside him and they huddled against the cab as the air filled with the stink of burning fuel.

"Hell yeah! You hit him."

Jo moved to stand up; Jed reached to pull her back down. "Sniper might still be able to see us. C'mon, we should get with the others."

***

"Direct hit, Jo. That's how you do it," Gallegos said as Welch and Jo joined them on the sidewalk. They all hugged the wall of the bus depot, staying low and keeping eyes on the street around them. Reeve was still at the end of the nearest bus, half hidden by their truck.

"Welch, take over for Reeve. Tell him to confirm they're out of action. Jo, Dom, Matty, follow me inside."

"Looks like your man is on his way already," Matty said, pointing toward the bus.

Gallegos followed his finger and saw Reeve's back

disappear around the bus.

"He's going to get his dumb ass shot off," she growled. "Y'all stay low. Keep covered here. Welch, on my six."

"Rah, Sergeant," he said, nodding.

Matty and Jo both grunted and took up positions next to the wall, crouching low and looking out. Matty had his pistol up. Jo still held the thumper. Dom just stood against the wall, staring into the empty air around him.

"Dom, get low and out of sight," Gallegos said.

He glanced back at the truck and his face fell, like he'd heard what she'd said but hadn't taken it in. Matty put a hand on his arm and guided him to a crouch beside him and Jo.

Gallegos stepped around the truck and moved to the back of the bus. She was ready to whip a quick look around the vehicle when Reeve's laughter filled the street.

***

Jed followed Sergeant G to the bus and kept an eye back down Lexington. If they'd finished off Tucker and his crew, that was one thing. But two hordes of sucker faces still roamed these streets. Sergeant G signaled for him to hold position before she swept around the tail end of the bus.

Taking slow steps and constantly roving his gaze back and forth, Jed crept around the end of the bus. Reeve was out there somewhere chuckling and Sergeant G was with him. Jed moved up and got a look at the street.

Reeve and Sergeant G had tucked up against the bus. She was scanning the street and angling for a look at the high rises. Jed slid back around the bus when he realized he could see the upper floors of the high rise. That meant any shooter up there should be able to see him as well. But nothing came his way. Reeve was still blowing out a laugh. Jed kept the SAW up, aimed high, and moved around the tail of the bus again. He got out in front, still eyeing the high rise for signs of enemy movement.

"Gotta give Jo a medal," Reeve said in between chuckles. "She went five hole with that shot. What a fucking yard sale."

Jed took his eyes off the high rise long enough to check out the truck. Jo's grenade had done its work all right. It had impacted in the road right in front of the truck, sending it over onto its side. The hood and grill were a tangled mess of jagged metal. Every window was missing and flames licked at the inside of the cab.

Bodies slumped in the seats up front and one was lying in the street. A third hung halfway out the passenger's side window in the rear cab. A helmet lay a few feet away. Two shotguns were in the street on that side.

"We're done here," Gallegos said. "Tucker's out of action. Let's get inside."

"Hey, one of them's still alive!" Reeve yelled. He charged forward, around the front of the truck, and climbed onto the rear cab. He yanked on the body hanging out of the window. Jed whipped the SAW up to cover the high rise in case he spotted any muzzle flashes. Shadows in the empty windows seemed to dare him to fire, but he held back, waiting for the enemy to reveal himself first.

Reeve gave a grunt and tugged again, bringing the dead

guy down to the pavement. Reeve climbed back onto the truck and reached into the window. He emerged with another man who managed to get himself out of the cab. Once they were on the ground together, Reeve grabbed the man around the throat and dragged him back to their position by the bus.

The whole time Reeve was out there, Jed expected sniper fire to take him down. But no rounds came in.

Maybe their shooter is coming down now. He had to see the truck get hit. So he knows he's on his own.

Reeve and Sergeant G hauled the surviving col-lab in Jed's direction.

"Back around the bus, Welch."

Jed retreated slowly, turned around, and cast one final look down Lexington in the direction they'd come from. He didn't see any movement in the shadows or along the length of the street. Nothing but rubble and ruin looked back at him as he moved back to the shelter behind the busses.

— 23 —

Back under cover by the depot, Gallegos called the squad to hold up. They stayed close to the building while she and Reeve stayed near the busses.

"We got a prisoner here," she said, letting her M4 hang on its sling and drawing her sidearm. The man lay slumped against the curb where Reeve had left him before he went to pace by the busses. He alternated between lifting his weapon and aiming at the man and letting his M4 hang on its sling.

The col-lab took ragged breaths and rocked on his side.

"The fuck do we do with him?" Reeve asked.

Gallegos checked the others. Welch was at the back of the bus, busy watching the street.

Dom was still hanging his head, hardly in the game anymore it seemed. Matty had it together, but was more concerned about keeping Dom on his feet than worrying about the col-lab they hadn't killed yet. Only Jo looked at the man with any kind of worry on her face.

"They took my son," the col-lab said. "Get him out of there, please."

"Why the fuck should we help you?" Gallegos asked. She stepped over to him, standing between him and Reeve.

"Nat Tucker and his son are down there with them."

"That ain't Tucker in the truck there?" Reeve asked.

"No. That was Allred and his boy up front. I didn't know the guys in back. They only joined us two days ago."

"Where'd they come from?" Gallegos asked.

"I don't know. They were soldiers, like you."

"Hardly, motherfucker," Reeve said. "For one thing, we're Marines. For another, they weren't shit."

"They were men like you and me. Just men trying to survive, and that gets harder every day. It's not our fault God sent these devils. It's people like—"

"If Tucker's not in the truck, where is he?" Gallegos asked.

The col-lab glared at her, but he swallowed whatever words he had on his tongue. His face fell and tears filled his eyes. "They got Nat and his boy when we were chasing you down. We stopped at one of the caches and got swarmed by the monsters. I always knew that would happen. Nat didn't want to believe it, but I knew."

"Caches, huh? Tell me where they are. You got ammo there? Food? Water?"

"All of that, yeah. But it ain't much. Don't think you'll get enough to make it out of this city alive."

"That makes two of us. Now tell me where the cache is at."

"Underground. In their lair. You get to it from the high rise. It's in a conduit tunnel. We had a deal, and Nat figured people like you would find anything we tried to hide above ground. So we hid our reserves down there."

"You dumb motherfuckers," Reeve said.

"Fuck you," the col-lab spat back. "I know you're going to kill me. I don't deserve any better. But they're still alive, all of them. The monsters keep them alive until they eat them. Everyone we gave them. And my son. My boy didn't want to help, but I made him do it. God forgive me, I made him. He never had his heart in it. Tucker would have given him up if he hadn't helped. Now he's—God forgive me. Carl, I'm so sorry. I'm—"

Gallegos pulled her sidearm and put one in the man's chest.

"Enough of your crying, *cabrón*," she said. "Tucker and them are with the sucker faces now? Good."

"What about his son?" Welch asked.

"His what?"

Gallegos turned around to see Welch had come closer, leaving his post by the bus. She stared hard into his eyes. Maybe it was the strain of battle, or losing Mahton, or Reeve and his *deke* bullshit. Whatever it was, Gallegos had to get her head clear about her squad. That meant they all had to pull their own weight and follow her orders. And right now, she didn't need Welch *the-guy-who-might-be-a-deke* fucking arguing about what she said they should do.

"You listen to me, Welch. I don't care who this motherfucker's son is or was, or where he is. What I do care about are the people who were with us three days ago and who aren't here now because this *pinche loco culero* and his friend Tucker gave them to the sucker faces. I care about Mahton, the man we lost trying to take Tucker down. The man who died to save my skin, and yours."

"I got people down there, too, Sergeant. I care about

getting them all out if we can."

"You got people?" Reeve asked, coming up close to Welch.

"Yeah," Welch said, and shifted back a step.

"Who? Who the fuck do you know who might be down there? Except maybe your guys who weren't in the truck that *Jo* took out?"

Welch reeled back like he'd been kicked in the dick.

"The fu—you think I'm with them? You still think that, man?"

"I've been thinking it since I met you, Welch. You're a fucking deke. Own it and take your medicine like your buddy here."

"He was never with Tucker," Jo said. "He couldn't have been. We'd have seen him before."

"You saw this dude before?" Gallegos asked, kicking at the dead man on the ground.

Jo took in a breath and let it out. She shook her head, and looked at the pavement.

***

Jed felt the ground drop out from under him. The col-lab said everyone was alive down there.

The monsters keep everyone alive until they eat them.

They'd just lost another man to sniper fire, but they'd finally taken out the col-labs in their truck. They knew where the others were, plus where they stored their gear. And for the first time, Jed thought he might actually see Meg Pratt again. He might be able to rescue her after all.

And here comes Reeve with his deke bullshit.

Jed was sure Jo would stand up for him. She trusted

him. She had to. But she dropped her eyes when Sergeant G asked her question. The other two firefighters were staying out of it, just huddling by the wall. Reeve looked about ready to chew his own teeth out, he was so pissed off. Sergeant G still had her sidearm out. She kept it by her side as she stepped closer to Jo.

"You said you'd know if Welch was with them because you'd have seen him. But you didn't see this man, did you?"

Jo shook her head again, but she quickly lifted her chin and stared Gallegos in the face.

"Jed's a good man. He could have let me fall out of the truck a hundred times, or get pulled out by the monsters. He didn't. He saved me more than once, and I'd do the same for him."

"Okay then. That's good enough for me," Sergeant G said, holstering her sidearm.

"Speak for yourself, Sergeant," Reeve said.

Quick as lightning, Sergeant G spun to stare Reeve in the face.

"I will speak for myself, PFC Reeve. And you'll remember that when I speak, it is your duty to listen."

Reeve looked ready to spit or fight or do anything but stand there and take an ass-chewing. Jed stepped up closer to him and Sergeant G. For her part, she was even more beat down than Reeve and looked twice as ready to forget about the mission and just take the man to the pavement with extreme prejudice.

"Y'all, this ain't how we survive. This ain't how we do it, oorah?"

Sergeant G blew out a breath. Without looking at Jed, she grunted an *Err* and stepped back from Reeve.

To Reeve she said, "Get your sight picture right, Private. Insubordination ain't part of my formation."

Jed stood ready to jump in between them, but Reeve backed away and shook himself. His face fell and he bit down hard on his bottom lip. When he recovered he looked at Sergeant G and nodded, squaring himself away and moving off the street toward the sidewalk.

"Good to have you back," Sergeant G said to him as he passed.

"Good to be back, Sergeant."

Sergeant G gave Reeve a nod, then ordered everyone off the street and inside the depot.

— 24 —

Gallegos led them into the hide and around the ruined stairwell to a back hallway. She and Reeve muscled a hole in a barricade they'd set up. The squad went through, with Welch at the rear. She told him and Reeve to close up the hole and had the others hold position in the hallway. She went forward and opened a mop closet underneath a firehole.

Reeve and Welch finished up, and Gallegos waved for everyone to join her by the closet. "I don't have the strength left to make the jump on the stairs, and I don't think the rest of y'all do either. We do this fast. In, regroup, and out. No bullshitting," she said, looking straight at Reeve and Welch.

They grunted a pair of near-silent *Errs* at her, but she was too beat to give them any shit about it.

One by one, starting with Reeve, they were hoisted up through the firehole she and Mahton had come down that morning. Matty went second, then Dom, Jo, and Welch. Gallegos closed the door behind her and reached for Matty's hand. He helped her up and she was home again, in an empty office that was down one floor from her gym and her bunk, and down the hall from the barracks where the men slept.

She tried not to think about Mahton's body lying in the hallway back at Tucker's stronghold. If it had been a different time and place, they would have taken him back to whatever served as a base of operations and washed him clean, dressed him in his traditional clothing, and cremated him. He deserved better than what he got. They could have at least brought him back here.

If they hadn't been running for their lives.

Just don't have the time or space to do right by the dead anymore. And every minute it seems to get harder to do right by the living.

Her squad stood in a wide circle around the firehole, with Welch and Reeve in opposite corners.

"Move out," Gallegos said. "Back to the barracks, everybody gets some chow. Reeve, Welch, take turns cleaning your weapons first. And I want the stairwell mined with the Claymores we got."

Welch took point and moved into the hallway leading to the hide. Dom and Matty followed with Jo bringing up the rear. At the entrance to the Stable, Welch held the squad up and double checked the room.

"Room's just like we left it, Sergeant," he called back. "Doesn't look like anybody's been in here."

"Everyone get inside. Eat, clean your weapons. Matty or Dom, there's an extra M4 in there. One of you take it. Double time," Gallegos said. "Me and Reeve are going to mine the stairs. Welch, come close the door after us, and be ready to let us back in. Two taps on the desk, rah?"

"Oorah, Sergeant," he said. He'd unloaded the SAW and began disassembling it, but now set it aside and stepped up to join them by the door. The firefighters sat around the barracks room ripping into MREs. Matty had already grabbed the spare M4.

"One of y'all always be on guard. Weapon up and ready while the others eat. Rah?"

They all nodded. Matty set aside his meal, lifted his weapon, and moved closer to the door.

"Let's go," Gallegos said, eyeing Reeve and Welch before she turned her back on the room and set off down the hall.

They rounded the corner and came face to face with the back of their barricade. It was intact and up to speed, just like they'd left it.

This can't last. They'll find a way in. Sooner or later. They'll get in.

Reeve and Welch muscled the desk out of the way, opening their passage to the hallway beyond. Gallegos went first and Reeve quickly followed after. She waited until Welch had the desk wedged into the space before moving on.

At the top of the stairwell, Gallegos posted against the wall, looking down into the cavern below. The place stank of piss and smoke and death.

Wasn't too long ago I didn't notice the smell.

She dropped her pack and helped Reeve get the mines set up. They positioned them at the mouth of the hallway, aiming toward the ruined stairwell, and ran the detonator into the first room in the hall.

"Anything comes up here, it'll get hit," Reeve said.

"We need someone watching the stairwell. I'll stay here."

"Negative, Sergeant. You've been on point all day. Let me take first watch."

"You want to check that attitude again, Reeve. Get your sight picture right. You're ready to cash out. I know I'm no better, but that comes with the job."

"I'll be good, Sergeant. Just throw my dinner down the hall. Gimmee that pork rib, rah?"

She watched him for a moment, checking for signs that the strains of combat were making their way back into his soul like they had outside.

We're at our limit. All of us.

"Be careful, Reeve. Don't let the sucker faces get the jump on you. You fire the mines the second you see them."

"Oorah. I ain't playing the hero today. Maybe next week. Depends on what the scriptwriters do, but my agent thinks I got at least another season before they take me out."

Gallegos barely held in her laugh. "That's the Reeve I remember. Here, swap mags with me. I'm full."

She handed him the magazine in her weapon and replaced it with his. Now she was down to maybe six rounds. Without anything more than a quiet *Err*, she left Reeve in the hallway and moved out to join the rest of her squad.

***

In the barracks, Jed cleaned the SAW while Jo and Dom ate and Matty sat guard by the door. They'd popped their eyes wide when they saw the stacked cases of MREs. Everyone had dug into the first bag Jed tossed them without asking for favorites. It was then that he realized they hadn't eaten a proper meal in who knew how long.

"What's the last thing y'all ate?" he asked as he slid the bolt back into his weapon.

In between bites, Jo told him it had been a mix of stale bread, cold canned beans, and the remains of frozen vegetables that they'd kept in the firehouse freezer.

"The power went out two or three days after the virus started. Our freezer stayed cold for a day or two after that, and we didn't start throwing out rotten food for at least a week. I guess somebody had the foresight to keep the power plant under wraps so the suckers couldn't get in."

"They got in anyway," Dom said.

Jo nodded and went back to her dinner. She finished it up and swapped out with Matty, who went back to his bag of chow. Jed wiped the feed tray one more time, set the bolt forward, and wiped a trail of CLP off the charging handle. He'd worked fast, and knew he could have spent another half hour on the weapon before he got all the carbon out of the thing. But Sergeant G or Reeve would be coming back soon, and he hadn't had any chow yet.

Jed grabbed an MRE and ate like a recruit with a DI barking down his neck. Matty was finishing up beside him. Dom and Jo kept watch on the hall.

"Y'all can have another if you want," Jed said. "We got plenty here, and we can't take it—"

Two metallic pings sounded and Jed was on his feet and out the door like a shot. He got to the barricade and hauled on the desk. It scraped a few inches before he lost his grip. He went back to it and tried again, but he could only get it an inch at a time until Matty joined him. Together they pulled it free.

Sergeant G crawled through the opening and stood on shaking legs, looking beat down and out of juice.

"Reeve's watching the stairs. We put the mines out and he'll blow 'em if he needs to. Meantime, somebody needs to run him his dinner."

"I'll do it," Dom said.

"He says to bring him the pork rib."

Matty went back to the Stable. He came around the corner a moment later with an MRE in his hand.

"Welch, go with him. I'll watch the door while you're out there."

"Oorah, Sergeant."

Jed joined Matty in crawling through the tunnel at the door. He gave Sergeant G an *Errr*, and sent a last look back at the corner, thinking about Jo and hoping she was okay.

***

Gallegos settled into her favorite spot around the trash hole and dug into a chicken dinner. Dom stood guard with the shotgun, by the door. Jo sat across from Gallegos, close to where Mahton used to sleep. She sipped from a canteen. Their water was running really low now they had three extra bodies to sustain with it.

"I sure hope Tucker's cache has what we need," Gallegos said around a mouthful of food.

"I hope we don't die trying to find it," Dom said. "Are you sure we need to?"

"We got people down there. Dead or alive, I don't know for sure. But until I do, I have to assume they're alive. That means I have to help them. The cache is secondary, but…"

"I feel the same way," Jo said, digging back into her meal. "I just don't like the thought of going underground where those things live. Out here on the streets it feels almost even, like we at least have a fighting chance. But down there, in their territory… I'm afraid we'll all be killed because we don't belong down there. That's their home now, so they'll be defending it better."

"Don't think of it like that. Think of it like any other mission. You're always going into unfamiliar territory. Enemy territory. But what you're bringing with you is a whole lot more than they've ever seen before. You're the variable they can't account for because you're foreign. They can't predict what you'll do."

"You make me want to believe we'll survive this," Jo said, halfway between crying and smiling. Her grin almost took hold, but it didn't make it to up to her eyes.

"So believe it. You'll be good out there, Jo. You were good on the way here, in the truck. You even took out the enemy's vehicle with the forty mike-mike. You too, Dominic. Rah?"

Dom nodded, but kept his attention on the hallway outside. Jo swallowed her food before saying, "Rah." Gallegos couldn't help but smile at that.

"So Welch taught you how to talk Marine."

"Yeah. I mean *Rah*."

"You think he's good people? Be straight with me."

"He's all right," Dom said. "I trust him."

Gallegos nodded at him, then looked at Jo, who held her gaze for a long breath, inhaling and exhaling fully before she replied. "I think he wants to survive just like the rest of us. I think he did something before this all happened, or he saw something that he needs to keep hidden. Whatever it is, I don't think it means he's working with Tucker or his people."

Jo went back to her meal.

"He's got bad paper," Gallegos said. "We know that much. But not what for."

"What's that mean?"

"Means he got discharged for something. Kicked out. He said it was bad conduct. Could've been drugs. Or he should've joined the Army instead."

"Why do you say that? If he got kicked out of the Marines… I don't get it."

Gallegos grinned and held up a finger for each part of her reply. "Ain't. Ready. To be Marines. Yet."

Jo took a moment to get it, and then her grin won the battle. She chuckled and shook her head.

"So it's true. The different branches never miss a chance to talk shit about each other."

"Rah. But at the end of the day, we're all on the same side. It's just doing the dozens, you know? Marines do it better, of course."

Jo shrugged, grinned, and mumbled something like *I guess,* as she took the last bite of her barbecue patty. Gallegos attacked her meal again, too, digging into the cold, mushy vegetables and stringy meat.

"This shit doesn't taste much like chicken, but I'm not sure I even remember what chicken tastes like."

Jo seemed about to reply when the telltale sound of two taps against the metal came into the room.

"That's them," Gallegos said, setting her meal pouch down. "I'll be right back."

— 25 —

Matty and Jed squeezed through the crawlspace. As soon as Jed's feet cleared the hole, Sergeant G started pushing the desk back.

"Reeve's coming in, Sergeant."

A second later and Reeve's goofy grin lit up the hall as he slid out of the crawlspace on his back.

"What's up, Reeve?" Sergeant G asked. "I thought you had watch on the stairs."

"I did. Then I figured I'd rather not die alone," he said, pulling the detonator's out of his vest pouch and setting them to the side of the crawlspace. The wires extended through the tunnel and around the hall. It had been Jed's idea to do it this way, but he didn't say anything to Sergeant G about it. Reeve kept it under his hat, and Jed figured it was best to do the same.

Together, the three Marines pushed the desk back into place before following Matty back to the Stable.

In the barracks, everyone topped off their water, emptying their last five-gallon jug. The firefighters each got a canteen from the spares that Sergeant G, Mahton, and Reeve had collected from the survivalist guy.

When everyone was saddled up, Sergeant G called them into a circle.

"Everyone get some rest. We take twenty-minute shifts in pairs. Power nap like you never have before. This might be the last sleep we all see for a while."

***

It felt like an hour or more had passed, but Gallegos knew it had just been a few minutes. She'd laid down next to the cases of chow and dropped into the deepest sleep she could remember. She'd snapped out of it just as fast. Across the room, Matty was lifting his face off his elbow while Dom was rocking his shoulder side to side.

"Looks like it's go time, Matty," he said.

Gallegos took a slug of water and tried to ignore how light her canteen was. She rubbed her eyes, strapped her helmet on and checked her squad. They'd all grabbed a little shuteye. She hoped it would be enough to recharge them for what lay ahead.

Reeve and Welch stood guard by the door. The firefighters stood in a line near Reeve's bunk, with Dom at the back, leaning against the wall. Gallegos wondered if she was crazy to try and take back survivors from the sucker faces. Then she remembered who was down there. Her fellow Marines. And some soldiers from the Army units that had come in with them for Reaper.

All warriors, every last one of them. Man and woman. All my brothers and sisters.

"We have some ammo," she said. "About two boxes for the SAW, plus those bandoliers. We're low on serviceable magazines, so if we spot any of those on the street, we need to collect them. Don't make that a higher priority than it needs to be. Keep your eyes out at all times, and never look at the ground for more than two steps. Suckers love to get the jump on you. Remember that."

She looked into every set of eyes staring back at her. To the last, they all had the same determination coupled with an undeniable fear. Gallegos felt it herself and took a second to send the fear packing. Her platoon leader had called it *Getting into your war mind*. She looked back to her squad, remembered her mission, and let everything else take a back seat.

"When we get to the high rise, everyone needs to be on top of their own shit and watching out for their teammate's back. We don't know how many numbers we're looking at down there, and that goes for friendly and enemy."

"Friendly?" Dom asked.

"The prisoners Tucker gave them. These are people who need our help, and some of them might need help dying. We all have to be ready for that."

"I'm ready as I gonna get," Dom said, holding up his pistol. They might have been tough words, but his eyes said he was about as ready as a sack of laundry.

"I mean ending a life out of mercy, Dom. You think you can do that? You need to tell me one way or the other. I can't have any dead weight on this mission. Either you are in, totally and one-hundred fucking percent, or you are out."

"What's 'out' mean?" he asked, and she didn't miss his eyes shifting side to side, checking everyone else's reaction to his question. Matty and Jo didn't seem to care, or hid their feelings if they did. They'd seen combat and were finally able to release the tension and adrenaline. Even Welch seemed cool with whatever Dom decided.

But Reeve put his eyes to the ceiling and moved his lips, like he was either praying or cursing himself. Given the mood of complacency from the others, Gallegos didn't known which would be worse.

"*Out* means you're staying here, Dom, with that pistol, by yourself, until we get back. And to be clear, I make no promises that we are coming back."

Matty put up a hand and Gallegos nodded at him to go ahead.

"I can't speak for Dom, or Jo either. But I'm good to go. I will say that I'd feel better if we had a full trauma bag with us. We have one IV, some bandages and iodine, one can of spray saline, a couple Sam Splints. Not much else. Any chance we could run for more first aid gear? There's a hospital not far from here."

"We can't afford the time or the risk. The sucker faces were more interested in securing territory than taking us out, but that isn't going to last. We all saw what happened with the two alphas. The one with the bone shirt came out on top, so we have to assume this neighborhood is back to the way it was before. Hunted and hopeless. I'm sorry we don't have more first aid, and I know these weapons aren't the usual tools of your trade. But it is what it is, no?"

The squad, including Dom, gave her their silent agreement.

"We have a few hours of daylight left. I say we go now, try to save whoever we can. If we make it out alive, we come back here with what we can grab from their cache. We get what's left of our supplies here, whatever we can carry to the truck. Then we get the fuck out of dodge, find someplace safer if we can as long as the truck has fuel to carry us."

"How long you think that is?" Matty asked.

"Not long," Reeve answered. "We got a quarter tank in it, maybe. I didn't spend much time looking at the dial, but when I did, it was well below half. If the damn thing starts again. Sniper put some holes in the engine and might have hit something critical."

Dom cleared his throat and stepped forward from his position by the wall. "Let's say we get back here with more survivors and we're able to get supplies to the truck, and it has enough gas to get us somewhere. Great. Where do we go? This is the safest I've been in a long time. I have a gun in my hand and nobody is threatening to throw me to the monsters for dinner."

"We could get on a boat," Matty said. "If we can find one, I can pilot it."

Jo answered that question. "My family had a fishing boat in the Jersey marina. Dad used to…"

Gallegos let Jo collect herself before she asked, "How big was the boat?"

Jo's face fell. "It's across the Hudson from the cruise ship terminal on the other side of Manhattan. It might as well be in Egypt. The truck might get us there, but if it runs out of gas, we'll never make it on foot."

"Says who?" Gallegos shot back. "You have three Marines with you, and your home team. Dom, and Matty. I honestly wasn't sure where we might go after this, but you just gave me the intel I needed.

"Now the mission changes. We get our people out of

the hive underground. If we make it out of there, and can get back here for supplies, we move out with a purpose for the Hudson. When we get there, we find transport to Jersey or we die trying."

When Gallegos was done speaking, Dom stood and stepped back from the group. He looked ready to choke. The others noticed the change in him. Matty reached a hand out, but Dom batted it away. Gallegos met his eyes and tried to see into his heart.

What's up, Dominic? What're you holding back?

A screech split the air, echoing through the hallways and into the room.

"Blow the front door!"

Reeve sped from the room. Gallegos felt the shudder of two explosions. Suckers faces shrieked and screamed in the aftermath.

"Lexington guard room! *Go!*" Gallegos commanded the squad as she rose to her feet. Matty, Welch, and Jo were on their game already, weapons up and eyes out. "Matty, get with Reeve first! Welch and Jo, upstairs!"

The trio moved fast, disappearing into the hallway like ghosts. Still more howls and screeches came from every direction.

"Where are they?" Matty shouted from the direction of the barricade.

"I can't tell where they're coming from!" Welch yelled back from farther down the hall.

"Keep your eyes the fuck out, people!" Gallegos yelled through the doorway. "Watch the windows and your six. They might find the fireholes and come up in the middle."

The stairwell door banged open, and Gallegos fought

the urge to race out of the room to join the others, make sure they were safe. The heavy *tromp* of boots on the stairs helped her breathe easier for the moment. Her people were getting to safety.

She'd be with them in a second, but had one last thing to do.

Behind her, Dom shifted beside the wall. She turned away from the door and sized him up. He held his pistol by his leg like it was a lunchbox or some other mundane object that couldn't possibly help him survive the next five minutes much less five seconds. It slipped from his grasp and clunked on the floor.

"Dominic, collect your weapon," she said.

He reached down and lifted the pistol off the floor. "Only got two left in it," he said, hefting it like was useless. Then he spit up a mouthful of what he'd just eaten, spattering the floor around his boots.

She'd seen it before in men and women who doubted themselves, or were just scared to death. And she did not need this shit now. But like her own leaders had done when she was a green recruit, Gallegos knew it was her task to give this man the right words. She had to say exactly what he needed to hear in order to get with the program.

"Dominic, *hermano*. You've done worse than this. You've been in worse places, doing more with less, saving people's lives, *sí?*"

He nodded as he wiped his mouth on his sleeve, but his eyes wouldn't meet hers, even as she paced to the side, trying to catch his gaze with hers. She stepped over to the stack of MREs and reached for a bandolier beside it.

"I need you here with me, Dom," she said.

Gallegos removed six flash bangs from the bandolier, one by one, and stuffed them into her vest.

Dom nodded at her again and eyeballed the grenades. She held one out for him.

"You need to carry this, too."

He took it, pocketed it, and heaved another mouthful onto the floor.

"I need you on your game, Dominic. *We* need you."

Dom straightened up, wiped his mouth again and rolled his neck and shoulders. But he looked more like a ragdoll than a fighter about to enter the ring.

"Okay," he said. "*Por mi corazon.* I'm good to go."

"That's how you do it," she said. "Do or die, rah?"

"Do or die. I—I got point," Dom said as he stepped around her to the doorway.

"I got your six," Gallegos said. *"Tranquilo, hermano."*

More howls and shrieks were coming down the halls now, resonating out of every crack in every wall, and through every broken window and doorway. Dom moved into the hall and Gallegos followed.

— 26 —

In the Lexington guard room, Jed tried not to focus on the pictures hanging around him, but they all stared back with eyes above gaping mouths that almost looked alive. Mahton had done more than just sketch the sucker faces when he'd been on duty. He'd turned them into art. Their bodies twisted across the sheets of paper hanging on the walls. The muscles bulged and stretched, and the faces—Jed couldn't help but think they'd already come to life and were the ones making all the noise now.

Shrill cries and barks of rage still roared through the building, sounding like they were coming from everywhere and nowhere at once. They would rise and fall in volume, but then go silent just as fast. It was almost like the suckers were toying with them.

"Why are they doing that?" Jo asked. She paced side to side, staying out of a direct path to the door, but trying to avoid corners, too, like she was afraid to get stuck in one. "Why can't we see them?"

"Probably don't want us to," Jed said. "I think they're fucking with us. Trying to freak us out."

"It's working. I feel like I'm buzzing all over, and I don't know if it's adrenaline or that I'm just scared to death."

"Probably both. But if it helps, I'm feeling the same way. I think they're trying to draw us out instead of fighting in here. They know we've got better chances inside, where we can control their avenues of approach."

"They *know*? How do you know that? What—"

"They're smart now. Whatever the Air Force dropped on them, it killed the dumb ones and left the smart ones alive."

Jo shook next to him and turned to look at the wall. She spun away from the pictures, shook herself again, and stepped closer to the window overlooking Lexington Avenue.

***

Gallegos caught up with Reeve and Matty at the stairwell. They'd stayed back while she got Dom into gear. When he saw her, Reeve slapped a hand on Matty's shoulder. The firefighter swept into the stairwell and banged up the steps to the next floor. Reeve hung by the door and motioned for Dom to go ahead of him.

"I got him, Reeve," Gallegos said. "Move out and keep up with Matty."

"Rah." Reeve was halfway up the stairs before the word left his mouth. The door on the upper landing banged open and the telltale sound of boots stomping into the hallway sounded back down the narrow space to Gallegos' ears.

The monsters' cries and howls kept coming in from

everywhere, but Gallegos had stopped worrying about them. They could have come into the building at any time. Now that she and her squad had been discovered, she figured they had seconds to live. But the sucker faces weren't attacking.

They're trying to drive us out. Well fuck this sucker face psy-ops bullshit. They want to play head games, fine. We'll play head shots.

"Dom, you still good to go? I'm taking point if you got any doubts."

"I'm good," he said. His sagging shoulders and slumped spine told a different story, but she'd rather have him falling down in front of her than falling out at her back.

"Move out then," she said.

He entered the stairwell and took lumbering steps upward. Gallegos held her M4 ready and flashed a look ahead and behind with every step, double-checking that her man was still in the game and making sure nothing caught them by surprise.

At the next floor, Dom rolled his neck and shoulders again. His moment of weakness seemed to have passed. She joined him on the landing and saw a new man behind his eyes. This one had some fight left, and she was glad as hell to see him.

"Lexington guard room is through that door and to the left," she said.

Dom held his pistol up by his cheek now, sighting as he moved to the door and reached for it with his free hand.

"You're breach man, Dom. On three. Pull the door open, step aside. I'll rush through and post on the opposite wall. You come in tight behind me. Check right as you go through the door and post this side of the hallway. If you see enemy, you fire. Don't tell me you see them. Just light them up and know that I'll be right behind you with more firepower. Rah?"

He nodded.

"Let me hear you say it."

"Rah," he said.

"You mean that, Dominic?"

"Rah!"

"Let's move, then. One. Two. *Three!*"

***

Jed had the SAW oriented on a zone of fire that included the window. Jo was beside him, staring at Mahton's art on the far wall now. She seemed to have got over whatever freaked her out about the pictures before.

A long screech cut through the air outside, but none of the scraping claws or clicking joint sounds followed it.

It's goddamned cat and mouse with the sucker faces now. And they're the cat.

Thumping footsteps led a trail down the hallway, coming closer to the guard room. Reeve and Matty came into the guard room and posted by the door.

"Sergeant G's back there still," Reeve said. "She's in the stairwell with Mr. Green Jeans."

"What the fuck's that supposed to mean?" Jo asked.

"That Dom ain't pulling his weight," Jed said. "You know? Green."

"Like the fucking grass in springtime, man," Reeve added. "Wait—here they come."

Jed moved so he could get a look down the hall. Jo

came to stand near him.

Sergeant G was back pedaling down the hall with her weapon up. Dom was even with her on the opposite side of the hall with his pistol up and ready. The hallway was empty except for the two figures moving as a team.

"Doesn't look green to me," Jo said.

Before Jed could say anything, Reeve looked at her over his shoulder. "So I was wrong. Take it up with my superior officer. Half his ass might be left out there somewhere, but the sucker faces got the rest."

Jo ignored him and went back to checking out Mahton's art while Jed watched the window. Sergeant G and Dom came in a beat later.

"They're fucking with us," she said. "Trying to push us out to the street."

"That's what Jed was saying," Jo added. "Are they really that smart now? Maybe they just don't know where we're hiding."

"That kind of thinking will get you and probably all of us killed," Sergeant G said.

Jed angled his view out the window, so he could see more of the street. "We got nothing out here, Sergeant."

A violent screech split the air and was followed by the sound of joints clicking and snapping outside. Jed stepped up closer and craned his neck to get sight of the exterior wall. Three sucker faces raced up the side of the building and were followed by a clutch of at least five more. They were all focused on following the leader of their little formation, but Jed ducked out of sight and stepped back from the window. He put an arm out toward Jo, waving her back toward the others.

"They're going for the roof."

"Then we move out fast and furious," Sergeant G said. "Closest firehole is two rooms down the hall. We move in teams of three. Clear the rooms as we go. First team is Reeve, Matty, and Jo. And you need to put that thumper to rest. Sidearm only for this operation, rah?"

Jo nodded and slung the grenade launcher around her shoulder. She drew her pistol and checked the safety was off.

"Good to go," she said.

"Then move out."

The three stepped out of the room without missing a beat. Reeve took point, Matty followed, and Jo brought up the rear. She looked back at Jed and gave him a thumbs up before stepping out of view.

***

Gallegos watched the other team depart before lining her men up for their turn.

"Welch, take our six. Dom, you're in the middle, behind me. We hear their banger, we move out and clear the next room. Then be ready to cover their movement. We leap frog like that to the firehole. Rah?"

Both men replied together.

"Let's go," she said and stepped out of the room. Shuffling boots behind her confirmed her men were in the game and on mission. The other team was a few yards ahead in the hallway, beside an open doorway. Reeve tossed the banger into the room and spun around the doorframe the instant the grenade went off. Matty and Jo followed him in with fast steps.

"Clear!" Reeve yelled out.

"On me," Gallegos told her men and took fast steps down the hall. She drew up outside the next door and repeated Reeve's action.

The banger went off and she was inside, posting against the near wall to leave room for the others. Dom was slow to follow her in. He stayed behind her while Welch pushed in and took a post on her right. Through the dust and smoke of the grenade she could just make out two shuddering forms in the far corner of the room. She fired twice and the figures went still. A broken window let in weak light. The smoke cleared away, revealing two dead suckers tangled up together.

"Clear!" Gallegos yelled.

"Moving!" Reeve shouted.

***

Jed waited for the hit. He knew it had to happen soon. They'd been too lucky so far, getting down to the second floor without any trouble. Reeve's team moved up the hallway now, heading for the firehole to the ground floor. Jed got a look at Matty and Jo as they went by.

Matty had his pistol up and his eyes were open, but he had to shuffle forward every couple steps. The trauma bag swung against his hip as he moved. Jo was on the opposite side of the hall, walking like she'd always been in combat, pistol up and near her cheek so she could hold a good sight picture. Her feet hit the floor just like Reeve's as she went by.

A single howl chased them from somewhere in the building, like the call of a ghost that wouldn't leave them alone. Jed couldn't stop the shakes that rippled through his arms and hands.

"Welch," Sergeant G said. "Welch, you with us?"

"Huh? Yeah, Sergeant. Yeah, rah. I'm here. Just…"

"Just what?"

"Them things are fucking with my head, Sergeant. They're playing with us and it's fucking with my head."

"Stay frosty, Marine. It ain't nothing but a thing."

Jed nodded and put his attention back on the hallway, doing his best to ignore the creeping feeling working its way up his spine.

A sharp clap burst through the air and Jed flinched, nearly losing his grip on the SAW.

Just the banger. Reeve and them just cleared the room with the firehole.

"Let's go!" Sergeant G shouted.

Jed peeled away from the wall and took the point position, running up to the firehole room. Dust spiraled in the air outside the door. He got there in time to see Jo helping Matty down the hole. The firefighter's head disappeared into the darkness as he dropped into the closet below. Jed posted outside the door while Sergeant G and Dom moved up the hall behind him.

Jo turned to face him from inside the room.

"You good, Jed?"

"Yeah. I'm good. Go on. I got your six."

Jo dropped to a crouch, swung her legs into the hole and slipped down and out of sight.

Crunching and scuffling sounds behind him were all Jed heard for a moment. Then the sucker faces started up their song and dance outside again.

They're just fucking with us. This has been their game all along, and now they're just fucking with us for fun.

His heart hammered as he entered the room and posted on the right. Dom and Sergeant G came in and posted on the left.

"Down the hole, Welch."

With shaking steps, Jed moved away from the wall and looked through the floor into the darkness of the mop closet.

One more floor and we'll be on the ground.

"Welch, time to move," Sergeant G said. He looked at her and nodded, then stepped forward, dropped down to his butt and swung his legs into the hole.

A screech and howl greeted him. Reeve's scream of agony followed.

Gallegos pushed Dom aside and dropped down the hole after Welch. Chatter from the SAW blasted through the building, punching holes in the silence that followed Reeve's scream.

I am not losing another man. Not today, not now.

She burst from the mop closet and slammed up against Welch's back. He staggered forward a step and caught himself, firing off a burst without missing a beat. He sent sustained fire down the hallway and she couldn't see what he was engaging. Across the hall, Jo, Matty, and Reeve were crouched in a tangle. Jo was working on Reeve while Matty split his attention between helping her and watching back down the hallway. A spray of fresh blood marked the wall above Reeve's body.

A sucker face lay slumped against the wall farther down the hall. It had three holes in its chest, and its claws were stained bright with blood. Beyond the body was one of the barricades she, Mahton, and Reeve had set up. The desks were covered in scratches and claw marks.

The barricade had been pulled apart.

That's why they were making all the noise. To cover their break-in. These motherfuckers got smart in a bad way.

Welch stopped firing and Gallegos got a better look at their AO. The barricade was all but useless now. If any more suckers came from that direction, her squad would be swarmed in seconds. Down the other way, a pile of at least a dozen dead monsters filled the hallway leading to the front of the building. More howling came from that direction, but nothing moved in the hall.

"Sergeant," Jo said.

Gallegos stepped up close to cover the firefighters and Reeve before she answered.

"How is he?" she asked while she monitored the ruins of their barricade. "Tell me I still have my Marine."

"I'm fine," Reeve said, but his voice cracked with pain at the end.

"How fine is fine, Reeve?"

"His AC joint is in pieces," Matty said. "The damn thing sliced right through it. And he took a few strikes to his ribs. It jumped on him and rode him to the ground before I could shoot it."

"I'm fine. Like I said. Fucking—*gahh!* Fuck. I'm fine."

"You don't sound fine," Gallegos said.

"He's can't use his arm," Jo said. "We can put some CELOX on it, but he needs a sling and we need to irrigate the wound. We only have a can of spray saline in the bag. How much water do we have?"

"Barely enough to drink," Gallegos said. "Use what you have to. We'll get you right, Reeve. Rah?"

"*Oo—rah,*" he choked out.

***

Jed kept his finger on the trigger and tucked the SAW in

tighter against his shoulder. Weaker howls and screeches found them, stealing into their position from every crack and crevice. Ahead in the hallway, three tall windows let in strips of light. Jed couldn't stop watching the dead sucker faces on the other side of the light.

Outside, the suckers kept shrieking and howling. They'd stopped hiding their movement. The sickening pop of their joints mixed with their screeches as they raced around in the street.

When's it going to stop? When are they just going to come in and get us? They broke in down here, and they're heading up to the roof. They know where we are. They have to.

Jed moved up to the first window and angled for a look outside. The city around them was empty and still. The sun seemed to drop fast in the sky, casting everything into an odd dance of light and shadow. Now and then a small shadow would detach itself from the ruins and scurry across the open street.

A sucker face's shriek would always come a few seconds later, making Jed think he was watching a movie with a lagging soundtrack. The alpha appeared, striding forward with a cluster of small ones around its legs. Jed couldn't miss it for its size, and as it passed, he saw the bones hanging off its back.

"Alpha's up here, Sergeant," he said. "The one with the bones on him."

"I don't want to hear about where they are, Welch. If they're in your sight picture and present a threat, you are cleared hot."

"*Errr,*" Jed said back.

Behind him, Reeve groaned while Jo and Matty took care of his arm. Dom came out from the mop closet and

Sergeant G told him to move up to join Jed. The firefighter had his pistol up and came to stand right next to Jed in the middle of the hall.

"Get behind me, man. Shoot over my shoulder if anything comes at us, and don't hit me, rah?"

"Yeah, rah," Dom said and stepped back a pace. He handed Jed a flash-bang a second later. Jed pocketed it without asking any questions.

If he's planning on going out, I'd rather have the firepower with me from the get go.

***

Gallegos kept watch down the hall while the firefighters got Reeve on his feet. They'd put his arm in a sling and wrapped his shoulder with bandages. Blood soaked the cloth and still oozed around the edges. Reeve's face paled and he took shaking breaths.

"You're gonna be okay, Reeve. We're moving out. Welch and Dom, you're at our six. I'll take point. Jo and Matty, you have our wounded man."

The firefighters lifted Reeve in a seat carry. When they had him settled, Jo asked, "Which way are we going?"

"We have to go out the back. Front door is compromised, but we have to expect enemy contact out the back, too. I have six bangers left, and we have at least three corners between here and the exit. What's everyone holding?"

"Two bangers on my person, and one box in the SAW, Sergeant," Welch said.

"We have two rounds left for the grenade launcher," Jo said.

"Couple in the pistols," Matty added. "Maybe a dozen between us if we're lucky."

"Use the bangers if the suckers get on our ass. Everyone conserve ammo. Fire only if you have no choice. Dom, take Reeve's weapon."

"I'm fine, Sergeant. I can shoot," Reeve said, holding his M4 with his good hand.

"Negative, Marine," she said, reaching for the weapon. Reeve let it go. She unclipped it from his sling and handed it to Dom. He handed his pistol to Reeve, who took it and let it rest in his lap.

"We're going outside at the rear of the building. That's where the busses pull in, so we have some cover at first. Once we're outside, we go for the high rises."

"On foot, Sergeant?" Welch asked.

"Truck's a lost cause. Suckers are out there, Welch, and you said the alpha was with them, rah?"

He nodded.

"That settles it," Gallegos said. "They'd be on us before we could get everyone in the truck and be moving."

Reeve grunted in pain next to her and she stepped up close to look him in the eye.

"You'll be good, Reeve. Just stay with us. Stay here. We got you and we're going somewhere we can get you right."

**

Jed backed down the hall with Dom behind him, guiding their movement with one hand on Jed's shoulder. He stayed focused on the squad's six as they backed through the corridors of the bus depot and around the ruins of the barricade. When they cleared the first corner, Jed caught the muzzle of the Dom's weapon drooping in his peripheral.

"We ain't out yet. Weapon up, man," he said. He breathed easier when Dom lifted the M4 in a steady grip.

"You're getting it, Dom. Keep on keeping on now."

"Rah," he said, holding his pace steady.

Sergeant G yelled back from her position that she was throwing a banger around the first corner.

Jed braced himself for the shock, but only felt it as a quick punch against his ears and gut.

"Move! Go!" Sergeant G yelled.

Dom tugged on Jed's vest as he led the two of them backwards and then around the corner. They stepped through the dust and smoke of the banger and across two bodies lying on the floor. Jed glanced down at them as he moved. Whoever they were, they'd still been people when they died. One of them was a man wearing a bus driver's dark blue sweater. The patches on the shoulders and elbows were stained with blood and soot.

Wish we had you with us, too, man. I'd give anything for a ride out of hell right now.

***

Gallegos held up a hand and the squad came to a halt behind her. The first corner had been easy. But now the sucker faces were pacing them. Their shrieks and screams bounced around the hallway, coming in from broken windows up ahead, and probably in the building somewhere above them.

The last of the firehole closets was just ahead on the left. Gallegos could swear the sucker faces were in the room above the hole and were just toying with the squad for shits and grins.

They could have rushed in and taken us down, but they just sent one through the barricade. It took Reeve out, and the others came from the opposite end of the hall. They're trying to weaken us. And it's working.

"Banger on three," she said over her shoulder as she readied the next grenade.

"One, t—"

Scraping claws and snapping joints resounded through the hallway and she tossed the banger around the corner, rolling back against the wall as it exploded and then rushing around with her weapon up, firing at everything that moved.

***

Jed spun around when Sergeant G cut off her count. He pushed Dom ahead of him as the grenade went off.

"Dom, get up there!" he yelled. "Sergeant G needs backup!"

She'd started firing right away and was still popping off rounds up ahead. Every shot cracked as loud as a thunderclap in the narrow space.

The firefighter stayed put for a beat, and then ran forward and around the corner. Two blasts from his weapon joined with Sergeant G's fire. Jed turned back to their six. The hall was clear. He pressed his shoulder up against Matty and Jo. They held Reeve between them. The man had his feet under him now, but his shoulder looked like hell and his face was drawn down in a grimace.

"Let's move," Jed said and nudged Matty to get them going. With slow steps, the whole group of them moved around the corner after Sergeant G. Jed split his attention between monitoring the path ahead and watching their six for movement.

Matty and Jo shouted and Jed turned back to see Reeve stumbling forward with an M9 in one hand.

He rounded the corner and was out of sight with Matty following after him.

"Move out, but stay with me; stay close," Jed said to Jo.

She kept tight with him and together they moved around the corner after the others.

Jed couldn't risk taking his eyes off their six. The sucker faces were playing fast and loose and changing the rules with every beat.

A roar filled the hallway behind them. Jed had one hand on his vest, reaching for a banger when a swarm of sucker faces poured around the last corner. Jed forgot about the grenade and yelled for Jo to run as he opened up.

— 28 —

The hallway in front of Gallegos was a bloodbath. Sucker faces lay in piles on both sides. Beside her, Dominic held his weapon by his side and breathed in heavy gasps, coughing from the dust.

A shout came from around the corner and Reeve staggered into view with a pistol in his hand. Gallegos reached for him, but he fell against the wall and cried out as his shoulder took his weight. He reeled away. Matty caught him and steadied him on his feet.

Welch hollered a beat later and Jo's face appeared. The chop of Welch's weapon followed Jo around the corner.

"Run!" she yelled and helped Matty get Reeve back on his feet. They stepped around Gallegos and Jo paused to look her in the eye.

"We have to go," Jo said. "They're coming in the windows. They're probably going to come in the back door in a second. We're going to die if we don't get moving!"

Gallegos felt like she was losing control of the situation. Jo was right. They'd let themselves get trapped. They'd treated the col-labs like the real threat, but it was always the suckers who had the game in hand.

Jo and Matty moved Reeve down the hall. Dom had the extra pistol tucked into his waistband and was stepping forward with the M4 held out like it could explode at any second. Back at their six, Welch was pumping out rapid fire bursts. He let out a *Whoop!* and came back pedaling around the corner.

"They're gone!" he yelled. "Fucking things ran away when I lit 'em up."

Jo and the others held up before the final corner that would take them to the back door. Gallegos grabbed Welch's shoulder as he came even with her in the hall.

"Throw a banger if they come in again, Welch. We don't have enough ammo left, and the sucker faces probably know it. They're going to weaken us until we have nothing left to fight with and then they'll come in for the kill."

Welch looked at her like she'd spoken gospel. He fished a banger out of his vest pouch and held it up. With a nod, she directed him to stay on their six while she moved up to join the firefighters and Reeve.

"Dom, I need you to open the door, just like on the stairs except you stand back this time while I toss the banger outside. Then it's you and me first. You take left; I take right. Rah?"

"Yeah. Rah," he said. "I can do this."

"Jo, Matty, you need to keep Reeve down and out of harm's way. You good?"

"We're good," Jo said. Matty nodded to confirm. Reeve's head hung limp on his neck but he managed a thumbs up with his good arm.

"Waiting on you, Dom," Gallegos said, as she picked the third flash bang out of her vest.

Two more left plus two with Welch. Salve nos Dios.

Dom stepped up to the corner, darted a look around it and came back. He stayed up against the wall, gave Gallegos a nod went around the corner. She stepped fast after him holding the banger against her chest.

The door was solid and made of metal. Bullet holes in it picked out dim glows of light from outside, but the door was whole and closed. Dom gave her a quiet count of three and yanked the door open.

***

Jed kept the flash bang grenade in his hand and waited for the clap of Sergeant G's to die down in his ears.

Mahton was right. You get used to it.

Jo and Matty struggled with Reeve to get around the corner. Jed stayed with his eyes on the route back down the hall, pivoting around the corner and finally pocketing the banger so he could hold the SAW with both hands.

An unnerving quiet and dim light greeted the squad as they emerged into the rear drive of the bus depot. No sucker faces raced in from the shadows. No big black trucks roared into the drives spitting death in their direction.

Sergeant G directed Jed to post by the railing across the driveway.

"Cover us from there, Welch. If you see enemy, banger first, then light up anything that moves that isn't us."

"*Errr*," he said and moved across the space, eyeballing every mound of debris as he went.

***

"Where the fuck are they?" Jo asked.

"Guess Welch was right. He scared them off back there," Gallegos said. "Maybe they're not as clever as I thought."

"If they're scared, that means they know better than to try us right now. That means they have fewer numbers than they used to, or they're trying to trick us into thinking that. I think you've been right all along. Those things are learning how to fight against us."

Reeve mumbled something and Matty chimed in. "Your man's right, if you ask me. They're not that intelligent anymore. They have tactics, but they're pack hunters. They might have some kind of strategy they follow, but they're not trained fighters like you all are."

"So what are they doing?" Jo asked. "It's like we're getting a reprieve. I don't like it. They don't have any compassion to spare. Just hunger. They should be coming after us right here, right now, and ending it."

"They're regrouping," Gallegos said. "Just like we did upstairs. We don't have time to argue about why we're not dead yet. Let's get moving."

She paced along the wall until she was at the end of the driveway. The wall stopped about a car-length from the street. A brick pillar supported the ceiling there. To her left, the driveway was open and clear, with another pillar at the opposite corner.

"Bring Reeve up behind me," she said to Jo and Matty. They moved slow to join her, half-carrying the wounded Marine between them.

"Dom, stay at their six. Welch, take that corner," Gallegos said, aiming a finger at the pillar opposite her position.

He stepped fast, following the railing beneath the windows. Gallegos watched over his head for any movement in the rooms there. All she saw were silent shadows.

"High rise is around the corner from Welch's position. Jo, Matty, and Reeve, you're first behind him. Dominic, stay tight with me. We'll be right behind your people. I got our six. Eyes out everybody. Let's move."

***

Jed pivoted away from the wall and sped across the street to the next corner. He roved the street with the SAW, scanning every shadow, anywhere the sucker faces could hide. But the street and city sent back only silence.

At the next corner, a high iron fence surrounded what used to be a small park at the bottom of the high rise. Jed followed it down 99th, keeping an eye on the depot across the street. If the suckers were going to come from anywhere, he figured they'd be on the roof and scrambling down the wall. And still nothing moved, no hit came out of the darkness.

The slanting afternoon light lit enough of the street for Jed to make out the bodies of suckers killed by the Air Force's last run.

And one block down there are seven soldiers lying in the street. Pivowitch and his squad. Tucker's last victims.

Thinking about their mission again put Jed's mind back where he wanted it. In the game and on point. He cast a quick look back to confirm Jo and Matty were still good. They had Reeve held in a seat carry with his M4 across his lap, held in his good hand. Jo gave a nod and Jed went back to leading them forward to the next objective.

He came around the end of the iron fence into a little patio beside the high rise. The area was clear so he pressed on to the back of the building. He held up beside a chain link fence that surrounded a heating and cooling unit there. A utility door was set into the building above a single low step. It looked like it might be open a few inches, but Jed couldn't be sure. He waved for Jo and Matty to pull in tight behind him. When they were well off the street and in the shadows, Jed moved closer to the utility door with the SAW up and ready to rock.

***

Gallegos and Dom swept into the patio and posted by the corner of the iron fence. She scanned the street behind them and looked up the depot wall across the way. Everything was still and quiet.

They're just taking their time about it, aren't they? Motherfuckers.

Welch had the others up near a chain link fence. Gallegos waved Dom forward to join them. She took three quick steps and posted by the iron fence that continued on the other side of the patio.

Nothing but the sound that death makes when it comes for you. We gotta get inside and get right.

"Welch, get everyone inside. Flash bang first."

He grunted an *Errr* back to her. A second later she

heard the telltale *ping* of the safety pin dropping on the concrete and then the explosive clap of the grenade.

The squad rushed in with Welch leading the way and Dom moving in right after him.

He's learning. It's a crash course in Battlefield 101, and he's learning. We might see tomorrow after all.

***

Jed went fast through the open door and nearly stumbled over a body. Dom had come in tight on his six and pushed him forward, forcing him to hop over the corpse. Jed had Dom take a position at the flight of steps going up to the next floor, then he bent down to examine the body. It was a woman, but he knew it had to be a col-lab. The body was torn to pieces by the sucker faces, and it was dressed in BDUs.

She'd been carrying a Ruger Mini-14. The weapon was lying at the base of the steps to Jed's right. It had an extended magazine and a scope mounted on it.

"Found our sniper," he said.

"The one that killed Luce?" Dom asked from behind him.

"Yeah man. Probably is. Cover them stairs."

Dom glared at the dead woman before turning his attention back to the staircase that wound upward into the tower.

Jed crept toward the steps leading down from the landing. Dim shadows greeted him in every direction except above. A slim blade of light leaked into the stairwell from a window on the next landing. Jed wished for a flashlight or something to illuminate the area, and then remembered his mom's favorite expression.

Wish in one hand and shit in the other, Jed. Tell me which one fills up first.

Jo and Matty carried Reeve in, and Sergeant G was right behind them.

"Sniper dead on the ground there, Sergeant."

Sergeant G went to the body, knelt, and checked it. She rifled through the pockets before standing up holding three magazines. She picked up the rifle, and took the weapon and ammo to Jo.

"Keep the thumper over your shoulder. Use this until we're out in the open again.

Reeve groaned and mumbled something about being able to walk.

"He's bleeding again," Matty said.

"How bad?" Sergeant G asked.

"Slow, but he needs a new bandage. We need to hole up somewhere so we can clean the wound and wrap it better. That hospital's sound better every second."

Reeve grunted at them through gritted teeth. "I said I can fucking walk. Now let me walk."

"Put him down," Sergeant G said. The firefighters slowly set Reeve onto his feet. He held his hand out for a weapon and Dom put the spare pistol into it.

"You're going to pass out if we don't get that bleeding under control," Jo said.

"We do that ASAFP," Sergeant G said. "First we get down those stairs. The col-lab said Tucker had a cache here, so let's get down there and find it. Might have more first aid we can use. Welch, how many bangers you got left?"

"One, Sergeant."

A screech split the air outside, resounding up and down the street.

"They're at it again," Jo said. "They've probably been watching us all along."

Sergeant G went to the door and brought her weapon up to cover the patio. "Maybe, maybe not. I don't see them anywhere," she said.

"What's this?" Dom asked.

Jed turned to see him holding up a small green box with wires running from it and out the door.

"Looks like a detonator," Jed said.

More shrieks and cries poured into the landing from outside.

"It's a distraction!" Dom shouted, and fired a burst at a trio that was slinking down the stairwell above. Jed expected more of the suckers to pour out of the darkness below his position, but the scraping of claws and snapping joints came from outside. Another crack from a pistol added to Dom's fire and three dead sucker faces landed on the steps in a heap. Reeve stood next to him aiming an M9 up the stairwell.

More small arms fire rattled the air, but this time it came from outside and rounds chipped away at the walls and doorframe. Sergeant G pushed Jo and Dom ahead of her toward Jed.

"Col-labs! Downstairs, people! Move!"

Jed took a step down, and then another, expecting death to come out of the darkness for him as more automatic fire popped from the outside.

A heavy explosion rocked the stairwell, followed by three more blasts. Jed looked back to see Reeve holding the detonator and standing near the door. He sagged against the door frame and was telling Sergeant G to get moving. She was saying the same to him.

A tornado of howls and screeches dropped down the stairwell from above and the whole squad looked up. Clicking joints added to the cacophony and dark shapes bounded across the space between each flight of stairs. The mass of monsters grew with each second until all light was blocked in the stairwell above.

"Run, people! Run!" Sergeant G screamed.

— 29 —

Jed slammed into the door at the bottom of the stairwell, hitting the crash bar and pushing through into a corridor. He came face to face with a man carrying a SAW and lit him up. Shattered glass cascaded down the wall and landed at Jed's feet. A mirror had been propped against the wall opposite the door. Jed shook off the distraction and moved into the corridor. It was clear to his left and blocked with broken conduits and tangles of telephone line to his right.

Weak light crept into the corridor from up ahead, and it was a sickly pale green.

He felt the squad come down the steps behind him, but he kept his eyes straight ahead, trying to pick out any details he could as he crept deeper into the darkness.

A hiss up ahead made him tense and he squeezed off a burst without thinking.

"You got enemy, Welch?" Sergeant G shouted up to him.

"Sounded like suckers, Sergeant. But I can't see anything up here!"

Small-arms fire rattled behind him.

"Col-labs aren't coming in," Sergeant G said. "They're

keeping us fucking pinned here, and suckers are coming down. Keep going."

Jed didn't move. Sergeant G fired twice more and she shouted to him again.

"Move it, Welch!"

He pushed forward, letting his eyes adjust to the weird green light. Shuffling sounds echoed down the tunnel. He couldn't tell if the sounds were from in front or behind him. He fired a quick burst. No cries or grunts came back to him. He had no idea what he was shooting at, or if he'd hit anything.

The odd green glow was brighter up ahead, but it wasn't enough to show him any details of the tunnel, much less who or what might be moving in it.

Shit, gotta get up to that light. Whatever it is. Gotta get where I can see.

A shriek came rolling down the tunnel in front of him. He couldn't tell how far away it was, and felt like he should fire, but he remembered Sergeant's G's order to conserve ammo. He kept moving, trusting his instincts, reaching out with everything he had and praying for safety for him and the whole squad. Another shot cracked at the back of their formation.

Is that Sergeant G or Dom? What are they shooting at? Are the sucker faces coming in now?

Jed kept moving, focusing on the path ahead and letting the green light guide him. He had to be under the lawn between the high rises now. He'd taken at least forty steps. Another shriek came toward him, but still he couldn't place it at a distance. Electrical conduit and water pipes lined the tunnel at eye level. The green glow reflected off the conduit lines.

Where the fuck is the light coming from? How long is this tunnel?

More gunfire popped in the tunnel behind him. Sergeant G was probably picking off sucker faces that tried to get in at the door. They'd be silhouetted at least a little bit. Jed paced forward another two steps and stopped.

"Holding here," he said to whoever was behind him. "Sound off back there, okay?"

They'd come into the tunnel so fast, he didn't know if it was Matty or Jo at his six. And he had no idea where Reeve was. Did he even make it to the steps?

Someone back there grunted. It might have been Jo, but he couldn't be sure. Sergeant G was still popping rounds off at their six.

How long until we're surrounded at both ends and just fucking killed?

***

Gallegos covered Jo while she reloaded the Mini-14 they'd picked off the dead col-lab. They stood side by side in the tunnel putting sucker faces down with single shots when they entered the corridor. Matty and Dom were a few yards farther along, carrying Reeve into the darkness behind Welch.

"Close it up," Gallegos said to Jo.

"They'll come in and swarm us," she said.

"I don't think so. They're not doing it now, and there's no reason they shouldn't. That tells me we've got breathing room."

"Or they've figured out how to set traps and they're

going to ambush us from the other end."

"Could be, but if it is, then it is. Right now it ain't, and we need more room if we have to use the thump gun. Close it up. I got our six."

Jo took a slow step backwards, then another. Gallegos aimed down the hall at the doorway where a mound of dead sucker faces blocked the entrance. More of them could easily crawl inside using the walls or ceiling, but they weren't just rushing forward.

It's like they're learning to avoid an obvious kill box.

If so, then they still have the upper hand. Either way, I hope I'm right.

***

Jed kept his eyes front, using the green glow to pick out shapes in the dark corridor. Footsteps slapped on the floor behind him.

"Who's back there?"

"Me and Dom," Matty said.

"You got Reeve with you?"

"Yeah, ya deke. I'm here."

Jed almost laughed, but the blast of a rifle behind them put him on alert.

"Sergeant G back there still? Why doesn't she come up? Where's Jo?"

"They're both back there," Dom said. "Let's keep going."

"I can't fucking see, man. This green shit helps, but only a little. What's it coming from?"

"Looks like the shit on the pipes is doing it," Matty said.

"Stay frosty, Welch," Reeve said. "Sergeant G wants us moving in case they need to use the thumper. So pinch it off and get going, rah?"

Jed bit his tongue. Reeve was making jokes when all Jed could think about was the hit he wouldn't see or hear coming.

He took a step forward and his foot landed in something sticky on the floor. He lifted up and almost stumbled when he had to use twice as much force to free his boot.

"There's something on the floor here, y'all. It's sticky as hell."

Dom and Matty said they'd watch out for it. Jed kept moving, one step at a time, deeper and deeper down the corridor.

A heavy silence wrapped around him as he walked in the darkness, and the green glow finally grew bright enough for him to make out more than the pipes running along the walls. He could see the ceiling better now, and when he did, he almost wished it had stayed dark.

***

Gallegos and Jo stepped back down the corridor, moving in tandem with their weapons up and aimed at the path back to the stairwell door. Jo had the thump gun slung still. The pile of sucker faces had grown by five more during the last few minutes.

"They're not coming in anymore," Jo said.

"I think they've learned not to."

"I'm starting to believe you guys. They aren't just monsters without any brains left. They can learn, and that scares the shit out of me."

"I'd think there was something wrong with you if it didn't," Gallegos said. "Let's catch up with the others."

Jo turned on her heel and went down the corridor. Gallegos followed, switching her view to their six with every other step.

Let my squad be safe. Let us get out of this alive.

The corridor stayed still and quiet between her and the stairwell door. As she stepped back, and the pile of dead suckers grew smaller and dimmer in her vision, the green glow around her revealed shapes in the walls. Lines of conduit and plumbing framed her path down the corridor.

"You back there, Sergeant G?" Welch's voice called to her through the dark.

"Rah. You got anything?"

"I got blood. A lot of it on the ceiling."

"Fresh? Old?"

"Can't say. It's like paint up here. And I think there's a patch of something else on the floor right behind us. Y'all watch your step coming up."

Yeah, we'll do that.

"How long does this tunnel go?"

"Looks like it opens up soon. This green shit—"

The chop of a machine gun broke through Welch's words. Gallegos dropped to her stomach yelling for everyone to hit the deck as bullets ricocheted down the corridor.

***

Jed stared into the darkness ahead. He and the rest of the

squad were all prone in the corridor. Nobody had been hit, but every few seconds a muzzle flash would light up the corridor and reveal a room maybe five yards ahead of their position. More rounds would come their way, but whoever was shooting at them didn't want to hit them. Or if they did, the darkness made it so they couldn't aim for shit. But with a machine gun, aim wasn't as much of a concern.

Volume of fire. It's all about filling the air with enough lead to make people too scared to move.

And it was working. Jed lifted his head between the bursts, straining to see into the room at the end of the corridor. But every time the gun fired, a series of ricochets forced him to suck the floor again.

Shuffling sounds in the room sparked Jed's trigger finger. He didn't even raise his head to look, just fired once and then once again. He caught more shuffling in the lull between his shots and risked lifting his head. He sent another burst into the space and spotted a figure running. The effect of the green glow was weakened by the constant muzzle flashes, but Jed could still make out shapes in the room and the outline of the doorway leading into the corridor in front of him.

Someone grunted in the room. A sound like an ammo box being slid across the floor came down the corridor. Jed fired again. Whoever was in there cried out and the scuffling sound stopped.

"He's down!" Jed said, lifting up to a high crawl. He flattened out again just as fast when another burst of machine gun fire lit up the hallway.

The chop from the weapon was heavier than a SAW.

Gotta be a 240 or something just as big. If it's a team weapon... Shit!

Like she was reading his mind, Sergeant G yelled up to him, "Welch, there's probably two of them! Sustained fire!"

Jed fired another burst into the room. Sergeant G slid up the floor at the edge of the corridor and stopped when she was even with his position. She kept her weapon aimed forward.

"Fire 'em up, Welch. Keep your sight picture to the left. I'm moving."

Jed lit up the room, sending rounds back in the direction of the enemy's fire. More lead came their way and the constant rattle and chop of both weapons turned the corridor into a frenzy of violent noise. Jed's ears felt like they were stuffed with cotton, but he could still make out the sound of a body going to the floor, followed by a gurgled cry. The gunfire stopped and Sergeant G slapped Jed on his back.

"Move up, low and slow. I'm with you."

"Who's got our six?"

"Jo's back there. Let's move, Welch," she said.

Jed crawled forward, sliding the SAW ahead of him. He kept his finger on the trigger guard, ready to snap it back and light up anything that moved.

Shuffling and scraping sounds came from the room. Jed was only a couple meters away now. The green glow made it easier to see. Shards of another mirror lay against the wall near the door, reflecting the green glow. It was stronger here and Jed finally figured out what it was.

Fucking black light paint. They used the mirrors to bring daylight into the hall to light it up.

The shuffling up ahead stopped, then the room filled with scurrying and dragging noises like boots and a body being pulled across stone. A click of a door latch was followed by light slicing into the room.

Fuck! That's gotta be Tucker and he's running away!

Jed picked up and ran forward to the doorway, sending a burst into the room and sweeping to his left, firing a second burst at a door that was swinging shut.

— 30 —

Welch fired off two bursts as he ran forward. He stopped at the end of the corridor and dropped his ammo box.

"Fuck! I'm empty!"

Gallegos was on her feet and charging forward with her weapon up, aiming into the room beyond. Nothing moved.

Welch backed away a step. Gallegos reached for her last magazine and handed it to him.

"Get the others up here," she said. Welch slapped the magazine into his weapon and shuffled backwards down the corridor.

Gallegos stepped into the room. She swept left and right, looking into every corner and possible hiding spot. There weren't many to speak of. The room was empty as far as she could tell, with only an easy chair shoved into the corner to her left.

The glowing green light was stronger in the room. She could make out a cupboard on the far wall, and a janitor's sink and mop bucket to their left. Two cans of paint and brushes sat on the sink. She could just make out their shape from where she stood inside the door.

Smears of something trailed along the floor from near the mop sink, going toward the door. Gallegos crouched and felt it with her fingers.

Fresh blood. We hit them. But not hard enough.

"Bet that's the glow paint," Welch said, moving in beside her. He chuckled. "That's what they used for night vision down here. Fucking raver glow paint."

"This is their blood, Welch," Gallegos said, standing up.

The others moved into the room behind him, with Matty and Dom holding Reeve in a seat carry again. Jo entered last, covering their path back into the darkness.

"Where's the machine gun?" Reeve asked, shifting off of the firefighters' hands and stepping closer to her position. "I heard a *240* in here. Had to be."

"It's gone. Whoever was in here got away. Welch hit 'em, so they're carrying wounded just like us. Let's take advantage of that."

The squad got in step behind her as she moved to the door leading out. Reeve sat back into Matty and Dom's carry. He put his good arm around Matty's shoulders.

"Thanks for the ride, y'all, but next time I'll just call a cab."

"Still full of shit, Reeve," Gallegos said. "Keep it up. It tells me you're still alive."

"Oorah," he said, and let out a short chuckle that turned into a groan of pain.

At the door leading out, Gallegos had Welch position himself opposite the opening.

"I'll breach. Throw your banger first, then go in hot. I'm on your six."

"Rah, Sergeant," Welch said and lifted his last banger

out of his vest.

Gallegos tested the knob first to make sure it turned. When it did, she opened it a few inches. Welch threw his grenade and turned away. She pushed the door shut as the banger went off, then yanked the door open again. Welch stormed through and she followed him in.

***

Jed rushed forward with the SAW up, roving his muzzle around the space beyond the door. He'd come into a landing like the one at the other end of the utility corridor, only this one didn't have a mound of dead sucker faces on the floor. But it did have streaks of blood leading up the stairs.

And it had something much worse.

"What the fuck is this?" Sergeant G asked from behind him. Matty, Dom, Reeve, and Jo were at the door, slowly moving into the space.

The underside of the stairs and the wall above the door were coated in some kind of glue or webbing. Sergeant G got closer to it and reached a hand out. Her fingers caught on it and she had to tug them back.

"Fuck, that shit's like hot glue," she said.

Jed looked at the stuff and shuddered when he realized what he was seeing. Here and there in the tangled sticky pulp, he could make out hollows in the substance that would have held arms or legs. Some could have been for shoulders or hips.

Jo let out a shout of disgust. "It's like a meat locker. This must be where they kept the prisoners."

Jed moved closer to where Sergeant G was standing

and reeled away when he saw a strip of skin hanging from the empty casing.

"Whatever this shit is, you don't want to get it on you."

The more he looked, the more he wanted to get away from the stuff. Spots and sprays of blood marked the hollows, along with strips of skin still embedded in the sticky material.

The stairwell beside them led up to another landing and a door to the outside. It was open and Jed moved away from the crap on the walls to check their path out of the building.

"Hold up, Welch," Sergeant G said. He turned back to see her kneeling and pawing at the blood on the floor. Dark smears coated the tips of her fingers.

"We definitely hit Tucker, or whoever that was back there shooting at us."

A groan outside snapped everyone's attention to the door. Jed moved like he'd go through it, but he stopped short at the threshold.

"What do you got, Welch?"

"It's him, Sergeant. It's Tucker out there. Gotta be."

"You got eyes on him?"

"Negative, Sergeant. But I can hear him. He's close by."

"Stay frosty. We don't know who else or what else is out there, or if that's even him."

"What about his cache?" Matty said. "Remember that man said they had a stash of gear under these buildings? Ammo, food, and water. Right? Or did I hallucinate the last twenty-four hours?"

"It's not here is it?" Reeve asked.

"Nothing's here," Dom said. "The prisoners aren't here. The monsters aren't even here. I don't like it. They're playing with us again, like they did at the bus station. I knew we—"

"You knew shit, Dominic," Sergeant G cut in.

"I got eyes on him, Sergeant," Jed said. "Our man's getting away. Well, he's crawling away."

"So go stop him, Welch."

***

Gallegos had Jo keep the squad covered with the Mini-14. Dom and Matty set Reeve down and Dom joined her at the door. He held Reeve's M4 at the ready. It wasn't like having a Marine at her side, but Dom had done all right so far. Most of his shots went into walls, but he'd hit some sucker faces back at the other building. Or he'd sent them scrambling away, making it easier for her and Jo to pick them off.

"Good to see you stepping up with that weapon, Dominic," she said.

He mumbled something that sounded like *thanks* and she left it at that.

As long as he doesn't get friendly with his fire.

Through the doorway, she could just see Welch crouched by a park bench in the middle of the lawn between the two high rises. Rubble and ash covered almost everything around them, but this little area had been spared destruction.

Welch was looking back toward the other building. Gallegos put a foot outside and said to Dom, "Stay here and cover me. Watch high and low for any movement."

Gallegos moved out to join Welch. He pointed back the way he'd been looking. A body was lying in the ash and debris up against the side of the building. The figure slumped against a weapon on a bipod. It looked like an M240 and had a belt of ammo hanging out of it. The person's hands were flat on the ground like he was dead.

"Cover me, Welch," Gallegos said, and stepped forward with her weapon up and aimed at the col-lab's head.

— 31 —

Gallegos moved fast until she was a step away from the body. She prayed the col-lab hadn't set a trap for them with a grenade under his chest. When she got closer, she caught the ragged breaths of a dying man.

"We need the medics out here, on me," Gallegos said. "Jo, stay with Reeve and keep watch on our six."

A few grunts and an *Errr* came back from the direction of the door. Welch was behind her, scanning the area. Gallegos put her attention back on the col-lab. Even though she expected sucker faces to come ripping down the walls or flying out of a doorway hidden under the debris, she knew better than to ignore a wounded enemy.

Matty rushed up to her position with the trauma bag. She kept one hand on her weapon and helped Matty slowly turn the col-lab over with the other. When they had him lifted up high enough, she jammed her hand under his chest, feeling for a grenade. All she felt was warm blood. The guy groaned and coughed. He spit off to the side next to his weapon.

"Wish we had better light," Matty said. "I only have a pen light and the batteries are about dusted."

"Flashlight—in my pocket," the col-lab said.

While Matty opened his kit, Gallegos kept her weapon on the col-lab and dug into his clothing with her free hand. She found a mini-mag in his cargo pocket. It even had a red lens in it. She clicked it on and aimed it at the col-lab's torso. He'd been hit at least once that she could see. Blood soaked into the BDU top he wore.

Matty went to work, cutting the guy's clothing away from his wound. He'd taken one to the gut and had pushed a wad of something under his shirt and against the hole.

"Gotta take that off, son," Matty said.

The col-lab groaned again and clenched his teeth as Matty lifted the makeshift dressing away from the wound. Gallegos held the light steady, but kept her eyes on the night around them. Any second, she expected sucker faces to swarm their perimeter.

What little perimeter we have. I got a man with a SAW and almost no ammo left for it. I got a wounded man who can't use a weapon, and a newbie with a boom stick who might hit one of us if I'm not careful where I put him.

And now we got this sack of dead weight on the ground.

"Are you Tucker?"

"No—I'm…" The guy sucked in air. "I didn't want to—"

"Where are they then? Tucker and the others. Where'd they go?"

"What others?"

"The other col-labs, like you. The motherfuckers who gave us up to the sucker faces."

"I—I don't know… Don't care. He's just got Jacob with him. They…left me here to kill—"

"To kill us? How'd that work out for you the first time?"

"Wasn't me. He was shooting. He made me go for the ammo. You shot me."

"Why didn't you stop him instead of following his orders?"

"He's—fucking crazy. Made a deal with the bone collector."

"Why? No, don't answer that. Just tell me where he went and where they took our people."

"Your people?"

"The prisoners. The ones that used to be hung up inside like meat in a freezer. Where the fuck did they go?"

The guy coughed twice and groaned. Bloody spittle coated his lips and ran down his cheek.

"The bone collector took everyone. He let us stay— We promised him more food."

"What the fuck is wrong with you?" Gallegos demanded. "These are monsters from hell and you're feeding them your own people—"

"It was—shit! That *hurts!*"

"Just keep talking. You'll be fine," Matty said. He had a new dressing over the wound and was applying pressure with one hand.

"Hold this tight," Matty told the col-lab. The guy weakly laid a hand over the bandage. Matty prepared a wrap to hold the dressing over the wound.

"Waiting to hear more from you," Gallegos told the col-lab.

"What?"

"Don't need your attitude, you piece of shit, just the four-one-one. Where did Tucker go?"

"The boat."

"And where is 'the boat'?" Gallegos demanded, pushing her muzzle closer to the col-lab's face.

"Shoot me," he said, and then coughed more blood and spit onto the grass beside his head. "I don't care. He isn't here anymore."

In that moment Gallegos realized the col-lab was just a kid, maybe fifteen or sixteen years old. Matty had the wrap around him once and was working on getting it around a second time.

Is this the other guy's son? I don't know why I care. I just know that I do.

"You got less time than you think, *mijo*, so if you want to go somewhere better after you die, this might be your chance. Tell us where Tucker is and where to find our people. Maybe God will grant you mercy."

"I don't know where they took the people."

"So tell us about Tucker. At least give us that much."

The kid rallied a bit, got some strength back in his voice when he let loose about Tucker. "He's fucking *crazy*. He was talking to the things since it started. They ate his girlfriend—*right in front of him*! He thinks they're here to help cleanse the world. It was my dad's idea, but Tucker...he agreed. Had all the guns. Him and Jacob and Mary."

"Who're they?"

"My friends—his son and daughter—I—"

The boy coughed up more blood and shook.

"He's dying," Matty said.

"You don't—have to save me," the boy said through choking coughs. "I know I'm going to die. They—they keep the boat up river."

"Harlem River?"

The boy nodded.

"All right. Now how about our people? You sure you don't know where they took them?" Gallegos asked.

The boy shook again and coughed up more blood. Matty had the bandage wrapped up good, but it wouldn't be enough. The boy was going to die and they couldn't stop it.

"Your dad was in the truck. Your name's Carl, right?" she asked.

The boy nodded again. Tears streamed down his face as he looked at her. He mouthed *I'm sorry* and she put her hand on his brow and said a prayer for him as his face went still and his breath sighed out for the final time.

"Welch, come here."

He moved fast and came over next to Matty. She had him take the col-lab's weapon. The belt hung off it with maybe a dozen rounds left. A soft ammo bag sat in the dirt next to Carl's body. She gave that to Welch, took her mag back from the SAW, and told him to disable the weapon.

"Take the bolt out. We'll lose it somewhere on the way. Harlem River's at least three blocks from here, straight down 99th Street. Reeve, can you walk?"

"Rah. I can make it. Just give me something to shoot with. This *9* is empty."

"You can have mine," she said, walking to his position and handing over her sidearm.

Reeve leaned on Jo's shoulder while Dom stood nearby, swiveling his head back and forth and holding Reeve's M4 with the muzzle up, aimed at the buildings around them.

"We still need to do better for Reeve," Matty said. "Met Hospital is two blocks away on 99ᵗʰ. We're down on bandages and saline. Who knows if anything is still useful or, God knows, sterile. But something's better than nothing."

"Oorah on that," Gallegos said. "When we get there, everyone keep an eye out. We'll stop only as long as we have to. Everyone ready?"

Grunts and a couple *Rahs* came back.

"Jo, stay on our six with Dom. Welch, Matty, either side of Reeve in the middle. Y'all follow me," she said, stepping away from the building and heading toward the street.

***

Jed walked fast through the darkness pivoting every few steps to watch behind them. He worried about sucker faces coming down from the high rise they'd just left, and the street around them was full of threatening shadows. It didn't matter where he looked. All he saw were avenues of attack.

When they passed the block where he'd seen Pivowitch and his squad, Jed whispered his promise to finally avenge their deaths. He knew they lay there in the dark, where he'd left them the day before, with their eyes closed and hands over their hearts.

Sergeant G was at least five yards ahead, pushing them hard to catch up with Tucker. If he was on foot, they had a good chance of catching him, and that thought gave Jed a boost of energy that made his legs feel like they could climb a mountain. His arms ached with the extra weight of the M240, but the fire of their mission pushed him on and drove him forward.

After a full day of chasing this motherfucker, we're finally close enough to have him in our sight picture.

He was sure they'd catch Tucker soon, even with Reeve stumbling now and then. He grunted and growled with every step, but he kept up like the rest of them. They made good time, getting two blocks along without seeing anything or hearing any signs of the sucker faces. As scary as that was, Jed felt something shift in the dead city.

The ruins and streets around them were full of smashed vehicles, craters, and debris, and 99th was no different.

But the sucker faces had pulled back and gone to ground. They weren't up here chasing Jed and the squad to their deaths. He could almost smile at the freedom of walking the streets again, until he remembered the suckers had taken their prisoners with them.

Jed cursed Tucker's name over and over again, with every step he took.

If we can't save them, we can at least stop you.

The squad raced across an open intersection with the wreckage of apartment projects behind them. On the next block, the remains of another apartment building sat in a mess of ash and splintered wood to their left. Three wrecked sedans filled the street to their right. Across the street, the towering bulk of the hospital threatened to crumble into the road. Parts of the building near the intersection had been knocked into dust and rubble, but father along the building stood proud in the darkness.

A small motor coughed to life somewhere up ahead and rattled at an idle. Jed spun to the side, bringing his weapon around to orient on the sound. The others had stopped short around him. Jed pivoted to take in the apartment ruins at his back, then moved into the street and set the bipod on top of the nearest sedan. Light and shadow shifted in the hospital ruins across the street. He roved his sight picture through the remains of the building.

Was that a sucker face on the wall or just a shadow? Shit. I can't tell if I'm seeing things or not.

Jed's heart beat fast as he scanned the area. Nothing moved, and the rattle of the motor kept echoing through the empty night.

Sergeant G posted with her weapon on the sedan next to him.

"You got contact, Welch?"

"Nothing, Sergeant. I thought—"

"Nothing to see, nothing to shoot. Let's go."

"Tucker's up ahead somewhere, Sergeant. He's got wheels now."

"I can hear that, but I can't see it. Move out, Welch."

Off to their left, the motor revved and then clattered a steady rhythm.

"Go!" Sergeant G shouted and set off at a run.

Jed hefted the *240* and followed. Dom was next to him, matching his pace. Matty, Jo, and Reeve had to be at their six, but right now all Jed cared about was getting eyes on Tucker. From the sound of the motor, Jed figured Tucker had found a Gator in the hospital lot up ahead. The things weren't that fast, but Tucker could still put distance between them.

***

The motor chattered loud in the empty night as Gallegos put everything she had left into running through the wreckage of New York on the trail of the worst monster she had ever known.

You are not getting away. Not now. Not this time.

Twin beams of light lanced out of the dim evening air ahead of her. They tracked across the ruins to her left and swung away, toward the river that was still a couple hundred yards from their position. The hospital ended before the next intersection, with a parking lot at the corner. Mounds of debris and smashed up cars and trucks filled the lot as best as she could tell.

She was twenty yards from the lot when a black square detached itself from the mass of debris and swung into the roadway.

Gallegos dropped to a knee, sighted, and opened fire.

32

Jed sped forward, leaving Dom behind him. He dropped down next to Sergeant G, who was still firing at the Gator.

"Stop him, Welch!" she shouted as she sent round after round in Tucker's direction. Jed charged the 240 and opened up, thrilling to the sound of his shots impacting on the Gator. The little vehicle swerved right, then toppled over. A figure rolled out of Jed's zone of fire and disappeared into the shadows up there. Another figure weakly crawled away from the Gator.

Sergeant G was already on her feet and rushing ahead. Jed lifted up as Dom sped past him. Jed was on his knees, hoisting his weapon when Matty shouted up to them.

"We got suckers on us!"

Jed spun around. In the dim light, he could just make out Jo, Matty, and Reeve about twenty yards back. Behind them, a clutch of shadowy figures sprang from the ruined hospital wing, scrambling over rubble and dirt as they came racing after Jed's squad mates. Their hisses and clicking joints froze Jed's heart.

"Go left!" he shouted as he dropped down with the machine gun. "Get clear!"

***

Gallegos and Dom came up behind the Gator at the same time. Dom stopped near the back end of the truck. Gallegos held a hand up, signaling him to hold position there. He nodded like he understood, so she went around to the front. As she came around the vehicle, she sighted on the body of a man that had crawled a few feet from the overturned truck. The man's limp form was sprawled in the street with blood pooling around his chest.

"Dom, come around the other side. Cover me while I check him."

The firefighter stepped around the truck and brought his weapon up. Gallegos paced forward slowly until she was in point blank range of the body.

A shout whipped her attention from the dead col-lab. She turned and saw her squad tearing away from a group of sucker faces springing out of the shadows around them.

She forgot about the body and Tucker and everything else as she yelled for Dom to follow her back to the others.

***

Jed sent a burst into the sucker faces jumping from the debris. He caught two of them, but at least half a dozen others charged toward the street, screeching and hissing as they moved. Jo separated from Matty and Reeve and turned around with her weapon up, taking shots at the monsters.

Jed held his aim and waited for a clear shot. Jo was still too close to his zone of fire.

"Jo! Get clear! Get clear!"

Matty and Reeve had moved to the opposite sidewalk, coming around a mound of dirt and rubble and setting down to Jed's right. Jo back pedaled as she fired, but the best she was doing was giving the sucker faces something to aim for. Four of them converged on her position and Jed shifted his aim.

"Jo, get out of the way!" he yelled.

The sucker faces were almost on her. Two of them leaped into the air. Jed got a clear shot at a third and put it down. The two in the air tackled Jo, but she fired and one instantly rolled away dead. The other one grappled with her and grabbed at her weapon, then it bit down on her arm. It reared back and howled and Jed blasted it off of her with a fast burst. The remaining sucker faces were stalking Matty and Reeve on the sidewalk, crawling around the debris pile in teams of two.

Matty lifted up from the dirt with a pistol and fired into the suckers' heads, putting two of them down. The other two raced up the dirt pile. Shots fired from behind Jed lit up the monsters before they reached the top.

He rolled over to see Sergeant G and Dom running with their weapons up. Jed lifted off the ground, struggling to a knee with the heavy weapon. He got to his feet and ran forward to Jo. She was rolling side to side in the street and crying out in pain.

Please be okay. Please be okay!

***

Gallegos sent a burst at the suckers climbing the dirt pile. Matty had taken the other two out and her shots finished the job.

"Help her!" Welch yelled from further up the street. He was a few yards back from where Jo went down. Matty half tumbled off the dirt pile with his trauma bag flopping against his hip. Reeve was out of sight somewhere. Gallegos knew she should check on him, but Jo was lying in the street, holding her arm and crying out.

Welch got to her just as Matty was dropping his trauma bag and flicking on the flashlight they'd taken from the col-lab kid. Gallegos went to the dirt pile, slapping Dom on the shoulder as she stepped past him.

"On me. Cover my six. I'm checking Reeve."

***

Jed stood over Jo as Matty went to work. Red light bathed her bloodied arm. The sucker had taken a deep bite out of her muscle near the elbow. She was shivering and crying. Jed kept one hand on the 240's grip as he took a knee beside her head. He rested the weapon on his leg and put his free hand on her brow.

"You're gonna be okay, Jo. Matty's got you. He's a good doc. Right, Matty? You got her?"

"I got her, man, now chill the fuck out. What is it you guys say? Stay frosty, right? Let me work."

Jed forced himself to focus on the night around them, on the street leading back into Harlem, on the dirt and the ruined buildings. He looked at anything and everything except Jo's arm. Her head shuddered under his hand, and he steeled himself again to stay on point and on mission.

Get your sight picture right, Jed Welch. Get it right and make sure this is the last time somebody gets hurt on your watch.

***

Gallegos rounded the dirt mount slowly. She heard a gurgling noise and feared what she would find. But she had a man back here, and whatever condition he was in, she needed to confirm his status and give him whatever aid she could provide.

Reeve was on his back, lying against the pile of earth and chunks of concrete that had been blasted out by a bomb. Reeve shifted his position and his head flopped to the side. Gallegos took two steps forward and lowered her weapon. Reeve hadn't shifted his position. His body had moved because of the sucker face that was eating him.

It had its mouth clamped onto his neck and was pulling back when it noticed her. She lifted her weapon and blasted it between the eyes. It fell away from Reeve and Gallegos staggered back, slipping to one knee against the dirt pile. She stared at Reeve, the last member of her platoon. The last one from their company to have survived this long.

The last Marine I knew before the end.

***

Jed heard the crack of an M4 behind him. He spun back for a quick look at their six, but didn't see anything

272

moving. Dom stood in the street near the dirt pile with his weapon aimed off to the side.

What the hell's he shooting at? Where's Sergeant G?

Beside Jed, Matty worked to wrap Jo's arm. She was holding in her pain now, biting down and glaring at the sky above her. Jed kept swiveling his head back and forth so he could keep an eye on her and their six, as well as their immediate AO.

"You can walk right, Jo?" Matty asked.

She nodded but kept her teeth tight together.

"Let's get you up now. C'mon."

He put an arm around her shoulders and got her standing. Jed stood with them and Dom joined them a beat later.

"Where's Reeve and Sergeant G?" Jed asked him.

"Back there, I think," he said, pointing at the pile of dirt where Matty and Reeve had been. Jed told them all to follow him as he set off, weapon up.

"Reeve! Sergeant G! Sergeant, you back there?"

***

Welch called her name again, and Gallegos wiped at her eyes, shook herself and stood up. The impression of her body in the dirt pile looked just like the casings they'd found in the high rise. She'd laid down next to Reeve and wished for God to take her as well. Being the last Marine alive in New York City was more than she could handle after the day they'd had. The warfare she'd seen overseas was nothing compared to surviving, unaided, for two days in a city that had become hell itself.

Then Welch's voice cut through the gathering night.

Gallegos remembered she wasn't alone, and she wasn't the only Marine alive.

"I'm good, Welch," she called out.

He came around the dirt pile with the heavy gun slung around his neck.

"Reeve—"

"Suckers got him, Welch. Just you and me now."

"And them, Sergeant," he said, nodding his head back over his shoulder.

Dom and Matty came around the dirt mound. Matty went over to Reeve, hauling the dead sucker face out of the way.

"He's gone," Gallegos said.

"There's an ambulance in the drive across the street," Dom said. "We should see what's in it and go find Tucker, right?"

"Right you are, Dom," Gallegos said. *"Charlie-Mike.* Honor our fallen by staying on mission."

***

Jed had point position as they crossed the street to where the Gator went over. While Matty, Dom, and Jo went to the ambulance, Jed approached the body in the street and gently nudged it with his weapon. The guy was well past dead.

"Bled out," he said as Sergeant G joined him.

Jed did a quick scan of the Gator and spotted a bag lying up against the steering wheel. He checked it and found a couple of full canteens, three mags of 5.56, and a pistol that felt like it had a full mag in it.

"Ain't much, but it gives us a leg up."

"Oorah, Welch. He had some ammo on his person, too," Sergeant G said, kicking at the body. Jed knelt down and lifted a belt of soft pouches off the man's shoulder. Two of them hung on the belt from loops of *550*-cord. Jed opened one.

"It's 7.62, Sergeant."

"Ain't sure why I should care about that, Welch. Tucker's gone. He got away."

Jed was surprised to hear her say that. She'd been on mission the whole day, calling shots and taking them. She'd just told them all to *Charlie-Mike*, but now she sounded like she'd run out of gas.

Who can blame her? Shit, I'd have been ate up hours ago trying to run the game the way she did.

"We can still catch him, Sergeant. He's wounded."

Jed pointed at a trail of blood leading away from the crashed Gator. It followed a winding path toward the hospital drive.

Her voice picked up when she stepped away from the body and said, "Secure that gear, Welch, and let's see what they got from the ambulance."

***

Matty and Dom were helping Jo to the ambulance when Gallegos and Welch got there. The vehicle sat at the edge of the drive, up against a low concrete wall and tangled chain link fence. Gallegos had Welch post by the front while she moved to the back, ready to fire on anything that moved. She rounded the open doors and relaxed.

Everything inside was torn apart and covered in blood. The stretcher was still there, with the straps hanging off like they'd been shredded by a sucker face.

Must have been one of the first ones. Someone got infected and changed while they were in here.

Dom pawed through the inside of the vehicle. He cursed a few times, throwing useless oxygen masks and gloves out of the back until he dug up a serviceable trauma kit. He opened it, but Gallegos didn't let him waste time confirming what was in it, just that they got something useful.

"Assume it's got stuff we need. Let's go."

She called for them to follow her and set off at a jog down 99th, away from the ruins of the hospital and away from the last person the sucker faces would take from her.

It's all of us or none of us now. But if anyone's going down, it's Tucker first.

33

Gallegos led the remains of her squad past trees that were nothing but charred sticks now. They passed the mounded wreckage of cars, vans, and emergency vehicles. A roadblock had been prepared at the intersection past the hospital, but it was all shoved aside and sent into the buildings by a bomb that had fallen on the street up ahead.

They crossed 1st Avenue, skirted the crater in the middle of 99th, and followed the weak trail of blood that Tucker left behind him. It was only drops now.

Gallegos figured they'd winged him or hit something non-vital. Any hit from a 7.62 would slow a body down, but Tucker clearly had enough stamina and resolve to get through a lot of shit and keep going. He had all the makings of a Marine except for honor and loyalty.

A staccato of footsteps erupted from the street in front of her. Gallegos couldn't see the runner, but she beat her own rapid pace as she set out in pursuit. The street ended maybe thirty yards ahead, t-boning with a wide road along the riverside.

"You got eyes on him, Sergeant?" Welch called up from behind her. She didn't take the time to reply, only waved her arm and hoped the others could see her signal in the fading evening light.

***

Jed and Dom moved out after Sergeant G. She'd gone ahead to the street by the river and was turning the corner.

Shit, she's going after him by herself. One is none, Sergeant. Shit!

He pushed himself to run faster and slapped Dom in the shoulder to keep the steam on. Matty and Jo stayed with them for a bit, but quickly fell back. Dom pulled up by a smashed car and Jed had no choice but to join him. If the suckers came after them again, they'd need the firepower from the 240.

But she's out for blood by herself. Dammit, what do I do?

"Dom, wait for Matty and Jo. Cover them. Sergeant G's on her own. I gotta—"

Small arms fire rattled into the evening air. Jed yelled for Jo and Matty to catch up fast before he sped off.

***

Rounds came in her direction and Gallegos reeled away from the wall behind her, taking up a crouched position beside a newspaper box that had strangely remained undamaged, except for cracks in the glass. The front page still showed images of a football player that had been convicted of murder.

Gallegos focused on her surroundings again, and duck-walked forward, toward the roadway. She huddled behind a crumpled SUV and smaller car that had impacted head on. The SUV had lifted onto the hood of the other vehicle. A low dividing concrete barrier ran down the length of the road, and the cars were tight up against it. The best cover Gallegos could get in this area was right beside the cars. That assumed Tucker wasn't up or down the road, but across it somewhere.

The only hint she had about his location was the direction his fire had come from. But that changed with each burst he sent her way. Chips of stone flew off the building at her back and one round pinged into the newspaper box.

Gallegos fired a burst up the street in the direction of Tucker's fire.

If that's where he is.

He'd spotted her first and she had no idea where he was hiding.

Bodies of dead suckers filled the street around her. A crater filled what used to be a parking lot at the intersection of 99th and the riverside drive. She slid and crawled over the shattered pavement, keeping low behind the vehicles as Tucker fired at her again. This time the rounds pattered against the hood of the SUV.

Another volley came in, puncturing the SUV's driver side door with heavy *thunks*. Gallegos had a better idea where her foe was hiding now. She moved to her left, using the vehicle and dividing wall as cover and hoping that Tucker didn't have the sense to anticipate her movement. He'd proven his conviction to his cause, but that didn't mean he could read a battlefield. The insurgents Gallegos had tangled with were just as ready to do or die for what they believed in.

And they'd died just as easily as this motherfucker will.

The evening light had faded to dusk now, and Gallegos knew that meant she was all but invisible if she stayed still.

Unless he's got night vision.

The blasted and shattered waterfront roadway filled with shadows as the sun dropped behind what was left of New York City.

Just this one last job to do. Just one last enemy to remove from the equation.

Tucker fired again, puncturing the doors of both cars this time. His burst was met with return fire from back the way Gallegos had come.

"Sergeant G!" Welch yelled from the shadows. "I got eyes on him! He's behind the dirt pile! Covering you!"

Welch's weapon chopped at the evening air and Tucker responded in kind. Gallegos spun around the rear end of the SUV and brought her weapon up. Rounds impacted on a debris pile in the street and Gallegos stepped into the open, following the line of the concrete dividing wall and making sure Welch could see her as she moved.

Keep up the fire, Welch.

More rounds peppered the earth and concrete. She advanced to the dividing wall and crouched there. Welch lit up the col-lab's hiding spot with sustained bursts. Gallegos spotted movement, like a leg being tucked out of view around the mound of earth. Welch fired another volley and the dirt pile turned into a spray of pebbles, soil, and chips of shattered pavement.

Gallegos quickly mounted the dividing wall and dropped into a crouch on the other side, weapon up and focus open.

A rifle lifted over the dirt pile and sent a burst in Welch's direction.

Gallegos stood and circled to flank the debris pile. She took a step to her left and looked through her sights into the eyes of a man wearing faded BDUs, a bandana around his head, and belts of ammunition crossed over his chest. Blood trailed down his neck and she could make out a furrow of angry red along his collar.

The man was aiming an old M16 in her direction.

She squeezed her trigger and felt her weapon kick just as she felt another, stronger kick against her left hip.

Gallegos spun around and fell onto her side. She screamed as searing pain exploded into her gut and down her left leg.

***

Jed picked up from his prone position and charged forward, roaring with rage. He stopped once to fire a burst at the pile of dirt where Tucker had been hiding, then put everything he had into getting to Sergeant G. She'd fallen in the street and screamed out.

Tucker shot her. He fucking shot her. But she's still good. She's gotta be good. She's alive. She's not dead.

He all but fell to his knees beside her, setting down in a rush and slamming his weapon onto the pavement next to Sergeant G's shoulder. He checked her wound. She'd been hit high in her leg on the outside, and it was bleeding like hell.

"Medic!" Jed hollered as loud as he could while he clamped his hands over the wound. She cried out and rolled away, but he held firm, clamping pressure around the bloodied area. He could feel her life welling and slipping between his fingers as he squeezed and he prayed.

Where the fuck is Dom? Why didn't they stay closer? Shit!

"Did—did I get him, Welch? Tell me I got him."

Jed remembered where Tucker had been hiding. He grabbed with one hand for his weapon and flashed a look at the dirt pile. A pair of legs stuck out from behind it. They weren't moving.

"You got him, Sergeant. He's dead. *Medic!*" he yelled again, clamping back down on her wound. He no longer cared if the sucker faces were about to come scrambling out of the shadows and eat him alive. Sergeant G's life was all that mattered and saving it was the only thought Jed would allow in his mind.

Racing footsteps pattered in the street behind him. Matty or Dom was coming.

"Hang tight, Sergeant. Help's coming," he said as he pressed his hands tighter around the wound. Sergeant G groaned loud and angry, but she added her own hands to the task, pressing down on Jed's.

***

Welch kept pressure on the wound, and Gallegos did what she could to help him. Matty or Dom dropped down beside her head and she heard velcro, zippers, and pouches being torn and then the pressure released around her hip. She gritted her teeth and growled against the pain as they cut her uniform away from the wound. Cold water splashed against her skin again and again.

She knew the round had tumbled or split up inside her. Her hip and abdomen burned an angry hot, like a blazing knife had been shoved into her side.

Jo shouted, "*Get CELOX on it!*"

Matty or Dom grunted something in reply. Words and sounds faded in Gallegos' hearing. All she heard was a constant hum and scraping sound.

Finally a dressing was pushed onto the bullet hole and she realized she'd been grinding her teeth together so hard they hurt. Gallegos forced herself to lie still, letting the pain wash through her in waves.

"Give her some water," Matty said.

Welch was there with a canteen that he tipped over her mouth, letting a trickle of cold water spill out.

"More," she said and Welch complied.

Gallegos let the squad do their job. She'd done hers. They'd caught up to Tucker and taken him out. He got one last lucky shot in, but that was it. He was dead. The col-labs were all dead.

A loud pop came from behind her head. Then another.

One pair of hands that was holding the dressing over her wound fell away. Matty and Jo both screamed with fury. Gallegos pawed at her M4, trying to get it around to fire back toward the dirt pile, but she couldn't move it. Something pressed against the barrel and held it down.

Welch had gone somewhere, out of her sight. Gallegos didn't know where he was or who was around her anymore, and her hip was on fire.

Her vision clouded with shadows. A dull ache spread into her throat and rolled her eyes back until she fell into the darkness.

***

Jed leaped for Tucker when he fired his first shot. It hit Dom in the chest and he slumped sideways, and then Jed was on top of the col-lab. Tucker got another shot off, but Jed had his hands around the man's face and brought a knee up into his groin. Jed hit him with every pound of force and rage he'd been holding since he first saw the col-labs giving prisoners to the sucker faces. Tucker folded in on himself, trying to cover his dick, but Jed was faster and brought his knee up again in between Tucker's hands.

"You killed them!" Jed roared. He lifted the col-lab's head up and slammed it back down into the earth and rubble.

"You're a shit! A fucking shit!"

"*Jed!*" Jo screamed behind him. He kept his grip on Tucker's head, but turned and looked over his shoulder. Sergeant G was lying still on the ground. Dom was on his face beside her with blood pooling around him. Matty was taking care of Sergeant G, and Jo was holding an M9, aimed at Jed.

"Move out of the way, Jed," she said.

He did, rolling off to the side and grabbing the revolver Tucker had shot Dom with. Sergeant G's shot had hit his right arm. Blood soaked his sleeve and he held the arm limply against his side. His M16 was on the ground beside his hip. Jed snatched it away before the col-lab could reach for it.

"Only wanted to protect my boy," Tucker said. "Only wanted to make sure he survived and—"

Jo shot him in the chest. He slumped sideways and looked at her like he couldn't believe what just happened.

"We felt the same way about everyone who died trying to stop you."

"You're a—medic," Tucker said. He sucked in a gurgling breath. "You...you're supposed to save me."

Jo shot him again, in the head this time. She threw the pistol toward the river with a roar. Then she fell to a crouch, slid down on her heels, and sobbed. Jed crawled over and put his arms around her, holding her while she howled and rocked and cried.

— 34 —

Jed laid Dominic's body down next to Sergeant G, then took a knee and rested his weapon on his raised leg. Jo sat on her hip, next to him, with her rifle slung. She was monitoring Sergeant G's breathing.

"She seems okay for now. But I'm worried about blood loss. The wound may reopen when we move her, and we don't know how bad it is. She could be bleeding internally."

Jed couldn't get any words out in reply. He maintained his post, guarding his injured squad leader and praying she would be okay.

Matty had dug some keys out of Tucker's pocket, then offered to go back to the ambulance for a litter. He'd taken an M4 with him, just in case. Jed wasn't dumb enough to think everything was going to work out, but the suckers hadn't come after them yet. With all the shooting and shouting they'd been doing, that could only mean the monsters were somewhere else.

Still, he roved the night with the *240*, looking into the growing shadows for signs of movement. Empty, dead buildings, and piles of rubble and ruin stared back at him.

You used to be such a great city. I'm sorry we did this to you.

Jed knew he meant the apology for the city itself, but in that moment he remembered Meg Pratt. The firefighter who'd saved his life and whose life he'd failed to save.

I'm sorry, Meg. I'm so sorry I couldn't do more right then. If you're still alive…

He couldn't let himself hope like that. Whatever chance he had of saving Meg's life, he knew it was crazy to think he'd ever see her alive again.

Matty appeared at the corner, wheeling a stretcher down the road. Jo stood, holding her injured arm close against her chest. She steadied herself on her feet and walked to meet Matty halfway. Jed kept an eye out, still dreading the hit he wouldn't hear coming. He watched them come back up the street together, jogging beside the stretcher like they were characters in one of those hospital shows.

Except this is real, and they're not actors.

Jo and Matty stopped beside Jed. He stood aside as they lowered the stretcher and lifted Sergeant G, with Matty doing most of the work. They slid her on and Matty tightened two straps to hold her legs and chest still. The other straps were too ripped up to be useful, but Matty tied them in a knot over Sergeant G's chest. He and Jo raised the stretcher together, making sure it stayed steady on the uneven ground.

"Got Reeve's tags," Matty said to Jed. He pulled two sets of the slender chains out of his pocket. "Mahton's, too."

Jed accepted them, put them in his pocket, and turned around to look at their path ahead. The riverside drive stretched into darkness, winding along the edge of the dead city like a failed suture. Here and there, Jed could make out debris, vehicles, and bodies that spilled off the roadway and into the water.

"The boat's supposed to be up this way. Let's move out."

Jo gave him an *Errr* and they all set off at a trot, with Jed quietly damning Tucker's memory as they left the dead col-lab behind them.

***

The boat was at a covered pier half a mile up the road. They wheeled Sergeant G the whole way on a footpath that ran along the riverside, dodging carefully around rubble and corpses that littered the area. At the pier they had to navigate around bodies of dead sucker faces and the people they'd killed before the chemical bombs came down.

Graying vines crawled over the pier roof, making Jed think of the sucker faces and the way they would scramble and slink along every surface like a swarm of ants that would kill you as soon as look at you.

And so many had died to get him to this point.

Every step made Jed wish he'd done better by the people around him. He couldn't stop thinking about times when he hadn't aimed well enough or been fast enough or alert enough to stop someone getting hurt or killed.

But you got there for Sergeant G. We found the boat and now we can get the hell out of this city. I don't know where we'll go, but anywhere has to be better.

The boat was a long sport fisher type with an open

cabin. Stacks of boxes and cases of water lined the walls. Jed let Jo and Matty get Sergeant G into the vessel. They had to move slow because of Jo's arm, but they managed by dropping one end of the stretcher and sliding her down head first. Jo controlled her movement from above while Matty caught her shoulders and brought her onto the boat.

Jed snapped his attention back to his surroundings and scanned the pier for signs of the monsters. The vines hung on the pier cover, winding tight around the poles supporting the roof and drooping from above. Nothing moved in the still early night air. For a moment, only the steady beat of the water against the boat's hull told Jed he was still alive.

Sergeant G was safely on board, and Jo was with her. Matty came back to offer Jed a hand onto the craft. He turned away from the pier, climbed aboard, and took a seat next to Sergeant G. She was breathing steady. Her eyes were closed, but she was conscious. She muttered a weak *Thanks* as he settled himself near her.

"I'll get us into the water," Matty said, moving to the console.

The motor coughed at first, then grumbled into life. Jed cast them off and then they were on the water, leaving New York behind them and heading toward the East River.

— 35 —

Jed sat on his ass, with his back against a stack of boxes on the port side. He stared at the deepening night, watching it for any sign of threat. But he knew he was too numb and exhausted to stand much less fight back against anything that came their way.

Matty pushed the boat at a good pace. New York vanished into the darkness behind them as they came around Randall's Island. Jo had laid down beside a stack of boxes and was snoring lightly. Jed let the night take care of itself and kept vigil over Sergeant G while Matty steered them through the dark water. The bulk of Rikers Island appeared off the starboard side, above Jo's sleeping form. Jed looked behind them at their wake and watched the water cascade as nightfall finally came like a final note of loss.

Took our people, took our city. You took everything, even the light. But you didn't take us.

Sergeant G's eyes fluttered open and she instantly cried out, clutching at her side.

"Sergeant!"

Jed was next to her in a flash, looking into her eyes for some sign that she was okay. She flicked her gaze side to side and didn't focus on him when he stared right into her eyes.

"I think she's going into shock!"

Jo shook herself and crawled across to join him beside Sergeant G.

"She needs fluids. She's bleeding internally. Matty, where's our IV?"

"Bag's right here! Top pouch!" he yelled back from the console.

Jed pitched forward and grabbed the trauma bag from beside Matty's leg. He dragged it back to Sergeant G and opened the first pouch his hand touched on top. It had bandages and other small packets in it, but no IV.

He unzipped the top flap and grabbed at the clear bag held there by a velcro strap. He tugged the strap open and held the IV out to Jo.

"You have to do it, Jed," Jo said, cradling her injured arm. "I can't trust my hand to stay steady."

Jed shook with fright. He'd trained for this before, but it had been years. He knew the *don'ts*, but could barely remember the *dos*.

"Cut her sleeve open," Jo said. "Shears are in the bag, there." She pointed at the flap he'd pulled the IV from. Jed grabbed the shears from their strap and cut a slit in Sergeant G's sleeve right above her elbow.

"Iodine," Jo said, and her voice was the calmest sound Jed had heard in as long as he could remember. He reached for the bag, but it was too dark for him to make out which pouch was which.

"Pen light is in the top pouch, the first one you opened."

Jo's coaching settled his nerves and he breathed in and

out, feeling his lungs swell first, and then shrink in a smooth rhythm. The pen light was where she said it would be. He flicked it on and found a box of iodine wipes.

"Wipe the whole area, and use more than one if you need to. We can't risk introducing infection."

He did as she said, cleaning Sergeant G's arm again before he got the IV ready to go in. When he had the needle above her vein, the boat rocked in the water. He thought for sure he would miss or collapse the vein, but Jo's even voice and confident coaching got him through the shakes.

Jed breathed in and out, steadied his hands, and laid the needle against Sergeant G's vein. He gave a push and watched it slide under her skin. Pressure against the needle told him he was above the vein. He angled down, pushed again, and felt it slide home.

Jo told him to open the drip.

"Start it slow."

He did, and together he and Jo held their patient steady as the boat pushed through swells in Long Island Sound. Jo soaked a bandage with a bottle of water and swabbed Sergeant G's forehead. Jed put his hand on Jo's shoulder and thanked her.

"Couldn't have done it without you, Jo. Oorah."

"Oorah, Jed. You did good."

Sergeant G rolled her head to face him. He thought she said *Errr* before her eyes closed and her face went still.

"Sergeant G! Sergeant!"

"She's good, Jed," Jo said. "She's breathing steady. You did it."

Jed held the IV bag up in one hand and sat back on his ass. He looked at the woman who saved his life, and whose life he finally saved.

You did good, Jed. You did good.

***

The coastline of Long Island was a dark slice at the bottom of the sky as they pushed farther out from the city.

Lights flashed on the water ahead and Jed thought it was a nautical signal. He just didn't know which one.

"Could be someone good, could be someone bad," Matty said. "I'm turning our lights off and moving out of their path. Just in case."

A loudspeaker crackled to their starboard, but they were too far to make out the message clearly.

"What'd they say?" Jo asked. "It sounded like *enemy*."

Jed handed her the IV bag and picked up the *240*, moving to starboard. He set the bipod on top of the boxes there, hoping he'd know for sure who they were before he needed to fire.

Matty had their lights off and was idling the engine. The loudspeaker crackled again in the darkness.

"Are you friendly? Confirm ID."

"Sounds military to me," Jed said. "I bet they're okay. Get us closer, Matty."

"You sure, Jed? That asshole we chased all over the city might've been military himself. That didn't make him okay."

"I trust these guys," Jed said. "They sound legit. Get us closer. If they're bad people, I'll light 'em up."

Matty grunted something, but he brought them around to aim toward the other vessel. As they turned, a spotlight flared and blinded Jed. Three motors roared to life in the dark water and in seconds they were surrounded.

Jed held a hand up to block the spotlight. He couldn't see who it was, but he did see what they were sailing in. Three SOC-R craft floated in a perimeter, each with its armaments aimed in their direction.

"Friendly!" Jed shouted, lifting his other hand off the *240*. "US Marines! We got wounded!"

***

The welcoming party escorted them through Long Island Sound until their motor sputtered. With help from one of the SOC-R teams, they transferred Sergeant G and the supplies from Tucker's boat onto the other craft.

"We're from Plum Island," one of the Marines told Jed once they were underway. The whole crew wore protective gear, so the man's voice was muffled, but it still had the command and confidence Jed was familiar with.

Sounds a lot like Sergeant G.

"Where's Plum Island?" Jed asked.

"End of the sound. That's where you're going now. You'll be de-conned, treated, and interviewed. If you're lucky, they'll give you a new uniform. If you're unlucky, they'll feed you."

Jed wanted to laugh at the joke, but he couldn't. He looked at Sergeant G, who was lying on the deck, still and calm, like she could be dead or alive. Only the steady rise and fall of her chest told him what he needed to be true.

He got the other Marine's attention and pointed at Sergeant G.

"She saved my life, man. You gotta help her. Make sure she comes through."

"We have good doctors there. She'll get the best she possibly can."

Jed couldn't let it go.

Doesn't anybody care if she's okay?

Jo was sitting next to him. She put a hand on his shoulder and looked him in the eye.

"*You* saved *her* life, Jed. Oorah?"

Jed thought for a moment, feeling everything they'd been through that day like a smothering weight. He watched the team of Marines crewing the SOC-R as they sped over the water.

"Hey," he said to the one who'd spoken to him. The man stood behind a .50 cal turret. He turned to Jed and told him to get some rest.

"I will, but you gotta know—we had to leave some people behind," Jed told him in a rush. "There's people back there. The sucker faces have 'em. We couldn't get everybody out."

"Operation Liberty starts tomorrow morning. If they're alive, we'll find them and they'll be safe. Now make use of that fourth point of contact, Private."

Jed wanted to tell him the people were underground, but the guy had clearly ended the conversation, and the tone of his voice told Jed he'd already used his get out of hell free card.

As they raced through the sound toward Plum Island, Jed whispered into the night, saying a prayer for the people still in the city, and the people who had died so that he and the others could get out. Then he said a prayer for the people who would be going back tomorrow morning.

Good luck, and God bless you. The people we couldn't get out, they're down in the sewers and maintenance tunnels under buildings. If you see her down there...

If you see Meg, please get her out.

END OF BOOK TWO.

The story continues in

RESURGENCE

book 3 of the Redemption trilogy

Available at Amazon Books

About the Author, AJ Sikes

AJ Sikes is a freelance editor and author. His short stories have been published by Fox Spirit Books and Hamilton Springs Press. Sikes is a US Army veteran, father, and woodworker. If he's not at his desk, he's in his shop. Or possibly dealing with whatever the children or cats have gotten into.

Follow him on Twitter @AJSikes_Author
Join his spam free mailing list here: AJSikes.com

About the Author, Nicholas Sansbury Smith

Nicholas Sansbury Smith is the New York Times and USA Today bestselling author of the Hell Divers series. His other work includes the Extinction Cycle series, the Trackers series, and the Orbs series. He worked for Iowa Homeland Security and Emergency Management in disaster planning and mitigation before switching careers to focus on his one true passion—writing. When he isn't writing or daydreaming about the apocalypse, he enjoys running, biking, spending time with his family, and traveling the world. He is an Ironman triathlete and lives in Iowa with his wife, their dogs, and a house full of books.

Are you a Nicholas Sansbury Smith fan?
Join him on social media.
He would love to hear from you!

Facebook Fan Club: Join the NSS army!
Facebook Author Page: **Nicholas Sansbury Smith**
Twitter: @GreatWaveInk
Website: NicholasSansburySmith.com
Instagram: instagram.com/author_sansbury
Email: Greatwaveink@gmail.com